APRICOT MARMALADE
AND THE
EDMONDSON TRANSMITTAL

LON OREY

PAGE PUBLISHING, INC.
Conneaut Lake, PA

First originally published by Page Publishing 2021

ISBN 978-1-6624-1686-6 (hc)
ISBN 978-1-6624-1685-9 (digital)

Printed in the United States of America

PROLOGUE

The year was 1968. The war was not going well. The surprisingly effective Tet Offensive launched in late January had humbled and embarrassed the South Vietnamese and their American allies, sending a powerful message to the folks back home that this Vietnam thing was not going to be over anytime soon. The half million troops that the Lyndon Johnson administration had poured into this tiny Southeast Asian nation seemed to the world impotent, as their inability to subdue an outmanned and out-technologied adversary became increasingly apparent.

Johnson was haunted by the possibility that he might actually lose this war. There were things Johnson hated more than losing, but they were few in number, and as the days went by he tended to think of them less and less.

To make matters worse for Johnson, the US war effort was getting bad press on the home front. Some news sources reported that the war was not being waged effectively. Others argued that it should not be waged at all—at least not with US personnel. Americans in general were wearying of its intrusion into their living rooms every evening on the six o'clock news.

College students were protesting on campuses all across the country. Antiwar signs were everywhere, as were chalked-sidewalk denouncements and painted-wall condemnations, and that same sentiment served as the basis for songs that topped the record charts. ROTC buildings were torched or bombed on a regular basis, as were many other structures that were viewed as government symbols.

This was a lousy war, no question about it. World War II, Lyndon Johnson remembered almost fondly, had unified the people of the United States. It had inspired victory slogans and songs and had been a popular theme for books and movies. It had created a singleness of purpose for all Americans, leading to a strong sense of national pride. The Vietnam conflict, on the other hand, was tearing the country apart. It was also tearing Lyndon Johnson apart. And it made him old.

Meanwhile, in Bangkok, Thailand, five hundred miles away from the battleground, the special agents assigned to the 187th Military Intelligence Detachment, the US Army's counterespionage arm, were dealing with the war and its implications for the rest of Southeast Asia in their own way...

Reynolds was not normally one to worry. He liked to think of himself as laid-back and easygoing, a glass-is-half-full kind of guy. But for some reason he was worrying now. His instincts were telling him that something bad was going to happen. Something *really* bad. He'd learned to trust his instincts. Ed Reynolds and Don Cooper were in Lopburi on an assignment. Reynolds hated Lopburi. Too many US servicemen. Too isolated. Too flat. Too boring. Too damned hot! Although it was only about an hour's drive north of Bangkok, Lopburi always seemed to him much hotter and more humid than the larger city—some sort of climactic aberration, he supposed. The fact that it was February, a time of year that Reynolds generally thought of as cold and icy, made the contrast all the more striking.

Today the sky was completely clear in every direction, sapphire blue as far as the eye could see. The sun was relentless. With absolutely no breeze to ease their discomfort, the air felt thick to Reynolds and Cooper, a hot blanket sitting heavily on their shoulders.

They had driven up in a green, government-issued Ford Falcon—vintage 1963—with two sack lunches and a .38 caliber Smith & Wesson revolver in the glove compartment. The hour was nearly twelve thirty, and they expected to be breaking out those lunches soon, bologna sandwiches and fried chicken. The Smith & Wesson, a Detective Special model, had been checked out early that morning from Captain Scharfenberg, the unit's heavily freckled, redheaded supply officer.

Leaning against the front fender of the car, each of the agents was drinking a Coca-Cola. For Ed Reynolds the Coke worked its magic. It refreshed him and helped him set aside his worrying instincts, at least for now. He grinned beneath blue eyes and curly, light-brown hair. He was dressed in faded jeans and an untucked Hawaiian shirt, as was Cooper. Reynolds was the taller of the two by a couple of inches, standing just a shade under six feet. "Thank God for American enterprise abroad," he gurgled between gulps.

"Amen, brother, and hallelujah," his friend agreed, wiping a drip from his chin. With a rounded but pleasant face and short dark hair featuring a clearly defined part, Don Cooper observed, "You can always get a Coke anywhere in this country." Coke stands were ubiquitous, it seemed, even in the remotest of jungles, usually manned by a Thai youngster with entrepreneurial ambitions. And unlike Thailand's water supply, Coca-Cola was entirely safe and drinkable.

Reynolds hopped onto the hood of the car, regretting it instantly. The dark metal surface seemed to hold the heat of a super-nova. Immediately he slid off, and as he looked back at the hood, he could almost see the paint blistering.

Lopburi, home of the primary training center for Thailand's Special Forces units, was also home to a large contingent of US Special Forces personnel functioning as instructors and advisors. Parachuting was a major activity and attraction of the area.

"Have you ever wondered about people who jump out of airplanes?" Cooper asked of Reynolds, his sturdy, green-tinged bottle already half-emptied of its contents.

"They've got to be loony tunes, all of them." On the eastern horizon, a few miles away, Reynolds could see a half dozen parachutes popping open in the approximate location he had seen an airplane earlier, and then swinging their way slowly earthward.

"There's no way you'd ever get me to do that. Hell, I'd rather have meningitis."

Reynolds was acutely aware of his friend's unrivaled hypochondria. Cooper was intractable in his conviction that he was destined to die from some exotic disease, probably sooner rather than later.

5

He fretted about it constantly and made frequent visits to the 603rd Medical Dispensary, located in a building in downtown Bangkok, leased by the US government. Cooper was usually referred to Doctor Swanson, who insisted on being addressed as *Captain* Doctor Swanson. Rumor had it that his wife expected to be addressed as *Mrs.* Captain Doctor Swanson.

Sergeant Mason McElroy would be under one of those parachutes, or so Reynolds and Cooper had been told when they inquired at headquarters some forty minutes earlier. They needed to speak with McElroy as part of an investigation they'd been assigned regarding twenty cases of infrared, telescopic rifle sights that had been stolen recently from a US Army warehouse located at the end of Ploenchit Road in Bangkok.

McElroy had been dating a supply sergeant stationed there. Sergeant Judy Nicholls had reported to her superiors, and then to Military Intelligence, that McElroy had been acting strangely in the last couple of weeks and that he'd been unusually inquisitive about the recent shipment of rifle scopes from the States. Now that the scopes had vanished, there was much concern that they might end up in Vietnam where they would be affixed to various weapons and pointed at various GIs.

Don Cooper swatted at a squadron of insects that suddenly seemed intent on dive-bombing his face. His normally innocent features took on a scowl.

Reynolds's attention shifted once again eastward. The plane that had dropped the original group made another pass just then, and four new figures appeared, alternately soaring and tumbling downward, seemingly having the time of their lives. Then three parachutes came open in rapid succession, big and billowy and white, set off in spectacular fashion by the background of crisp blue sky.

"I wonder what's wrong with that other guy," Reynolds commented.

"Huh?" With his left hand, Cooper shielded his eyes from the sun.

"The fourth guy. He hasn't opened his chute yet."

"Probably just clowning around."

"Yeah, I suppose so."

"Showing off for his friends."

"Right."

They watched for a few more minutes with increasing intensity. "C'mon, pal, pull that cord," Reynolds muttered.

"Pull the cord, you idiot," Cooper echoed in a whisper.

Ed Reynolds was struck just then by a horrible thought. "Maybe he already has."

"Oh god."

Soon the fourth figure disappeared behind a strand of trees about a mile away. "Jesus Christ," Reynolds breathed. It came out almost as a whistle.

Cooper said nothing. The Coke bottle, still a third full, slipped from his grasp and fell to the ground as if mimicking the action of the figure he'd been watching. A glazed look came to his eyes.

When they managed to pull themselves together, Reynolds and Cooper jumped into their car and searched for a route that might take them directly to the downed chutist. Finding none that would get them even close, they drove back to the headquarters building and raced up seven wooden stairs and then inside. At the end of the corridor to the left, they nearly slipped on the highly polished tile floor leading into the main office.

The door was open, and three men were behind the counter, two of them standing and the other seated behind a desk. One of the men who was upright turned toward the newcomers. An armband identified him as the duty officer.

Even before asking the obviously rattled man the name of the parachuting victim, they knew instinctively that his answer would be "Mason McElroy." They knew too that they were on the right track in their investigation of the stolen rifle scopes.

"Did he have a family?" Don asked the duty officer, a surprisingly young man with a great deal of visible compassion for a fallen comrade.

"Divorced. Two kids. Living with their mother in Detroit."

Cooper and Reynolds shook their heads sadly as they went back outside. "I need a *real* drink this time," Don commented. "I'll even buy." Reaching into his shirt pocket, he withdrew a package of

Rolaids. He squeezed a tablet loose and popped it into his mouth. Something he often did during times of stress.

Ed nodded acceptance of the invitation, and away they went in the Ford Falcon. They would not know until later that they were making a huge mistake.

At Chonchai's Bar and Grill, Cooper and Reynolds parked their car on the grass strip in front. Inside, they found the place dingy, cramped, and smelling of unwashed field workers. The walls were unpainted, and only one of them had a window. Four black Naugahyde stools at the bar were accessorized in the middle of the room by six rickety tables and a number of equally rickety chairs. A ceiling fan didn't quite do the job of keeping the place cool.

From an old, stooped waitress with sad eyes, Reynolds ordered a scotch on the rocks and Cooper ordered Krating Tong beer, his go-to beverage. When the drinks arrived, Cooper took a big swallow, while Reynolds began nursing his scotch. He'd always found that he enjoyed adult beverages more if he drank them slowly. Mason McElroy was soon forgotten, even if only temporarily.

The pair, close friends for what seemed a long time, talked of many things. They talked of life, of politics, of philosophy, of religion, and of women. They talked of Don Cooper's post-army aspirations. With an undergraduate degree in psychology from San Diego State University already under his belt, Don had plans to go on for a master's and maybe even a PhD.

His aim was to become a clinical counseling psychologist, set up his own practice, or go into partnership with two or three other like-minded folks. He liked helping people, and he saw this as his means for doing that. Perhaps he could even help himself in some ways, as he was very much aware that he had a few neuroses of his own. Reynolds was struck by the way Cooper's eyes lit up as he talked about the future.

"Now all you have to do is survive the 187th MI Detachment," Ed interjected. "If you can get through that, you can get through anything."

"Yeah, I guess you're right about that."

They talked of their friends and fellow special agents, Marilyn Dunn and Doug Wilson. "I think I see a romance in the making," Cooper remarked. "Love in bloom."

"Well, I know they spend a lot of time together, but they're just good friends."

"My crystal ball doesn't lie." Don laughed. "You mark my words."

A young man, tall for a Thai, entered the bar and walked past their table. As he passed, he shot them an icy glare that seemed to lower the temperature in the room a good thirty degrees. He joined three others already seated at a table on the other side of the room. There, a quiet conversation ensued.

"What do you suppose they're talking about?" Cooper asked of Reynolds in a curious whisper. "You speak the language. Can you zero in on anything?" Before his assignment to the 187th in Bangkok, Ed Reynolds had completed a yearlong course in Thai at the Defense Language Institute in Monterey, California.

Reynolds experienced a moment of anxiety as his straining ears picked out a phrase or two. "I think they're talking about us...and they don't sound like fans."

"Terrific."

Reynolds listened further. "The tall one—the others call him Prachar—is saying something about giving the country back to the Thais and other peoples of Asia...eliminating all Western influence and interference."

With thoughts of malaria and other tropical diseases common to Southeast Asia flashing through Cooper's mind, he grumbled, "That would suit *me*."

"Shhh." Reynolds inclined his head in the direction of the conversation. It was amazing the things people would say when they assumed you didn't understand their language. "Now one of them is talking about rifles...and infrared rifle scopes...and getting them into the hands of true freedom fighters...the Vietcong."

"Hmmm, small world."

Reynolds strained harder, hoping to avoid being too conspicuous in his posture. Only a couple of additional minutes had gone by when he turned to Cooper and, in a hushed tone, said, "All right, very calmly now, you need to finish your beer, and then we're getting out of here…Not too fast. Let's not make any sudden moves." He plunked down some money on the table.

Cooper could not keep his eyes from darting about, and his breathing accelerated, but he did as his friend instructed and downed the last three sips of his Krating Tong. Silently sliding their chairs back, they stood and with equal silence made for the door. They heard a commotion behind them as they exited. Less concerned now with stealth, the two Americans sprinted for the Falcon and piled in, with Cooper at the wheel.

"Hit it, buddy!" Reynolds shouted.

The car fishtailed out of its grassy parking spot. They picked up speed rapidly but both of them knew, as if by radar, that there was a bright-blue Datsun not far behind.

Two and a half kilometers of two-lane, dust-covered, gravel roads went by. Cooper had established a good pace and a comfortable lead, raising a rooster tail of dust in the process. A glance in the rearview mirror revealed nothing more than a small blue dot, shrinking by the minute. "We're going about Mach 2!" he shouted, looking now at the speedometer. "We're gonna beat those bastards!"

Reynolds began to breathe a little easier. "Hey, man, I'll tell you what. When we get back to Bangkok, I'm going to buy you a big New York steak—cooked medium rare, just the way you like it—and two pitchers of Krating Tong beer. Whattaya say?"

Then it happened! Blowout! Right front tire! Despite Cooper's efforts to hold it steady and brake to a controlled stop, the Falcon pulled hard to the right and slammed into a ditch alongside the road, planting itself there as though it had always longed to be a tree.

Cursing Goodyear and various members of his family, Ed Reynolds grabbed the .38 revolver from the glove compartment. A quick flip and a scan of the cylinder told him it contained five rounds. Then he and Cooper jumped out and high-stepped their way into a field of tall grass. The ground was wet and marshy as though recently irrigated or rained on. Reynolds noticed that his shoes were making a puck-like sound with each stride. The Americans were about a hundred meters into the field when they heard car doors slam somewhere behind them. Two shots were fired. Reynolds swore. Hearing more shots seconds later, they ran all the harder, each correctly sensing a feeling of desperation coming over the other.

The grass was shorter and more sporadic here. There was no place to hide, no objective they could pick out, no real hope of escape. The field seemed to extend forever, blending into the horizon, green fading into blue.

Again shots sounded, a burst of four cracking through the air.

Reynolds hurdled over a mound of earth about two feet high, a rare exception to the flatness of the field. "Get down," he barked at Cooper who followed an instant later. They both went prone onto their stomachs behind the mound, grateful for its presence.

Reynolds took a strategic position and leveled the .38 carefully, studying the situation. Two men were coming directly at them, firing their pistols approximately every third step. They were hunched over, trying to keep low. One more was angling out to the left, a fourth angling right. These two were carrying semiautomatic rifles, most likely retrieved from the trunk of the blue Datsun. Soon the two Americans would be surrounded.

Now Reynolds fired, more to let everyone know they were armed than with hopes of actually hitting anything. Marksmanship had never been one of his strengths, no matter how much he worked at it. A sensitivity to loud noises invariably caused him to flinch slightly with each squeeze of the trigger. He would have passed the .38 to Cooper but for the realization that his aim was even poorer.

One of their pursuers dropped to the ground but only momentarily. Soon they were all advancing and shooting again. Reynolds fired another round with a tentative finger while Cooper attempted to burrow into a hole that wasn't there. The enemy closed in steadily, confidently.

Reynolds squeezed off two more rounds but he knew it was hopeless. "We're in trouble."

"No kidding," Cooper acknowledged.

"These guys mean business. I give them about two minutes before they blow us to bits."

"Oh, Christ."

Feeling the end rapidly approaching, Don Cooper wondered if his life soon would be flashing before his eyes. If so, he hoped it would be the *Reader's Digest* version.

"We'd better surrender," Reynolds announced finally. "Otherwise, we're goners."

Cooper nodded weakly.

Ed Reynolds looked around, patted his pockets. "We need something to use as a white flag—a handkerchief maybe…I don't have one. Do you?"

"No." Cooper rarely carried a handkerchief, although he usually kept a surgical mask in his hip pocket. You just couldn't be too careful about germs. Today he was without even that.

"Wonderful. We can't even give up… Hey, Don, you wear white boxer shorts, don't you?"

"Yeah," Cooper answered belligerently. "What of it?"

"Take off your pants."

"What?"

"You heard me. Get 'em off."

"Huh-uh."

"Come on, buddy. It's the only way."

"No."

"Would you rather get shot?"

A deep sigh. Then, grumbling, Cooper removed his trousers.

"That's good. Now your shorts."

"Oh, for Chrissake," Cooper growled, but he did as he'd been told. Off came the shorts. A bullet kicked up dirt nearby as he was about to get back into his trousers.

"We haven't got time for that," Reynolds insisted. "Start waving those boxers."

Cooper straightened slowly, naked from the waist down, and waved his shorts in high, wide, sweeping movements. When another shot sounded, his waving became more frantic.

Then the shooting stopped, and the Americans moved cautiously toward their adversaries, who also stood and began closing the gap. About halfway there, Don Cooper, his arm aching now from creating huge arcs, asked of Ed Reynolds, "Hey, what color are *your* shorts, anyway?"

"White."

A half turn of the head, followed by a whispered "You rotten son of a bitch."

A dog barked in the distance as though angered by some other creature invading its territory. Several hours had passed. The sun was disappearing slowly behind a low range of hills to the northwest, casting long, jagged shadows all about the clearing. Although it wasn't visible, the smell of smoke from some distant blaze hung in the air, a campfire perhaps. Surrounded by four men with most unfriendly faces, Ed Reynolds and Don Cooper were sitting on either end of a decaying log, hands tied behind their backs so tightly that Cooper's had gone numb. At least their captors had found his pants for him and had the decency to return them so he could put them back on. Thank heavens for small favors.

The two Americans had been marched some six kilometers in the heat of the day to this secluded, quiet, heavily wooded area, mostly oil palms and rubber trees. On top of everything else, they were exhausted.

A trickle of blood had made its way down the side of Cooper's face, a zealous questioner having left his mark. "*Puud*," the man was saying, his hands filled with the front of Don's Hawaiian shirt.

"Talk!" another echoed. "Talk, you filthy American pig! Who are you? What you doing here?" Although Don was not normally one to criticize, he couldn't help but notice that the man's hands were dirty and that his breath smelled like a dozen eggs gone bad. But then, nobody's perfect.

"I told you before—my name is Elvin Bradley. I'm a graduate student at Chulalongkorn University in Bangkok...majoring in political science. I did my undergraduate work at the University of Colorado in the United States...and I decided it would be exciting to come to a different part of the world for graduate school. I'm here in Lopburi to conduct some research on the municipal government." Canned stuff in preparation for the trip. Rule number one for MI agents: always have a cover story ready.

The man who had asked the question appeared not to understand the reply. Undoubtedly, he would not have believed it anyway. "You lie, damn bastard!" he spat. "You lie, damn bastard!"

"You American Special Forces, *chai mai*?" This question came from another man, the tall one, and it was directed at Reynolds, who had been hit several times during the last few minutes.

"Hell, no," Ed retorted. "I don't know anything about Special Forces. I wouldn't jump out of an airplane on a bet. Besides, I don't look good in a beret. Now maybe a tan fedora—"

The man struck him across the face with the back of his hand. "You spy, *chai mai*?"

"You've got to be kidding. Come on now, do I look like a spy? My name is Benjamin Richards. I'm a graduate student, like my friend here. Good old Chulalongkorn U. You know, rah-rah-siss-boom-bah and all that good stuff."

The man struck him again, this time with the other hand and it was balled into a fist. Ed's eye began to swell shut. His mouth felt like it was full of cotton. But he was sticking to his story, and he was sure that Cooper would too.

"You lie, damn shit bastard!"

"I'm telling the truth. I swear it. And please don't yell. It hurts my ears."

Ed Reynolds was hopeful that he could talk his way out of this, but he knew it was a wasted hope. This time the man slapped him repeatedly, first with his right hand, then with the left. Then came a clenched-fist blow delivered squarely to the breastbone.

Reynolds had never known such agony, nor had he even suspected it was possible. He was convinced something must be broken as a low-pitched moan tunneled upward through his throat, sounding to him as though it were coming from someone and someplace else. Out of the corner of his eye, Reynolds could see the blurred outline of a rifle butt coming at his head. If only he had the strength to avoid it...

✄

Consciousness did not come easily to Ed Reynolds. He had to work for it. Inch by inch, he pulled himself into a state of awareness, constantly fighting the temptation to slip back into the abyss. He didn't know how much time had passed. Hours? Days? Hell, he supposed, it could have been a week.

He was lying on the ground, and his hands were still tied. So he strained at the ropes, twisting his wrists back and forth, but he couldn't free himself. A distinct taste of blood was in his mouth. His face hurt and his head throbbed. His brain remained foggy.

The sun made him squint. It had the feel of morning. He blinked a few times while his eyes adjusted to the light. Looking around him, he realized that he had not been moved, for all of his surroundings were familiar. There was the log he had been forced to sit on, and the gulley directly behind it that grew deeper as it stretched to his left carrying the slenderest stream of water. And the trees ringing the clearing—those were well known to him too.

But the people—where were the people? Where was Don Cooper? He forced himself to sit up. "Don, you crazy-ass lunatic! Where the hell are you?"

No reply.

"Hey, Cooper!" he tried again. Nothing.

Suddenly, it struck him that noise might be an enemy. Noise might do him in. Maybe their attackers were still within earshot. Or maybe there were bandits in the area on the lookout for prospective victims, a common situation in this part of the country. And then, of course, there was the possibility of attracting the attention of wild animals. Tigers, the most feared animals in Southeast Asia, were not unheard of in these parts.

He sealed all potential sounds within him and awaited the crack of a rifle or the rustle of approaching footsteps, be they human or animal. He suppressed a need to belch, concerned even *that* might create too much noise.

After fifteen minutes or so, he allowed himself to think that he might be safe, and he went to work again on the ropes, pulling, twisting, tugging, struggling. This time there was some give. Gradually, over what was probably an hour or more, he worked himself loose. Then, defiantly, he heaved the rope as far as he could throw it. Rubbing his wrists together, he massaged each of them gently to restore the circulation. They ached, and much of the skin was raw.

Reynolds struggled to his feet, and cautiously he probed his surroundings in ever-expanding circles. Maybe he would be able to find out what happened. Maybe he would be able to find Cooper. But then, surveying his own battered body, it occurred to him that it might be better if he didn't. The possibility of finding his best friend bloodied and dead sent a shiver up his spine and turned his stomach queasy.

He did not find Cooper or anyone else, but as he moved about, his sense of security increased. For reasons unknown to him, his tormentors had departed, leaving him behind, perhaps mistaking him for dead. But it looked like they had taken Cooper with them.

Eventually, after maybe three or four hours of searching, Reynolds stumbled upon the main road. And not far away was the green Ford Falcon, one of its front tires limp and lifeless. Reynolds removed the keys from the ignition, using one of them to open the trunk. He pulled out the jack and the spare tire and went to work, focusing all his energy on the physical movements of the task at hand. Somehow, these simple activities helped him feel more confident, and that he was living in a more normal world. He did his best to push his anxieties deep down below the surface. There would be plenty of time to deal with them later.

When he finished, he drove to the Special Forces headquarters building to report Cooper's apparent kidnapping, thinking they might be able to help find him. The duty officer listened to all that Reynolds could tell him.

Ed realized that his speech was halting and his voice was heavy with emotion. After all, he was talking about a friend whom he valued as much as any he'd ever had.

"We'll do everything we can," the young officer promised.

"Thank you."

It was late afternoon by the time Reynolds made his way out onto the highway. Into the glare of the eye-level sun, he drove. And then the road curved, and the sun was on his right.

When he reached Bangkok, darkness was settling over the city. Minutes later he was in his apartment, home and glad to be. He dragged himself into the bathroom, and with extreme care, he washed the dirt and dried blood from his body. As best he could, he doctored his wounds, evaluating each for possible need of professional attention. Indeed, such attention would be required.

But what of his friend? What of Don Cooper? Would he ever see him again? Ed Reynolds didn't know. And he could not be glad about that.

Reynolds stretched out on his living room couch. He reflected on the early days of their friendship, a bond that had formed quickly, beginning in the middle of 1967. Before either of them had heard of, or even thought about, infrared rifle scopes. Or a sabotaged parachute. Or the Edmondson transmittal.

PART ONE

THE ARREST

CHAPTER ONE

Ed Reynolds was halfway through his twenty-fourth year when he discovered pineapples. Not the tart, sliced, or diced kind that come in cans and laden US-supermarket shelves. Nor the imported, unhusked version to be found occasionally in the produce section. Nor even the straight-from-the-plantation variety available at the Dole pineapple stands of Hawaii. No, Ed Reynolds discovered the *Thai* pineapple. Without a doubt, the very finest pineapple in the world! Sweet, sinfully succulent, totally wonderful! There was simply no other taste that could compare with it. Reynolds would take thirty of them back with him in his luggage, he vowed, when he returned to the US and separated from active duty in August. August of 1968, that is. A lifetime away.

Three of his friends were returning today, their tours of duty completed. Reynolds and Don Cooper had driven them to Bangkok's Don Muang Airport. Reynolds had known the three for only a few months, himself a relatively new arrival here—and Cooper was almost as new—but friendships could form quickly under circumstances like these. Good little soldiers, more or less, these three had put in their time and would be separating from the service after their arrival at Travis Air Force Base in California some twenty-two hours from now. Lucky bastards! Reynolds drooled at the thought.

There was Texas Stanley Gillespie. Texas Stan, as everyone knew, liked to screw outdoors dressed only in cowboy boots, a Stetson, and a big red bandanna. It reminded him, he said, of his college days and of those wild nights out on the prairie under the stars with various members of the Texas Central cheerleading squad. He appreciated the fact that Thailand was free of cactus. Reynolds would miss Texas Stan.

There was Big Bob Burgess, who worked out daily and who could bench press twice his weight. His muscles had muscles. And there was Barry Henderson. Henderson was a nonconformist in every way, although he never would have called himself that because he hated labels of any kind. Reynolds would miss these friends too.

Gillespie, Burgess, and Henderson—they were about to board a Boeing 707 marked "Saturn Airlines," destination California. Reynolds bade the three of them goodbye, as did Cooper, sharing a handshake and a pat on the shoulder with each. They were rotating stateside. They were getting out of the army. Reynolds envied the hell out of them. He was thirteen months away from separation. This fact made him occasionally crazy.

At two-thirty the next morning, the telephone in his apartment rang. These calls always came at two thirty in the morning. You could set your watch by them. Reynolds was suddenly glad that his new girlfriend, Kanlaya Chanyangam, hadn't stayed the night to be subjected to this indignity.

With the unsteady hand that comes of being jolted into awareness against one's will, Reynolds reached across to the nightstand, yanked the receiver from its cradle, and spoke into it. "Hello goddammit, Finsky, you prick!" His voice was wide awake, even if the rest of him lagged behind.

"Apricot marmalade," Specialist Fourth Class Al Finsky said in a mirthful tone.

Finsky had been a bugler once, Reynolds was sure of it. "Fuck you," Ed replied.

"Come on, Eddie boy. The countersign. Let's have it."

Reynolds hated this game. More than he hated stewed tomatoes, he hated this game. He knew, though, that he had no choice but to play it. "English muffins and apple jelly," he mumbled, wishing he were talking about breakfast.

"Beg pardon? I didn't quite catch that. Could you speak up?"

"English muffins and apple jelly, you goddamned son of a bitch!" Reynolds screamed into the phone. Trained in the Thai language while stationed at the Defense Language Institute in Monterey, California immediately prior to his assignment to the 187th MI Detachment, Reynolds found that a few Thai obscenities were coming to mind. Then he realized they would be wasted on Al Finsky, who could barely handle English.

"That's my boy, Eddie baby. The CO wants you here in fifteen minutes. And I quote, 'Tell Sergeant Reynolds to get the lead out.'" Ed had no doubt that was a direct quote from the commanding officer.

"Yeah, sure, you prick." It was common knowledge among the members of the 187th that Alexander Finsky—a specialist fourth class with the working title of intelligence coordinator, and with a brown brush cut, an abundance of pimples, a pair of chrome-rimmed spectacles, a permanently affixed smirk, and a knack for repairing anything mechanical—was a prick. Reynolds was certain that even Finsky himself would not have denied it, probably regarding it as a badge of honor.

Still half asleep, Reynolds stumbled into the closet of his one-bedroom apartment on the outskirts of town, and got dressed. There were no US military bases within or close to Bangkok, and all the agents of the 187th lived in civilian accommodations of their own choosing, supported by a modest housing allowance from the US government. They also wore civilian clothes, and that was all Ed's closet held.

By the time he had the Ford Falcon running and in gear, Ed Reynolds was awake. And he was furious! This was the fifth apricot marmalade drill Colonel Morgan had activated this month. The situation was getting ridiculous! How was a guy supposed to get any sleep?

As he drove past the guard responsible for manning the front gate of Ed's apartment compound, he would have sworn the man flipped him off. It was subtle but clear enough. Apparently, Ed Reynolds wasn't the only one who didn't like being awakened in the middle of the night.

Frequent apricot marmalade exercises seemed to have become Colonel Morgan's unique way of supporting the war effort, and he'd become fanatical about it. "All right, gentlemen, we've got to cut down on our response time," the commanding officer would proclaim as he reviewed the troops, each wearing civilian clothes, each standing at attention beside his gear bag, together forming two neat rows just outside the "ready room," most of them wishing they could be somewhere else.

Ed Reynolds, invariably the last to arrive at the eighth floor of the Chairanee Building, home of the 187th MI Detachment, was typically singled out for special attention. "And you, Sergeant Reynolds, had damn well better get your head out of your ass!" Bellowing in drill sergeant fashion was one of the CO's strong suits.

"Yes, sir. Right away, sir."

Reynolds often joked about this distasteful apricot marmalade business with Don Cooper, fellow special agent, close friend, and kindred spirit. Colonel Spencer Morgan—a *lieutenant* colonel by actual rank—had chanced to overhear Reynolds's end of one of these exchanges, something about Reynolds being all-state on his high school marmalade team.

The following morning, Reynolds was instructed by the first sergeant to report to Colonel Morgan's office. Major Orville Harris, the operations officer, was already seated there, smoking a cigarette, looking grim and reproachful. The CO often looked to Major Harris for moral support and backup. Harris was a West Point man with a Dick Tracy jaw.

Colonel Morgan, a colorless, odorless, tasteless man of average height and build and closely cropped graying hair, pointed to a chair, and Reynolds sat. Next, the colonel challenged him with. "You're trying to undermine the US mission here in Thailand, Sergeant. Why is that?"

"But I'm not, sir. Scout's honor." Reynolds held up the first two fingers of his right hand in Boy Scout fashion. He was not surprised by the CO's accusation. It was nothing new. It didn't take much, he'd come to realize, to end up on Colonel Morgan's list of subversives.

"Bullshit, Sergeant. You'd damn well better shape your ass *up*, or I'm gonna damn well ship it *out*. Is that clear?"

"Oh. You bet, sir."

Major Harris gave a contemptuous snort, viewing Reynolds through humorless eyes. With dark hair and thick, dark eyebrows, Harris's mood and countenance were even darker. And to Reynolds at least, there was something downright sinister about the man.

Ed couldn't quite put his finger on it, but he believed it nonetheless. Perhaps it was the way one of the eyebrows—the right one—arched a bit more than the other. Perhaps it was a smile that more often resembled a sneer. Perhaps it was a laugh, although rarely displayed, that was low in volume and seemed to emanate from deep in the throat. Or perhaps it was the fact that the major took obvious delight whenever delivering bad news. Whatever it was, Ed Reynolds couldn't help but feel that this man was capable of great evil.

"You're dismissed, Sergeant," the colonel informed him, scowling as Ed got to his feet and made for the door. Major Harris scowled too, something he was quite good at, and he mumbled, "I'll be watching you, motherfucker."

Although Ed wasn't disturbed by the colonel's assertion about undermining the mission—an inaccurate assumption and certainly not the first time he'd heard it—what *did* disturb him was being referred to by his rank. Civilian clothes, the great equalizer, had dissolved or at least blurred most distinctions of rank. As MI special agents or intelligence coordinators, the members of the 187th all dressed in civvies.

The typical look for the unit consisted of short-sleeved white shirt, narrow diagonally striped necktie, dark slacks, and either black or brown loafers. Shirts with short sleeves were an accommodation to the climate, not particularly stylish but comfortable and functional. In the case of First Sergeant Barnett, the shirt covered a great deal of belt overhang.

In addition, the special agents carried MI credentials identifying them as such, unless they were on a covert operation of some sort. The unit also featured three intelligence coordinators, who did not carry credentials.

Nearly everyone was on a first-name basis with nearly everyone else, and Reynolds liked it that way. It seemed to lend itself to a sense of "team-ness." Colonel Morgan, on the other hand, preferred to see rank distinctions preserved, despite the civilian clothes attire. "Military protocol" and all that.

The necessity for continued apricot marmalade drills wasn't widely understood nor accepted. Colonel Morgan's explanation whenever asked, which almost never happened anymore, was always the same: preparation for a possible emergency that would require immediate mobilization. "You never can tell, for instance, when we might all have to take to the jungle. We damn well need to be ready. Any damn sonofabitch who isn't ready can damn well expect to be court-martialed, damn it!"

That explanation had sounded almost plausible to Reynolds the first time he'd heard it. And certainly the court-martialing part had gotten his attention. It was true that if communist terrorists (usually referred to as "CTs") were to pour into the country from the north or the northeast—both considered to be vulnerable areas, particularly given their proximity to Vietnam—there wouldn't be much room in Bangkok for the 187th. They'd have to go someplace. Why not the jungle? They were packed for it.

Supervised by Major Harris and First Sergeant Ernest Barnett—a fat, bald, not-too-bright baritone and the ranking NCO—every member of the unit had efficiently packed a gear bag with two pairs of fatigues, one steel helmet, one helmet liner, one pair of boots, five pairs of socks, four sets of underwear, one small ax, one bottle of malaria tablets, one can of insect repellent, fifteen chocolate bars, three rolls of toilet paper, and a folded-up, one-man tent. The gear bags, stored alphabetically in the "ready room," enabled the troops to be exactly that—ready.

But then Reynolds zeroed in on some flaws in the commanding officer's grand plan. First of all, he was struck by the realization that practically no one in the outfit knew a blessed thing about the jungle, let alone how to survive in it. The single exception was Irv Bonner, who'd spent a lot of time recently in several parts of the jungle on various assignments. But Irv was scared out of his skull over snakes. While Ed found that to be an entirely understandable phobia, it limited Bonner's usefulness. Secondly, if the CTs ever *did* manage a takeover of the country, even the deepest of jungles would offer little cover for a group of Yankees. Thirdly, where in God's name could they go from there? Laos? Cambodia? Vietnam? The prospects were not exactly thrilling.

Reynolds had pointed out these concerns once to the CO. Colonel Morgan had immediately accused him of attempting to undermine the mission. Then, with hazel eyes narrowing in a flat, puffy face, Morgan threw in, "They still have firing squads, Sergeant."

J. Edgar Reynolds. That was how he signed his name. His parents had named him after that famous FBI fellow. They hadn't given him a first name, only the initial "J," not realizing the FBI guy actually was named John. After reading and being impressed by *The Great Gatsby* for a college course, Ed had toyed with the idea of announcing to the world that he would be known henceforth as "J," or perhaps as "Jay." Later, he considered "J. E." But, invariably, he returned to the fact that he was simply "Ed." That's where his comfort zone was and always would be.

His parents had done something else to him too. Early in his life, they instilled in him an acute sensitivity to loud noises. When he was two years old, he'd climbed onto a coffee table. His mother, concerned that he might fall and hurt himself, tiptoed up behind him and clapped her hands smartly just inches from his ear, simultaneously shouting, "No!"

His head snapped around, mouth falling open as a brief deafness came over him. This was followed by fearful wailing and by trembling that did not stop for several hours. His parents—Ellen and Henry—noticed that their son didn't go near the coffee table anymore, and they began to use this obviously effective technique often to generate a broad range of wished-for behavioral changes.

Ed hated it. He grew to hate other loud sounds as well. To the extent possible, he stayed away from barking dogs, firecrackers, sonic booms, motorcycles, and cars with faulty mufflers.

When he hit US Army basic training, he discovered that this part of his life was to hold many high-volume noises that would be difficult or impossible to escape. Shouting drill sergeants bellowing at point-blank range. Rifle ranges. Mortar shells. Hand grenades. As if basic training weren't tough enough all by itself, it was mighty damned loud!

CHAPTER TWO

"You have the sensitivity of a porcupine," one of Reynolds's former girlfriends had told him in his collegiate days. Both had been journalism majors and had several classes together.

What was her name anyway? Joyce something or other. Now that he had matured enough to be able to look at himself more objectively, Ed could acknowledge that she probably was right.

Although he regarded himself as basically a good, decent, and caring person, he realized that he always had been characterized by bluntness. The direct approach. Laying it on the line. No holds barred. There were times when this trait served him well. There were others when it got him into trouble. For starters, Joyce what's-her-name had dumped him because of it.

There were people around him with sensitivity. Irv Bonner, as an example, had a bundle of it. A kind, compassionate guy, it seemed to Ed that Irv was always conscious of the feelings of others and looking out for their best interests. Doug Wilson was a sensitive person as well, sympathetic and supportive. Even Don Cooper had his fair share of sensitivity. Marilyn Dunn, on the other hand, was more like Ed, typically quick to speak her mind without regard for the consequences.

Kanlaya Chanyangam, Ed knew whenever he saw himself reflected in her eyes, was not one who shared Joyce what's-her-name's viewpoint. There, in those large, lovely, brown eyes, he saw only admiration and deep caring. He was glad.

Kanlaya—he'd taken to calling her Connie—was intelligent. She was also warm and charming, with an infectious laugh. She was poised. She was polished. She spoke English superbly, probably as the result of her father's role as professor of languages at Chulalongkorn University. The professor's language skills must have rubbed off. She might well have sounded like a Yankee if it weren't for the fact that she completely avoided contractions. Thus, "aren't" was always "are not" and "wouldn't" was always "would not." Connie was a management trainee at the National Bank of Siam, and it was clear to Ed that she was destined for great things.

As if all that were not enough, she was blessed with a flawless beauty and a dazzling smile that attracted stares wherever she went. She was mesmerizing. And whenever she and Ed were together, it was as though they had invented sex.

In spite of years of conditioning to the contrary, Ed could feel himself falling in love. True, he had only known her for three months. But it had been a highly intense and meaningful three months, with the pair of them spending every possible moment together: dinner at some of Bangkok's finest restaurants and at some of its worst, movies, the zoo, tours of the majestic and colorful temples, Sunday afternoons strolling through Lumpini Park listening to Ed's portable radio and songs like *Moon River* by Andy Williams.

Sometimes she even went with him to the gym of Chulalongkorn University to watch him play basketball, something he did routinely to stay in shape. "If you could learn to move to your left better," she had once told him, "you would be much more effective."

"Yeah, right. Thanks." Easier said than done.

"I hope you will find it useful information."

Love might not be such a good idea right now, Ed knew. A complication he hadn't planned on. From time to time, thoughts of retreat went through his head, but he doubted that he could find it within himself to follow through with them.

"I like the hair on your chest," she told him one Saturday morning while the two of them lay in bed.

"It kind of turns you on, does it?"

Kanlaya continued to run her fingers through it as though her hand were a comb. "Well, I would not say that I am a fanatic about it."

"That's good, Connie, because it's actually a toupee," Ed told her. "Oh?"

"Yep. Good old Sears and Roebuck. On sale for twenty-nine ninety-five."

She clobbered him with a pillow.

Five feet eleven and a hundred seventy-five pounds, Ed Reynolds had a trim but sturdy build. Not classically handsome, he did seem to appeal to a reasonable percentage of women. That may have been because of his curly, brown-blond hair, blue eyes, and crescent-shaped dimples. At least he'd heard comments to that effect in recent years.

Kanlaya Chanyangam seemed particularly intrigued by his dimples. "Thai men do not have dimples," she had told him. "At least none that I have observed."

Ed kept in shape by lifting weights three evenings a week and by playing basketball on the two weekdays in between, the university gym serving nicely in both respects. Ed had been a basketball player in high school—starting guard for the Jefferson Patriots.

"*Nothing but net*" was his nickname in those days. Or maybe he'd simply wanted it to be. He couldn't recall exactly. Then, as now, it was an inability to drive to his left that kept him from greatness. Life could be so unfair sometimes.

❧

Ed Reynolds liked Bangkok but he also enjoyed getting out of the city and experiencing other parts of the country as well. Unexpectedly, he learned of such an opportunity on the morning of November 14. As was his custom, he arrived for work a few minutes late, parking his 1963 Ford Falcon—one of a fleet of eight owned by the detachment, all 1963s but in varying colors—in its reserved parking space alongside the Chairanee Building. They also owned four Land Rovers, stored at a parking lot on the edge of town.

A ninth space next to the Chairanee was reserved for Orville Harris's bright-red 1967 Mercedes Benz. Reynolds shook his head in amazement every time he saw it. He knew that Harris had arranged for the glove compartment to be equipped with a two-way radio and had received authorization from the CO to use the vehicle in surveillances and other covert MI operations, bringing a whole new meaning to the word *discreet*.

"Stupid bastard," Reynolds would mutter to himself whenever he thought of the major and his car, which he did as infrequently as he could manage.

It was widely known that the Mercedes, purchased in California immediately prior to the major's departure for Thailand, was his one true love. He'd paid several hundred dollars of his own money to have it shipped from Los Angeles to Bangkok, draining most of his discretionary funds and leaving him without money for auto insurance. Orville Harris loved his Mercedes deeply. He fawned over it. He doted on it. He did everything possible to protect it from the elements and from birds and from people. Twice a week, he washed it and waxed it, creating a luster that in the noonday Bangkok sun caused passersby to turn away rather than risk blindness.

The 187th MI Detachment operated out of a spacious suite of offices leased by the US Army and took up the entire eighth floor of the Chairanee. The National Bank of Thailand owned the building, located near the corner of Sukhumvit and Rajadamnern, and did business on the ground floor. Space on the remaining floors was taken up by engineering firms, travel agencies, and an assortment of other small businesses.

This was the heart of the downtown area. The Chairanee stood in the midst of dozens of other tall office buildings. A single exception was a small, one-story building—a hardware store owned by an elderly Chinese couple who consistently refused to sell their establishment to any of the business conglomerates interested in buying it. "You can buy it from our children when we are dead," they were fond of saying. The hardware store was directly across Sukhumvit from the Chairanee.

Reynolds took the elevator to the eighth floor and entered the suite of the 187th. He nodded as he passed Al Finsky, who was seated at the reception desk smoking a cigarette and evidently repairing some sort of electrical gadget. It seemed that Finsky was always tinkering with something electrical or mechanical. He neither looked up nor acknowledged Ed's nod. Ed sauntered on.

Even though Ed had no great love for certain members of the 187th, he experienced a reluctant admiration for the facilities in which they all worked. For an overseas duty station, the whole layout could be regarded as nothing short of plush. "So this is where the tax-payers' money goes," he would sometimes grumble, but if the truth were known, he too appreciated their comfortable surroundings.

A dozen sumptuously furnished offices were distributed along three of the outer walls. Punctuating the fourth wall were the entrance to a high-security file room used for storage of top secret documents; a tech room boasting the latest in electronic gadgetry—the kind of place Q would have hung out had James Bond worked here; the ready room; a small break room with a coffee pot, a few chairs, and a view of the street below; and a reception area immediately inside the suite's entrance.

Al Finsky was responsible for reception duties but also spent a lot of time in the tech room. In addition, he handled apricot marma-lade telephone chores, and did so with obvious glee.

"G'mornin', Eddie boy," Finsky said, suddenly at Reynolds's ear. "Did I happen to mention the CO wants to see you and Cooper pronto. By the way, I'd hurry if I were you. He's already pissed off about you bein' late again."

"Yeah, okay." Ed turned to see Al Finsky with a cigarette in his mouth and jangling keys in his pants pocket. An avid tobacco user, Finsky liked to use the expression "Smoke 'em if ya got 'em."

"Just thought you oughta know." Finsky lumbered off. Whenever he walked, he was all arms and legs and wasted motion. Whenever he was seated, one of his legs would be crossed over the other, and the knee of the top leg would bounce ceaselessly. Al Finsky was the personification of nervous energy.

Reynolds made his way to the coffee pot in the break room, pouring himself a cup. Then he swung by to pick up Cooper, and the two of them went past the first sergeant's cubicle and then on in to see the colonel.

"You wanted to see us, sir?" Ed blew across the surface of his coffee to cool it.

Lieutenant Colonel Spencer G. Morgan's office, occupying the northwest corner of the suite, had a roominess to it that reminded Reynolds of a hotel lobby—the Waldorf Astoria, perhaps. That lobby look was enhanced by the presence of a soft leather pecan-colored couch, a matching pair of overstuffed armchairs, and a substantial teak desk with a leather-padded swivel chair. Approximately three-quarters of the beige tile floor was covered by a luxurious area rug, thick, buoyant and a rich shade of tan.

The walls were an eggshell color, and they were laden with a score of framed certificates and awards, indicators of Morgan's various military achievements over the years, most of which Ed considered to be inconsequential. A large window behind the couch afforded a sweeping view of much of the city. As usual, the room smelled of cigar smoke.

"Uh-huh," Morgan replied. "Sit down."

Reynolds and Cooper seated themselves in the twin armchairs and looked across at the colonel. He was seated behind the desk with fingers steepled in front of his chin, creating a look of wisdom that Ed knew was at odds with reality.

Morgan continued in a gruff tone, "I'm sending the two of you to Hua Hin on an assignment. You'll take the train first thing in the morning."

"Hua Hin, sir?" Reynolds inclined his head. This sounded too good to be true. Hua Hin was considered to be one of the two finest beach resorts in all of Thailand, Pattaya being the other. They were located on opposite sides of the Gulf of Siam. These were the places that tourists with money went, not a pair of penniless GIs.

"Great!" This from Cooper.

"It's against my better judgment," the colonel went on, looking directly at Cooper, "but I don't have much choice. Our more reliable agents are busy with assignments of their own."

"You're too kind, sir," Reynolds countered with a broad but insincere smile.

"It's not a matter of kindness. It's a matter of necessity."

Reynolds had no doubt that Colonel Morgan indeed had selected them as a last resort. All the other agents were tied up with other activities, just as he had stated.

"I want you to keep an eye on a Russian woman by the name of Tania Kolovich," Morgan said, walking over to hand Reynolds a photograph, then returning to his chair.

Reynolds gave a soft whistle. "A gorgeous lady." He reached over to hand the photo to Don Cooper.

"Ohh," Cooper murmured, eyes widening.

A few moments passed, and then Reynolds said to his friend, "You hang on to that, Don. It looks like it means a lot to you."

"Okay." Cooper slipped it into his shirt pocket.

It was Colonel Morgan who spoke next. "She's an employee of TASS, the Soviet news agency… But we're pretty well convinced she's also a GRU agent." The GRU was the USSR's intelligence gathering arm, the flip side of the KGB and the Soviet equivalent of the CIA.

"A GRU agent? What a waste." This from Reynolds.

"Since she isn't attached to the USSR embassy, like most of their agents are, she doesn't have diplomatic immunity. That makes her *extremely* vulnerable. She's going to be in Hua Hin for the next couple of weeks, presumably on vacation."

"That's where we come in?"

"Uh-huh. I'm willing to bet she's planning more than fun in the sun. I want someone there to nail her, and nail her hard, as soon as she tips her hand." He leaned forward and pointed an index finger. "That'll be you two. We've made train and hotel reservations for you. You'll leave tomorrow at 0800 hours."

"If you insist."

Then the colonel focused his attention solely on Reynolds, regarding him with cold eyes. "And let me be clear about this, Sergeant. If you screw this up, you'll damn well be trading in your cloak and dagger for a poncho and bayonet." Morgan, suddenly struck by the humor of his remark, leaned back in his chair and laughed uproariously.

Cooper threw a nervous glance toward Reynolds, and in spite of himself, Ed winced. He could only hope it didn't show.

At two thirty that night, the telephone in Ed's apartment rang, awakening him from a sound sleep. Ed reached across to the nightstand, pulled the telephone handset from its cradle, sat about half upright, and spoke into it with as much volume as he could muster at that hour. "Hello, goddammit. Finsky, you prick!"

"Apricot marmalade, Eddie boy," chortled Al Finsky.

"English muffins and apple jelly, you goddamned son of a bitch!"

CHAPTER THREE

Hua Hin, lying along the western shore of the Gulf of Siam, was nearly a full day's train ride south from Bangkok and seemed to Reynolds and Cooper even longer, primarily because of the small, wooden seats and windows that could not keep out an endless supply of dust but did a fine job of keeping in the heat.

They chatted about a number of things throughout the journey. As they were nearing their destination, Don revealed something about himself that Ed hadn't previously known. "There's a song stuck in my head that I can't get rid of."

"Really?"

"It's been there for weeks, and it's driving me crazy." He ran a hand down the back of his neck.

"What is it?"

"Well, you remember I told you that I took a ten-day leave after finishing up MI training at Fort Holabird and before reporting for duty at the 187th. Right?"

"Yeah, I recall that."

"My parents met me in Southern California and, sort of as a graduation present, took me around to some of the tourist attractions there. One of them was Disneyland, which I loved, by the way. It's fun for grown-ups, as well as for kids."

"I've heard that."

"Anyway, there's a ride there called It's a Small World. It takes you on a boat through a number of scenes representing several different countries. And for each country there are children singing this song in their own language. It starts in English and then, after going through many other languages, it ends in English."

"How does it go?"

Cooper sang the primary lyrics a couple of times, causing the heads of a few of the other passengers to turn. Then he stopped. "Well, you get the idea. So it's stuck in here." He tapped his forehead.

"Have you tried replacing it with something else?"

"Yeah, many times. Usually it works for about a day, and then *bam*, 'It's A Small World' comes right back. Once I thought I was really on to something. I substituted 'Viva Las Vegas,' and that lasted about four days. But then..." He shrugged his shoulders.

Just then, the train drew into the station. Reynolds and Cooper pulled their suitcases down from the overhead rack, and they began their slow exit. They took a pedicab from the train station to the Hua Hin Hotel. An appealing structure, it was surrounded on three sides by acres of lawn and large shrubs and hedges skillfully manicured into animal shapes—elephants, tigers, giraffes, and more—a topiary menagerie of sorts. The fourth side, the back actually, ran along the edge of the beach. The building was large and white and elegant, and it had the look of a place where rich people stay.

Reynolds and Cooper registered under cover names—Benjamin Richards and Elvin Bradley. Reynolds enjoyed using a cover identity. To him it was kind of like being at a costume party but without the costume.

In their rooms, 224 and 237, Reynolds and Cooper deposited their luggage, changing quickly into swimsuits and flip-flops. And then it was onward to the beach equipped with towels and suntan lotion, Cooper mumbling something about needing to lose a couple of pounds, Reynolds complaining about how badly his tan had faded. There would only be a couple of hours of good sun left. So they had to move along. Work could wait.

Ed Reynolds and Don Cooper had visited Pattaya previously, over a long weekend, but this was their first chance at Hua Hin, and they were determined to make the most of it. They were taking the assignment seriously, but wine, women, and relaxation were also on their agenda. Ed found the sight of the beach irresistible! It offered the cleanest, whitest sand and the bluest ocean he had ever seen, and it appeared to stretch on forever.

After a late breakfast the following morning, they put on swim-suits and returned to the beach, spreading a couple of huge towels on the sand. While Cooper dozed and Reynolds fended off herds of mosquitoes, Ed shielded his eyes from the sun and then fixed his gaze upon an approaching female figure.

He poked Cooper in the ribs. "Hey, wake up."

"Huh? Wha—"

"Over there. In the green one-piece. Tania Kolovich." He indi-cated a tall, shapely woman with medium-length brown hair.

"Oh."

As she drew nearer, Reynolds found her captivating. With eyes that were brown and bold, lips that were full and flirtatious, cheekbones that were high and haughty, and a nose that was capri-ciously curved, she exuded an electricity that at once enraptured and engulfed. She had an aristocratic bearing, and she walked with a pro-found self-assurance that reminded Reynolds of Marilyn Dunn.

Cooper looked her way as she passed within a few feet, and a strange fascination came over him. "Wow," he breathed. His eyes were suddenly glazed.

"Easy, guy," Reynolds cautioned. "This part of the trip is strictly business. She's the enemy. You remember that, okay?"

"Oh, uh-huh."

"Snap out of it."

"I'll be fine," Cooper insisted, although he continued to gape, and his breathing became ragged.

"Let's follow her."

"You bet." Cooper stood and immediately realized his mistake. The crotch of his red-and-blue striped swimsuit bulged grotesquely.

Embarrassed, he promptly sat back down in the sand and took a hurried look around to see who might have noticed. Several feet to his right, a pair of Thai youngsters, a girl and a boy, pointed and laughed. The girl said something to the boy, holding her hands in front of her about a foot and a half apart. The boy laughed again and nodded.

"Jesus," Reynolds said to Cooper with a grin, "you can't go anywhere like that." Don's face, he noticed, had turned an amazing shade of crimson.

"Huh-uh," Don agreed.

"You stay here. I'll follow her alone." Letting out a chuckle, Ed added, "And for God's sake, cover yourself with something. You're disgusting. Let's have a little dignity around here."

Don Cooper began to bury himself in the sand while Reynolds grabbed his towel and took up the surveillance. Tania Kolovich walked slowly along the beach. Stooping at one point to pick up a pebble, she pitched it sidearm into the surf and watched it disappear. She stood in that one spot for several moments, gazing out at the ocean, evidently admiring its beauty, allowing some of its soft, white foam to wrap itself around her ankles.

Then she was moving again. She led Reynolds into the hotel and up the stairs to Room 248, meaning she was a neighbor of Reynolds and Cooper. When she entered her room, Ed waited for her beside a window at the end of the hallway, pretending to watch the ocean and the seagulls.

Three European men—Germans, Ed thought—walked by in colorful shorts and Hawaiian shirts. One was remarkably fat with chins numbering somewhere between five and nine, depending on the angle of his head. He reminded Ed of Gert Frobe who played the villain in the movie *Goldfinger.*

As always, Ed felt awkward in the stationary phase of a foot surveillance. He felt big and obvious. He wished he had pockets, so he could thrust his hands into them.

"My kingdom for a pocket," he muttered half aloud once he determined that the Europeans were out of earshot. He still clung to his beach towel, and now he spread it across his shoulders. Then he began to whistle softly the tune from "If You're Going to San Francisco." He checked his watch. It was now officially afternoon.

At last, Tania Kolovich reappeared. Wearing a black cocktail dress, she made her way down the stairs and into the lounge. Reynolds followed her discreetly and sat two tables away, unconcerned that he was wearing only swimming trunks and flip-flops, as several others around him were similarly attired. He laid his towel across the back of an adjacent chair.

Charging it to Room 224, he ordered a whiskey sour, and when it arrived he took a sip. He didn't like it—light on whiskey and heavy on sour. Then he glanced about the room. The cocktail lounge was large and comfortable with an emphasis on browns and reds and supple leather. Four immense, expensive-looking Persian rugs covered the quadrants of the floor,

The instrumental version of a Beatles tune was being piped at low volume into the room. Reynolds detected a faint garlic smell drifting in from the nearby kitchen. Thai cooking, it seemed, often took on the aroma of garlic.

Soon, Tania Kolovich was joined by a tall man with a blond, military-style haircut and a bright-red Hawaiian shirt. The two obviously knew each other, though each seemed surprised at the other's presence here. Ed suspected that in Tania's case, the surprised look was an act.

Straining to overhear their conversation, he was able to catch bits and pieces. Both were speaking in English, clearly native to the man. And Tania herself was nearly as fluent. Cocktails were ordered and later replenished.

From what Reynolds could hear during the next hour and a half or so, he concluded that the pair had met in Bangkok several weeks ago, that the man was an officer in the US Air Force, and that he was here in Hua Hin on a four-day leave. It appeared to Ed that Tania was pumping the man, in a subtle and seductive way, for military information. Something about F-111s, their number and placement, and why did he suppose the Air Force had been losing so many of them lately through malfunctions and crashes?

"Sabotage," the man replied. "Gotta be."

"Oh?" A demure smile. She leaned in.

"The F-111 is an excellent piece of machinery. Too damned good for this many mishaps to happen by chance." He shook his head sadly.

He did not appear to be suspicious over these questions, and even though he answered most of them in vague terms, he was not uncooperative. He also was not sober.

Then there was conversation about Hua Hin—the town, the resort, the hotel. "It is all so lovely, is it not?" She smiled fetchingly.

"It sure is," the man agreed, moving his chair closer to hers.

"I'm afraid the Soviet Union has little to compare with it."

"I'm afraid you could say the same for Wichita, Kansas." The man's words were slurring noticeably.

"I would like to see your Wichita, Kansas someday." Her smile broadened, disclosing beautiful white teeth and sparkling eyes.

He smiled too. "Honey, I don't think Wichita is ready for you."

She cocked her head inquiringly for a moment, then said, "I think I shall take that as a compliment."

"You might as well. That's the way I meant it."

"You are very kind."

"I just call 'em like I see 'em. And lady, from what I've seen so far, *you* are gorgeous."

"How you Americans do flatter."

After that she leaned across to kiss him and, rising, said her goodbyes. She would see him again during their stay, she promised, hinting with a twinkle in her eye that it might well be under more intimate circumstances next time. She departed with graceful, sensuous, willowy movements.

Reynolds gave her about twenty seconds, during which he finished his barely tolerable drink and rattled the ice in his glass a bit, and then he followed. He caught sight of her just as she turned the corner at the foot of the stairs, lovely from any angle. But when he reached that spot, she was not to be seen.

Swiftly, he checked the nearest exit to see if she might have taken that. Evidently, she hadn't. *Damn,* he thought, *I've slowed down a step in my old age.*

With a slight shrugging of his shoulders, Reynolds headed out onto the beach in search of Don Cooper. He discovered that the number of swimmers and sunbathers had increased since he'd last been outside. There was scarcely room for him to pick his way across the warm, white sand, detouring around bodies and towels and blankets and colorful beach umbrellas.

Reynolds found Cooper precisely where he'd left him but buried under a mound of sand with only his head and neck and one arm protruding. "Well, how's the patient?" Ed asked. "Has the swelling gone down yet?"

Cooper grinned sheepishly. "I'm afraid to look," he said.

Ed then recounted for Don's benefit the conversation between Tania Kolovich and the American.

"It sounds like Colonel Morgan was on to something," Don remarked.

"Yeah, I suppose there's a first time for everything. I guess what we ought to do is give the lady a chance to hang herself."

"How do we do that?"

Reynolds laid out a plan he had conceived in his walk across the sand.

Don Cooper liked it. He asked only, "When?"

"Check the bar this evening. I have a hunch she'll be there. And by the way," Reynolds added, "if this works out the way I think it might, you are going to owe me a very big favor."

As it turned out, he couldn't have been more wrong.

CHAPTER FOUR

Tania Kolovich was indeed in the cocktail lounge that evening, and Don Cooper was as stunned by her as he had been before. Wearing a sleek blue evening dress, open at the bodice and accented by a single strand of pearls, she was so beautiful that Don blinked twice to be certain his eyes were reporting accurately.

Walking over to her table, he found himself gaping for a time, but then he managed a "Hello there, mind if I join you?"

She smiled up at him. Long lashes fluttered, opening and closing huge brown eyes as their mistress spoke. "Not at all. I am happy to have the company, I am Tania Kolovich. What do I call you?"

"Elvin Bradley." At least he remembered his cover name. That was a good sign. He sat down. He detected the scent of her perfume, faint and yet stimulating. "Tania Kolovich, eh? Are you from—"

"The Soviet Union? Yes. Does that bother you?"

"Huh-uh. I think it's kind of exciting. I've never talked with a Russian before." God, she was lovely. "Are you working here in Thailand, or are you a tourist?" Don asked, amazed that the anxiety he was experiencing hadn't cut off his powers of speech.

"I work for TASS."

"Ah yes, the Soviet news agency." She had a very fine body.

"Actually, my occupation is—how you say—dull."

"I'm sure you're being modest." The waitress came by then, and Tania ordered Chardonnay. Don followed suit.

"And you, Elvin? What do you do?"

"Me? I'm with the 83rd Radio Research Special Operations Unit in Bangkok. That's an army outfit. I'm a first lieutenant."

Her eyes lit up. "Yes, I've heard of your...outfit. What sort of work is it that you do there?"

"Well, right now I'm working on a special project, as part of a handpicked technical team." He lowered his voice to a whisper. "It has to do with interception of North Vietnamese communications, but I really can't talk about it." Play hard to get. That was the ticket. "It's all very hush-hush."

"Oh, I understand." She placed her hand on his. "It all sounds so exciting and—how you say—mysterious. Perhaps you could tell me *just a bit* about it. I like to have new experiences and learn new things." As Don's had, her voice dropped to a conspiratorial whisper. "I shall not breathe a word of it to anyone."

Don wrinkled his brow for half a minute or so, as though weighing the merits of her request. "Well, I guess I could tell you a couple of things without hurting anything."

She smiled, mostly with her eyes. The waitress brought two glasses of wine and collected for them. Tania insisted on paying.

Don took a big gulp of wine and then leaned in toward her. "Like, for instance, there's this Captain Jorgensen, and he's developed this new transistor that boosts the energy of our listening equipment by 50 percent."

"Fifty percent? Such an achievement."

For the next fifteen minutes, Don Cooper used his very best creative skills, throwing in a pinch of this and a smidgen of that, pulling from his memory every bit of communications data and jargon he could, being careful not to overdo it. Her facial expression told him she was buying it all. If she'd had pencil and paper, he was sure she would have been taking notes.

The conversation gradually shifted to more general topics, such as travel. Tania regaled Don Cooper with tales of journeys across Europe and also other parts of Asia. Don was mesmerized, although he once again found that the lyrics of "It's A Small World" were all floating through his head.

"Shall we go up to my room?" she suggested suddenly, her glass now empty. She tilted her head at an immensely pleasing angle.

"Uhh…" He hadn't expected that. Hoped, certainly, but not expected. "Sure, why not? You lead the way."

"All right. I shall."

Standing, Don worked to control a tremor in his knees and then followed close behind her. He realized that his problem of earlier in the day had returned and clasped his hands self-consciously in front of him.

Tania's room was much like his own. Pleasant décor. Whites and yellows mostly. Brightly tiled bathroom. Small kitchen. One chair made of teak. Vanity with mirror. Mosquito netting above the bed. Enticing view of the gulf. Also like his, the room offered up the faint smell of disinfectant, a smell he appreciated.

"Would you care for a drink?" the lady asked in a marvelously sensuous tone.

"Sure."

"Would vodka and tonic be all right? It is Russian vodka. The very best."

"Fine." With strains of "It's A Small World" dancing through his mind, he sat on the edge of the bed. Actually, he would have preferred a beer but thought she might consider him a peasant were he to say so.

"To your health," she said a moment later, handing him a drink and sitting next to him. "That is what you Americans say, is it not?"

"It sure is." When it came to toasts, that had always been Don's personal favorite. Anything having to do with health was always a big hit with him.

They sipped from their glasses for a while, not speaking, then set them on the floor. Don gazed into her eyes until he could stand it no more. Then, with all the smoothness he could muster, he took her face in his hands and kissed her a profound kiss. Tongues darted. Hands roamed. Clothes fell away. Drums rolled. Cymbals sounded. More clothes fell away.

"You want to—how you say—turn me on?" she whispered in his ear, which was now in the vicinity of her breasts.

"Uh-huh." He was enjoying the intoxicating scent of the perfume he had detected earlier.

"What I would really like, you know, is for you to bite my earlobe—gently, of course—and then suck on my neck. For me, it is the best foreplay."

"Bite your earlobe and then suck on your neck?" He wanted to make sure he had this right.

"It is the best way I can get—how you say—hot."

Immediately, Don Cooper went to work, alternately biting her earlobe and sucking on her neck, biting then sucking, then gasping for air, then more biting and sucking. He nearly had raised a welt on her neck when she insisted that he do his manly duty at once, which he did with considerable enthusiasm. She went wild, but to ensure her continued fervor, Don went right on biting and sucking. He was taking no chances.

After several more minutes and two position changes, they climaxed together in a frenzy, with screaming and shouting and swearing and scratching and limbs thrashing about. In the back of his mind, he realized she may be faking orgasm, but at this point, he wasn't about to question it.

When it was over, they lay on their sides facing each other, she still breathing unevenly, he feeling guilty for having screwed under an assumed identity.

Tania murmured, "That was wonderful."

"Mm-hmm, it sure was." Don had never known such bliss.

They both laughed for no other reason than the fact that they felt like it. "Making love is my favorite hobby," she told him."

"Everyone should have a hobby."

"I do have others. I must tell you about them sometime."

"I think I'd like that."

She raised herself up on one elbow as a sly look came to her face. "So tell me, Mr. Cooper," she said in a voice that had taken on a new quality, a toughness, "why is it that you wish to spy on me?"

"What? What do you mean?" He was caught off guard.

She hit him with a dazzling smile. "I know who you are. I have seen your picture many times in GRU photo albums. We have pictures of all American agents. You are not Elvin Bradley. You are Donald M. Cooper Jr."

"I am?" He knew it would be useless to deny it.

"You are."

"I see."

"I do not care to be spied upon."

"You don't?"

She went to the closet for a robe, a black silk number that looked as though it could have come from Frederick's of Hollywood. "No," she said, putting it on and tying the sash, returning about halfway back to the bed.

"But I'm not spying on you," he insisted, voice rasping over the words, brain churning for a way out of this. He hoped he sounded more convincing to her than he did to himself. "Honest, I'm not." His eyes darted around the room, and he began to sweat.

"Of course you are." From a pocket of the robe, Tania Kolovich produced a .32 caliber automatic pistol, which she leveled at his chest. "And now that you have given me what I want, I am forced to eliminate you."

Don's eyes went to the gun. A jolt of adrenaline exploded through his body. His throat had gone dry.

He tried to swallow, but it was impossible. "Look," he said finally, "you may think you got what you wanted from me, but you need to know that the information I gave you—that was all made-up stuff. None of it was true."

"You are right, of course." She laughed. "But I was not talking about the information."

"Oh." For a moment Don felt flattered, but only for a moment.

"I do have personal needs that require—how you say—attention from time to time. However, now I must return to business... and the matter at hand."

"Well, please don't go to any trouble on my account." Cooper gnawed at his lower lip, tasting perspiration as he did so. This was far more than he'd bargained for. Things like this just didn't happen. Not to him, anyway.

When Tania spoke again, there was a determined look on her face, and it seemed to Don Cooper that her voice was coming from a long way off. "It is clear that you have discovered my activities, mister counterespionage agent. Because I do not share in the diplomatic immunity protection afforded my comrades at the embassy, I am subject to prosecution by the Thai authorities. I could go to prison. For a very long time. I would not like that."

A nervous nod from Don. "I can't say I blame you. It doesn't sound like much fun." Sweat dripped from both of his temples.

"For that reason, I cannot permit you to live long enough to tell anyone. Please understand, it is nothing personal. In fact, I like you. But—"

"God Almighty," Cooper muttered, still unable to believe his senses. Then, trying a new tack, he said, "Say, I have an idea. Why don't we make a deal."

"A deal?"

"Yeah, a deal. *You* put the gun away, and then we'll kiss and make up, and *I'll* promise never to tell anybody about any of this."

Her beautiful brow furrowed.

He went on, "Listen, I'm going to do even better than that. I'll give you my word never to talk to anyone ever again...about anything...for the rest of my life. A vow of total silence..." He was rolling now. "Now, you can't beat a deal like that. What do you say? We'll put all this other business behind us and start over again."

"A fresh beginning?"

"Exactly."

She sat on the edge of the bed, about two feet away. "Well, I suppose I might consider it. If you were to make such a promise, that is."

"Oh, I would, I would. I do, I do."

"Not a word to anyone?"

"Not to a soul. I swear it." He was breathing easier now. The perspiration had ceased to flow. Things were looking up.

"And perhaps we could make love again sometime?"

"You bet. I'd like that a lot." He thought about that for a moment, then added, "I mean *really* a lot."

"I am sorry, Mr. Cooper, but your assurances are not enough." She had been toying with him. "I cannot afford to take the risk."

With chilling calmness, she took aim with the automatic, clearly preparing to use it in a most unpleasant way. In desperation, Cooper lunged at her, knocking her from the bed and onto the floor.

But she still had the gun. Racing for the door, Cooper yanked it open, and as his bare feet hit the floor of the corridor, a bullet carved out a chunk of wood from the doorway. Cooper cringed. Naked as a turnip, he lengthened his stride.

At Ed Reynolds's door moments later, Cooper stopped and pounded with both fists until it was opened. Reynolds's eyes widened at the sight of his friend, and he burst into laughter.

"Damn it," Cooper growled, bursting inside, slamming the door behind him, and locking it, "this isn't funny."

"What is it, buddy? What happened?"

Cooper explained quickly, all the while attempting to catch his breath, his pulse thundering so loudly he could barely hear himself talk. His face was flushed and the perspiration was back.

"Jesus Christ," Reynolds whistled when the explanation was complete. "I thought I heard a backfire a couple of minutes ago. I guess I was wrong."

Still out of breath, Cooper sputtered, "She tried to kill me once and she'll try again."

"Maybe, but you're safe here. Relax."

"Relax, he says. She knows all about me. She's seen my picture. And she wants to kill me. She probably knows about you too. Including what room you're staying in," Don whimpered. He scampered under the bed, wishing he could have some fatal disease instead. Anything would be better than this.

"Hey, Don, come on out. You're being silly, you know that. Everything's going to be okay."

Ed Reynolds felt that his friend was overreacting. In fact, he was convinced of it until two bullets smashed into the door in rapid succession.

Instantly, Reynolds dropped to the floor. For several seconds, the sound of those two shots reverberated inside his head, planting a pain there. Loud noises had that effect on him. "Shit," he muttered, angered as much by his own reaction as by the situation itself.

Ed generally found the cat-and-mouse, one-upsmanship games the US and Soviet intelligence services often played with each other to be stimulating and even enjoyable. Usually, participants on both sides approached these activities lightheartedly. But when the games involved bullets, they stopped being fun.

Four more bullets pelted against the door within the span of a few seconds. Then came a fifth. The pain in Ed Reynolds's head grew worse. He had to do something to make it stop. "What kind of gun is it?" he called to Cooper.

"A .32 automatic!" Cooper called back.

"Then she's empty."

Reynolds went to the door and opened it with such force, it almost came off its hinges. Leaping at Tania Kolovich, he knocked her over and swiftly disarmed her while she yelped, screamed, and struggled. Next, he dragged her into the room and pushed her into a chair.

Cooper crawled out from under the bed. Feeling bashful about his appearance, he clutched a blanket to him. "What'll we do with her?" he asked of Ed, casting a sideways glance toward the neutralized GRU agent.

"I'll keep an eye on her while you go back to your room and get dressed. Take the blanket with you, if you like." He laughed.

"Okay."

"Then you can make a long-distance call to Colonel Morgan. Tell him to get some Thai police over here in a hurry. We need someone with powers of arrest."

Nodding in agreement, Don noticed that Tania's robe had fallen open, exposing her breasts. He gaped. He salivated. And his erection problem began all over again. Readjusting the blanket, he left the room.

CHAPTER FIVE

At least twice each week, Ed Reynolds made a detour on his way to work so he could make a stop at the farmers' market on Sawan Road. This was a market specializing in fruits and vegetables imported from distant and exotic parts of the world. There was kiwi fruit from New Zealand. There were mangoes from India. There were figs from the Middle East. There were apples from the United States.

More specifically, there were apples from the state of Washington. Large red apples of the genus *delicious*. Crisp! Crunchy! Refreshing! Beautiful! Biting into one of those natural works of art was a great way to begin a day of combating espionage and catching spies.

Ed often thought longingly of his days in Washington State. "It doesn't rain as much in the Seattle area as people think it does," he was fond of saying to whomever might care to listen.

"Yeah, right. Whattaya call it—liquid sunshine?" was a typical response.

"No, seriously, it doesn't. I have to admit, though, it is overcast a lot of the time. It's not unusual to go three weeks without seeing the sun—sometimes even during the summer."

"Three weeks! Jesus!"

"But I have to tell you something. When the sun does come out, there's no more beautiful place on earth. There are views you can see on a perfectly clear day that are so incredible, you'd sell your soul for them."

"Really?"

"One of my favorites happens when you approach the city from the east. You've got the gorgeous Seattle skyline directly in front of you with the Space Needle off to the right. Behind that is the Olympic mountain range, snowcapped year-round. In the opposite direction, you can see the Cascade mountain range, also snowcapped year-round. And of course, the city is practically surrounded by water—Puget Sound. Lake Union. Lake Washington."

"Sounds beautiful."

"It's more than beautiful. It's stunning. It just absolutely takes your breath away."

"So how many times each year is it clear enough to see all that?"

"Five, maybe six," Ed would laugh. "But I'll tell you, if you could see it all just once in your lifetime, you could die happy."

Actually, contrary to Colonel Morgan's accusations, Ed Reynolds had no interest whatsoever in undermining the US mission in Thailand. He was far too busy focusing on ways to survive his three-year enlistment to give much thought to anything else, except for Connie that is, and maybe basketball. Scheduled to separate from duty on the 8th of August 1968, he had already begun marking off the days on a short-timer's calendar, although it was still many months away.

Way down deep, far beneath the surface, Ed Reynolds always had felt like an outsider. He was aware that what most people saw when they looked at him was a confident, almost-cocky extrovert. But there was more to him than that. Somehow, at every age, at every stage of his life, it seemed the "in crowd" was someplace else. Even when he was part of a group or club, it always seemed that some other group or club was more desirable or more important. Or cooler. A symptom of insecurity, no doubt. A character flaw. But a real feeling, nonetheless.

These days, the "in crowd" was back in the States protesting the war and staging sit-ins and other demonstrations. By way, of contrast, Ed was over here surrounded by lunatics and egomaniacs and participating in endless *apricot marmalade* drills.

He recalled his four-day stopover a few months ago at Oakland Army Base, processing station for troops about to cross the Pacific, most of them to Vietnam. On one of those days, during a lull of a couple of hours amid the forms and inoculations and the wait for a flight designation out of nearby Travis Air Force Base, Ed and a dozen or so of his fellow servicemen responded to a posted request for volunteers to donate blood. As instructed, they lined up outside the barracks at 1030 hours.

Feeling remarkably noble, they boarded a green bus with white stenciling on both sides that proclaimed *US Army*. The bus smelled old and stale, and the fabric of the seats was frayed in some places and nonexistent in others. The bus transported them to the medical center of the University of California, San Francisco, by way of the Haight-Ashbury district.

Ed had heard of Haight-Ashbury, of course, who hadn't? According to the songs, the legends, and the evening news, this district was the very heart of the counterculture. Ed wondered how accurate that image might be. As the bus made the turn onto Ashbury Street, the sidewalks were suddenly lined with "flower children," hundreds of them in tie-dyed shirts and denim vests and headbands and love beads. They shouted at the bus. They jeered. It appeared that they were angered at the intrusion of this symbol of war into their anti-war domain. Ed and his companions experienced a jolt of fear as the thought flashed through their minds that this might not be a safe situation. Tension and mumbled words of apprehension filled the air inside the bus.

Then, gradually, it appeared that the anger of those lining the street subsided, giving way to peace symbols—hand after hand held high with the first two fingers extended and separated to form a V. There were smiles too, and the occupants of the green bus started to breathe easier.

As the Haight-Ashbury district disappeared in the vehicle's rear-view mirror, Ed Reynolds tuned into his own feelings and beliefs. He loved his country, certainly, but he recognized the fact that its government was made up of human beings and was capable of occasional mistakes.

He found himself wondering how it had come to pass that the people who believed as he did were out there, and he was in here. How had that happened? He was inside, and they were outside. But clearly, once again, it was *he* who was the outsider.

⁂

Wearing a pink Hawaiian shirt and a pair of slacks that were a shade of green not found in nature, sucking on a Rolaids tablet, and with strains of "It's A Small World" dancing through his head, Don Cooper continued a description of his latest physical symptoms, speculating at some sort of kidney malfunction as the cause. His audience of Marilyn Dunn, Doug Wilson, and Ed Reynolds listened politely, taking occasional sips from their glasses of beer. This was their second after-working-hours stop this week at the Hollywood Bar on Petchburi Road. It was a clean, sparkling place with good food, good drinks, and good music. They had gone home after work and then reassembled here at 1930 hours.

Reynolds stroked his chin with an index finger. "This kidney thing—it sounds like it's mostly lower back pain?"

"Well, yeah."

"Tell me, did it begin about a week ago?"

Cooper pondered that for a moment. "Yeah, I guess so."

"About the time you and I were in Hua Hin?"

"Uh-huh. Maybe a day or two later."

"At the risk of seeming unsympathetic, let me offer an alternative explanation to your kidney-malfunction theory."

"What's that?"

"I believe the technical term is *sexus-over-extendis extremis*, resulting in strained muscles of the lower back." Reynolds did a quick scan of his surroundings to ensure no one outside of his intended audience could overhear his next comment. "Do you recall the name Tania Kolovich, former employee of TASS, currently residing in an AFSC detention center?" AFSC was Thailand's intelligence service.

Doug Wilson nodded his agreement with that diagnosis, as did Marilyn Dunn.

With a skeptical shrug of the shoulders, Cooper said, "I only wish it was that simple, but I can tell you I've got major surgery coming. I can feel it in my bones."

Wilson remarked, "Well then, I'll call Captain Doctor Swanson and tell him to start sharpening his scalpel."

Cooper shuddered and let out a short whine. "Oh. God," he whimpered.

"Aw, shut up and drink your beer," Reynolds told him with a playful poke on the arm.

"Don't look now," Wilson whispered through tight lips, "but three big, surly-looking guys just walked through the front door, and they're headed this way. Three middle linebackers tired of playing on a losing team, by the looks of them."

He indicated a trio of solidly built young men, two of them white and one black. All three had wide chests and well-developed biceps that strained at their short-sleeved sport shirts. And indeed, they did make their way straight through the crowded Hollywood Bar directly to the table of Dunn, Wilson, Cooper, and Reynolds.

But instead of confronting them as Wilson had hinted they might, one of them asked timidly, "You folks mind if we join ya? There don't seem to be any chairs left."

"Not at all," Reynolds replied. "Our table is your table."

"Hey, thanks," the young man said. "That's real nice of ya." He and his friends settled into the last remaining vacant chairs in the establishment. "I'm Randy Bowden. This here's Mike Scott," he added, nodding toward his black acquaintance. "And that's Bill Mathis over there."

Marilyn Dunn handled the introductions on behalf of the MI group. They shook hands all around with a "Nice to meet you" here and a "How ya doin'?" there. Reynolds signaled the waitress to bring another pitcher of beer and more glasses.

"Are you guys here on R & R from Vietnam?" Cooper asked.

"Is it that obvious?" Scott asked.

Wilson pointed out with a smile, "Almost everyone in here is on R & R from Vietnam. That's where these bars on Petchburi Road get most of their business. And even if it weren't for that, those spit-shined shoes would have given you away. How long are you going to be staying?"

"A week. We're stayin' at the Chavalit Hotel. We were supposed to stay at the Capitol Hotel, but they were full up." Both establishments had contracts with the US government, as did the Chao Pya Hotel.

"Where are you guys from?" Marilyn Dunn asked of the new arrivals.

Bowden answered, "I'm from Arkansas. Fayetteville. Scottie and Bill—they're from Oklahoma. Coupla' Boomer Sooners. Played football, matter o' fact."

"No kidding? What positions?" This from Doug Wilson.

"Linebackers, both of 'em. Mr. Inside and Mr. Outside."

Wilson cast a sidelong glance and a half wink at Ed Reynolds. "Linebackers, eh? Ever think about turning pro?"

"Nah," Mathis contributed. "We were good, but we weren't that good. Besides, we didn't play a full four years of ball. We had grade troubles, and then we lost our II-S deferment."

"Then Uncle Sam came to call," Scott chimed in. "And suddenly we found ourselves in Southeast fuckin' Asia."

Since his enlistment, Reynolds had become accustomed to hearing the word *fucking* used in a variety of imaginative ways. Two acquaintances from his days at Fort Holabird—New Jerseyites, as it turned out—took great pride in their ability to split words of three syllables or more and to insert the key word somewhere around the middle. Thus were born such artistic creations as "re-fuckin'-frigerator," "sub-fuckin'-marine," and "Massa-fuckin'-chusetts."

"So how do you like "Southeast fuckin' Asia so far?" Cooper asked of the R & R group.

"To tell you the truth," Scott said, "Thailand is nice, especially Bangkok. But Vietnam, man, that's a whole 'nother story. What it is—is heat and humidity and jungles and dysentery and mosquitoes and malaria. And to top it all off, they got these guys over there that shoot at you and try to blow you up with fuckin' bombs and land mines and hand grenades and shit like that."

"The man is tellin' it right," Bowden agreed. "It's the god-awful shits." He shook his head. A sad expression came across his face. "We lost a good buddy last month. He didn't make any sound. Just keeled over right there in front of us."

"Wow," Doug Wilson murmured. "How do you get over something like that?"

Mathis responded, "The really scary thing is we *did* get over it. Pretty fuckin' fast, matter o' fact. After a while, death gets to be kinda routine, y'know? People dyin' all around you constantly. And you kill a few yourself, of course. It gets so it's just no big deal any more. And that's the scary part, because it *should* be a big deal."

Reynolds bit his lip. Most of the time, the war seemed a million miles away. It was different people in a different place doing a different thing. Now, suddenly, it had all moved much closer. "How much longer?" he asked. "How much longer is this damned thing going to last?"

Mathis sighed. "Could be forever, the way things are goin'. We aren't making any progress, man. We take a little ground over here, and we lose a little ground over there. We kill a few guys in black pajamas, and they grow new ones faster'n we can kill the old ones. Charlie is everywhere, man. It's demoralizin'."

"But what about those astronomical body-count numbers we keep hearing about?" Cooper wanted to know. "It seems like we're eliminating their guys ten times faster than they're eliminating ours."

"Those numbers are bullshit, man." It was Scott. "Don't believe 'em for a minute. Ya gotta remember where they come from."

"Where's that?"

"Platoon leaders report 'em to their company commanders, and then the numbers go on up the line. Every commander from General Westy on down wants to hear big numbers. Only a damn fool would report little ones. Especially when they all do their own verifyin'." The "General Westy" comment was an obvious reference to General William Westmoreland, who headed up the US effort in Vietnam.

"Yeah, I can see it now," Bowden chimed in, "some colonel goes in to see the general and says just as proud as can be 'Sir, I'm happy to report we got us two enemy soldiers last week, plus one puny little guy in black PJs, one little old lady that we kept alive 'cause we thought she might know somethin', and three kinda suspicious-lookin' chickens.'"

That brought a laugh from the group. "Nobody's crazy enough to do that." This from Scott. "They'd have to have rice for brains."

"We can't win this war," Mathis contributed. "I don't care what anybody says. We could be there for another twenty fuckin' years and still not make a fuckin' bit of difference in anything. We might be fightin' against six-year-olds by then, but you can bet we'd still be fightin'."

Ed Reynolds was disheartened by this analysis, although he suspected it was accurate. Regardless of the rightness or wrongness of US involvement in the war, at least he'd always assumed we would win eventually. That assumption was now badly shaken. By the expressions on the faces of his colleagues from the 187th, he knew they shared this concern.

The group was ready for another pitcher. Reynolds waved to the waitress, who responded promptly.

At two-thirty that night, Reynolds was awakened from a sound sleep by the ringing of his telephone. Reynolds sat about half upright, grabbed the phone, and shouted into the mouthpiece, "Hello, goddammit, Finsky, you prick!"

"Apricot marmalade," chortled Al Finsky.

Even though still groggy, Reynolds managed what he considered to be the appropriate response. "English muffins and apple goddamn jelly, you goddamned son of a bitch!"

PART TWO

THE PRISONER
EXCHANGE

CHAPTER SIX

It is a well-established fact that since World War II, the army has been one of the United States' foremost equal opportunity employers. MI, a little slow getting started, as Ed Reynolds had noticed and commented on a number of times, began picking up steam in the mid-sixties. The 187th Military Intelligence Detachment, for example, counted an ethnic minority among its ranks. Not great but a start, at least.

First Lieutenant Douglas T. Wilson—tall, slender, and black—had his quirks, naturally. But then, who didn't? Doug was big on astrology. A Gemini himself, he knew the astrological signs of each of the other members of the unit and had worked up complete charts on several of them. He'd made a convert of Colonel Morgan, a Virgo. The CO rarely made an important decision anymore without first consulting Wilson.

"What do the stars say about it, Lieutenant?" the colonel would ask routinely.

"Jupiter is favorably disposed, sir," Wilson might respond, or "Uranus warns against it."

"That damned Uranus again," Morgan might grumble. "Always fucking things up."

Ed Reynolds, generally a skeptic where matters of the supernatural were concerned, was forced to concede that Morgan usually did a better job with Doug Wilson's counsel than without it. Reynolds liked to kid him about it, though, with frequent remarks along the lines of, "I see the CO nicked himself shaving this morning, Doug. Did you tell him to do it?"

"Nah, I told him to cut off his ear."

Wilson's ultimate goal was to become an author. He was confident that he understood the field of astrology well enough to write books on that topic. And somewhere down the road, he might even try his hand at fiction—a novel or two. That would be extremely fulfilling, and the prospect was a very exciting one!

On July 24, 1967, the 187th MI Detachment had taken one more equal-employment-opportunity plunge. They'd been assigned a special agent with the rank of sergeant and the name of Marilyn Dunn. Colonel Morgan had demonstrated his open-minded viewpoints about women by not packaging her up and shipping her back by parcel post, although Reynolds was almost certain he'd considered it.

Reynolds liked Marilyn Dunn. Even more than that, he admired her. She had self-confidence. She had a look of importance to her, especially around the eyes, and most especially when her dark hair was pulled back and she wore her reading glasses. Tall and lean, Marilyn's posture was flawless and commanding. In keeping with the customary attire of her male counterparts, Marilyn usually dressed in white or light-colored blouse and a dark skirt hitting just above the knee.

Physically, she reminded Ed of a girl he'd known in high school—Mindy Taylor. Though quite intelligent, Mindy's somewhat tongue-in-cheek motto had been "Live fast, die young, and leave a beautiful corpse." Ed had dated her for a few months and could vouch for the "live fast" part of the credo, but he'd lost track of her after high school, so he had no knowledge of the other elements.

In addition to Marilyn Dunn's other notable qualities, she had something Ed hadn't seen much of for a long time. She had brains! More than Ed himself, even. It wasn't just her doctoral degree in political science from Stanford University that impressed him. No, it was more than that. She had *street smarts*. She had moxie.

She also had a vision—a vision for how the world ought to be. She saw a world free of tension and strife, free of hunger, free of war, free of racial divisions. She saw a world in which a child in any land could expect to grow up healthy and contented in an environment of love and hope. Marilyn had political ambitions. She would make a run at congress as soon as she finished her military stint. That was the best way she could think of to advance her vision.

Her role model was Bobby Kennedy. First a fine attorney general and then a splendid senator, he would be president someday, she was sure of it. And a wonderful president he would be! If she eventually could possess half of his wisdom, a third of his integrity, a quarter of his oratory skills, and an eighth of his political savvy, that would be an achievement indeed!

Reynolds enjoyed chatting with this new special agent. Marilyn Dunn, he discovered, liked good plays, good movies (fewer and fewer these days), good books (particularly science fiction—a bit of a surprise to Ed), and good music. Her favorite writer was Frank Herbert, her favorite actor Gregory Peck (wasn't *To Kill a Mockingbird* a masterpiece?), and her taste in music ran the gamut from pop to blues to bluegrass.

Don Cooper liked Marilyn too. "How are things at the Bird these days?" Cooper had asked her one Tuesday morning shortly after her arrival. Fort Holabird had been her most recent duty station. The two were standing next to the coffee maker in the break room.

"Relative to what?"

While Reynolds found Dunn to be intelligent, Cooper found her amusing. "Relative to what." He guffawed. "That's beautiful."

"Well, as a matter of fact, nothing much has changed at the Bird," Marilyn told him, taking a sip of her coffee. She was wearing a dark-gray skirt and gold blouse. "I'm glad I'll be missing winter in Baltimore, though. I hear it can be a real bitch." It was common knowledge that at Fort Holabird, training ground for MI special agents and affectionately known as "the Bird," nothing much ever changed and winters were *always* a bitch.

Cooper replied, "Yeah, I caught the full blast of winter when I was there. Absolutely brutal. Freezing temperatures. High winds. Blizzards. Snowdrifts seven or eight feet high. It was miserable!" He tossed his now empty paper cup into the trash and then popped a Rolaids tablet into his mouth.

"I grew up in Sacramento, so that would have been a big adjustment for me. My only exposure to snow was the occasional ski trip to Tahoe."

She went back to his question of a few minutes ago. "Come to think of it, there *was* something kind of interesting that happened there just before I left."

"Oh really?"

"Yeah. An outbreak of meningitis."

"Meningitis?"

"Uh-huh."

Cooper felt suddenly strange. There was a numbness creeping slowly along his lower spine. "I see."

"My best friend had it. Almost died. I got a postcard from her yesterday, though, and she tells me she's fine now. Fortunately."

"Thank goodness."

She cocked her head. "You know, when you stop to think about it, I was pretty lucky to get away untouched. It's very contagious."

"Yeah, I've heard that. Say, what do you suppose the incubation period is for something like that, anyway?" His legs were starting to weaken. He felt a slight wobble in his right knee. He wanted very badly to sit down, but there wasn't a chair in sight. He caught the faint fragrance of Marilyn's perfume. Normally, he would have found it pleasant, but at this moment it seemed to be doing strange things to his stomach.

"I really don't know much about it, but I imagine it's a couple of weeks or thereabouts."

Cooper shifted his weight from one foot to the other, then back again, trying hard to keep from collapsing entirely. That would have erased any hope of retaining his dignity in the eyes of this new friend. "And you've been here—"

"Ten days."

"Ten days?"

"Uh-huh."

Cooper was desperate for a chair. A cot would have been even better. Finally settling for a nearby wall somewhat in need of paint, he leaned against it. "And you're sure you escaped untouched?"

"Definitely. Hmm, you know, I *did* feel a little queasy when I woke up this morning."

Cooper felt his palms go flat against the wall as dizziness swept over him. "Queasy, eh?"

"Probably just my cycle." She did a quick count on her fingers. "No, I guess it's a few days too early for that."

"Oh?" He had a pulsating headache and a cold pressure was tightening around the back of his neck. There was a ringing in his ears that made it difficult for him to hear his own voice, let alone hers. He could feel sweat emerging at his temples and on his palms. And there was a circus going on inside his stomach.

"Must have been something I ate last night," Dunn continued. "Actually, now that I think about it, I skipped dinner last night altogether, so it couldn't be that. Oh well, I'm sure it's nothing."

The following morning, Donald M. Cooper Jr. reported for sick call at the 603rd Medical Dispensary. Captain Doctor Swanson greeted him with "Well, Trooper Cooper, it's you again." The doctor folded his arms. "What is it this time?"

"Meningitis, sir."

CHAPTER SEVEN

Spencer Morgan and Ralph Owens hated each other. And yet, in another sense, they were the very best of friends. In still a third sense, they barely qualified as acquaintances.

They hated each other for belonging to competing US intelligence organizations. They were the best of friends in that they had much in common: both grew up in the Midwest—although Owens had migrated to New Haven to attend Yale University, both arrived in Thailand on the same date, and both hated communism passionately. And they scarcely knew each other in that they hadn't actually met until this very minute.

"Colonel Morgan, I presume," said Owens, rising and offering his hand to the MI man, who had just entered the conference room on the third floor of the US embassy, and who was the last of six attendees to arrive for this high-level meeting. The conference room was paneled all around in teak. A blackboard was at one end, and a large globe of the earth and a coffee pot sat on a credenza at the other. Colonel Morgan was made a bit uncomfortable by the fact that the room had no windows.

"Mr. Owens, it's a pleasure to meet you at last," Morgan said, which was the truth almost as much as it was a lie. "I've heard a lot about you." This was *entirely* true. Mostly, what he'd heard was that Owens was an egomaniac and that he couldn't be trusted.

Owens, the ranking Central Intelligence Agency operative in Thailand, was a short, balding man with gray-black hair which—Morgan noticed and found comical—resembled a wide, fuzzy horseshoe encircling the back of his head.

Morgan already knew the other individuals in the room, and he began shaking hands with them. There was General Daeng

Rachawang, commander of the Armed Forces Security Center (better known as AFSC), Thailand's intelligence arm. The general, Morgan knew, had contracted malaria several years earlier and still suffered occasional recurrences. Morgan was also aware that the general and his wife were "on the outs," verging on divorce.

"General Daeng, it's good to see you again." Morgan had always considered it strange that in the Thai culture, it is the first name, rather than the last, that is used to address someone when a formal title of any kind is involved. It had taken him a while to learn that, and even these days he occasionally embarrassed himself by slipping up.

"It is nice to see you, Colonel."

"I hope you are in good health."

"I am. It has been several weeks since my last relapse."

There was Major Panit Pattaratuma, also of AFSC, and the general's right-hand man. The major greeted him with "Good morning, Colonel. Nice day, isn't it?"

"Good morning, Major. Yes, it is."

There was Major Orville Harris, Morgan's own right-hand man, present at Morgan's invitation.

Also present at Morgan's invitation was Sergeant Ed Reynolds, the only agent with interpreter skills presently available within any of the three agencies represented at this gathering, and the only one whose hand the colonel did not bother to shake. Although both General Daeng and Major Panit spoke English, neither spoke it with much fluency. Reynolds would be called on to handle any difficult conversational problems that might arise.

Despite his diminutive stature, when Ralph Owens, the meeting's orchestrator, spoke it was with confidence and authority. "Gentlemen, thank you for coming. We have a matter of the utmost importance to discuss this morning."

All eyes turned toward the agency man.

"As you know, AFSC has taken Tania Kolovich into custody. She is due to stand trial shortly in a Thai court of law and undoubtedly will be found guilty of espionage." Owens talked slowly, so as not to lose the Asian members of the group. "That is, assuming we allow things to go that far."

Morgan arched an eyebrow inquiringly.

"One of the agency's key operatives is missing," Owens continued, getting to his feet and the point at the same time. "His name is Harold Edmondson, and we believe he was kidnapped by members of the Communist Party of Thailand."

"Why are you assuming it was the CPT?" Morgan asked.

"All the signs point to kidnapping. And to the CPT. Forced entry of his home, indications of a struggle, two sets of fingerprints inside the house which match up with known CPT agents." Noting puzzled expressions on the faces of General Daeng and Major Panit, Owens paused to allow Ed Reynolds to translate the last couple of exchanges.

Owens strode across to the blackboard, lifted a piece of chalk, and wrote the letters "CPT" such that they filled up nearly half the board. "*They* have him. And, gentlemen, *we* must get him back."

Orville Harris was next to speak. "What makes this guy so important?"

"Edmondson has been operating for the past ten months in Chiang Mai. During that period, he's turned up a tremendous amount of useful intelligence for us regarding the Communist Party of Thailand's insurgency activities in the northern sector." Apparently as an afterthought, he added, "Much of which we have deemed it appropriate to share with MI." He indicated Colonel Morgan with a nod—regarded by the latter to be a patronizing gesture—and then he sat down once again.

Spencer Morgan smiled, remembering how much the CIA had deemed it appropriate *not* to share. It seemed to him that cooperation among the various US intelligence services was at best poor, and at times nonexistent. Morgan regarded this condition as regrettable and stupid, and he typically dealt with specific instances by denying MI assistance to the offending organization.

Now seated, Owens went on, "Edmondson was about to transmit to us information of great significance when he disappeared." Suddenly, the agency man was on his feet again. "Gentlemen, not only can we ill afford to lose a man with Edmondson's contacts and capabilities, but we *must* have that information. It is *vital*."

More translation by Reynolds.

"What kind of information?" Harris wanted to know.

Owens threw the major a look that made him wilt. "For now at least, the matter is being handled strictly on a need-to-know basis."

Harris squirmed in his chair, turned red, said nothing.

No doubt thinking it odd that Harris's brief humiliation should bring a smile to the face of Ed Reynolds, Ralph Owens said, "What I propose is an exchange—Kolovich for Edmondson. Straight up."

Doubt registered on several faces as Owens sat down again, folding his arms. Spencer Morgan started to say something but thought better of it. Major Panit whispered something to the general.

Owens held out his palm, looking for all the world like a traffic cop. "Now I know what you're all thinking. You're thinking the CPT would have no possible interest in Tania Kolovich. And that is correct. However, I can assure you the *GRU* would be quite happy to have her back, so they can quietly spirit her out of the country."

"Not to mention the advantage they would gain for their government by avoiding a hell of a lot of negative publicity that a trial would bring," Morgan contributed. He saw where Owens was heading, and he was beginning to buy in.

Owens acknowledged Morgan's comment with a sideways nod. "I'm afraid it is also true that the Soviets and the CPT are not currently on the best of terms. That is unfortunate. But, gentlemen, this appears to be the only game in town. If you are in agreement, I will send a communiqué to the Soviet ambassador proposing such an exchange. He can relay the message to the GRU chief."

The GRU chief, Morgan was aware, used the cover identity of assistant army attaché for the USSR. "And after that?"

"After that we wait to see what the GRU can work out with the CPT."

"You are forgetting one thing." This from General Daeng Rachawang when Reynolds had finished translating for his benefit.

Owens couldn't imagine that he had forgotten anything. He had studied it all so carefully. "What do you mean, General?"

"We of AFSC have...not yet agreed to turn over our...prisoner to you. She has committed serious...crimes within the borders of our nation. Espionage and attempted murder. We have our own...interests to consider. In other words"—he paused, evidently searching for the right phrase—"what is in it for us?"

Grimacing, Ralph Owens cocked his head. "You want to know what's in it *for you?*"

"Correct." The general settled back into his chair, a look of smugness overtaking his face.

This was a complication Owens obviously had not foreseen, and he became visibly perplexed. A heavy sigh escaped from him as he slumped in his chair. Colonel Morgan leaned over and whispered something in his ear. Finally, Owens said to the general, "We will be prepared to make you an offer by tomorrow."

"Very good."

"We will all meet here again tomorrow at the same time."

"Of course."

They all went their separate ways, AFSC having put the bite on MI and the CIA, who wanted to make a trade with the GRU, who would probably end up putting the bite on the CPT, in order to enable them to complete the trade with MI and the CIA, which of course they would all very much want to do.

During the remainder of the day, while Spencer Morgan and Ralph Owens sat in Owens's austere and unfriendly office discussing possible approaches for bargaining with the Armed Forces Security Center, Morgan wondered what sort of information Harold Edmondson was about to transmit to the agency when kidnapped. Why was it so important that Owens was willing to go to any lengths to obtain it?

The agency man broke away long enough to dispatch a courier to the Soviet Ambassador with the communiqué decided on earlier. "We may as well get that part of the plan started. It'll take them a while to contact the CPT and make their arrangements."

"Good idea."

When Owens returned fifteen minutes later, he announced, "The communiqué is on its way."

"Great."

"Now, let's see what ideas we can come up with." Owens picked up a pen and a pad of paper, preparing to begin a list.

"Right."

A number of plans for obtaining Tania Kolovich were advanced. Included among the possibilities were: offering AFSC ten thousand dollars cash for her; offering five hundred shares of AT&T stock; kidnapping General Daeng and exchanging him for her; offering to share with AFSC certain key pieces of intelligence, hitherto an unheard of practice; or hijacking a Thai Airways jet and holding it for ransom.

Colonel Morgan wished that Lieutenant Wilson were available for an astrological consultation. He always felt more comfortable operating under Wilson's astrological guidance when confronted with important decisions.

Late that afternoon they agreed on a plan. It would be an offer of money plus a Land Rover. The AFSC folks had been envious for quite some time of MI's fleet of four Land Rovers, evidently unable to afford one themselves.

"We should have a secondary offer available, though," Owens stated, "in case they don't go for this one." He ran a hand from his forehead back over the crown of his head, a signal that his thought processes were fully engaged.

"You're right. It's always good to have a backup plan."

The alternative offer they agreed to was the sharing of all available information regarding insurgency activities in the southern sector, which had been selected simply because far less intelligence had been accumulated pertaining to this sector than any of the others.

At the meeting the next day, all parties were present, including Ed Reynolds. Greetings were exchanged, coffee was poured, and doughnuts were consumed. General Daeng Rachawang had four of the latter, then licked his fingers. "Delicious," he remarked.

The CIA and MI made their initial proposal. "Ten thousand dollars—that's two hundred thousand baht—and a Land Rover."

General Daeng shook his head.

"Very well," Owens said without missing a beat. "We have an alternative offer that I'll explain." Then he did so.

The general shook his head once again. "I am sorry. We cannot consider it." It was clear that he was enjoying this.

Owens let out a sigh of exasperation. "Then what *would* you consider."

Daeng did not hesitate. "All that you have offered is good. And that is what we want. *All* that you have offered."

Morgan threw a questioning glance at Owens, but General Daeng was not yet finished. "*And two* IBM typewriters."

Owens and Morgan held a hurried but private discussion. Then the former straightened and said to the general, "We will agree to everything but the Land Rover. And as far as the money is concerned, we will give you seven thousand dollars instead of ten."

General Daeng, obviously an old hand at the time-honored Thai tradition of *taw rakaa*, was not to be out-bartered. "We must have the Land Rover and the ten thousand dollars. We will give up one of the IBM typewriters."

"You must give up *both* of the IBM typewriters and two thousand dollars," Owens insisted, drumming his fingers on the table.

"We will give up one IBM typewriter and…five hundred dollars."

Owens looked at Morgan, who gave a slight shrug. "Oh Christ, all right. It's a deal."

"Very good."

Using Reynolds as interpreter, Owens and Morgan worked out the details with Major Panit. The goods would be delivered to AFSC headquarters at 1600 hours that afternoon. Tania Kolovich would be delivered to CIA headquarters, also known as the US embassy, at 1700 hours.

The embassy location had been insisted on by Ralph Owens. The original suggestion had been the Chairanee Building, home to the 187th but Owens, evidently fearing the possibility of a double-cross of a new kind from a new quarter, had nixed that. It appeared he was taking no chances.

That afternoon, Ed Reynolds started the engine of the agreed-upon Land Rover, an IBM electric typewriter beside him in the front seat. He headed in the direction of AFSC headquarters.

In a separate vehicle, Major Harris, accompanied by First Lieutenant Irving Bonner, swung by the US embassy to pick up an attaché case which Owens had left for them with the marine on duty at the front desk. In the case was ninety-five hundred dollars converted to Thai currency. The case also contained eight file folders filled with carbon copies of documents dealing with CPT activities in the southern sector of the country. Some were marked *confidential*, some *secret*, and others *top secret*.

Then Harris and Bonner too were off to AFSC. They parked immediately behind Reynolds and the Land Rover. Instead of waiting for the Americans to come inside, the AFSC general came out to greet them, wearing a large smile. "You are most generous," he said, bowing from the waist.

Harris was about to say something—something unpleasant, by the look of him. Irv Bonner wisely cut him off with "We'll trust you to keep your part of the bargain, General."

General Daeng bowed once again. "Of course."

At precisely five o'clock, a black Mercedes turned from Wireless Road into the driveway of the US embassy. Inside was Tania Kolovich, escorted by Major Panit and a corporal. The corporal was at the wheel. As the three got out of the car, Tania appeared to be irritated and confused by it all.

She demanded of Owens and Morgan, who greeted her at the front steps, "What is the necessity of shuffling me from place to place like an unwanted package?"

Owens's response was curt. "You're going to be part of a trade."

"What sort of trade is this you speak of? Apples for oranges? Lettuce for tomatoes? An old automobile for a new?" She gave him the sharpest of stares. "Do I appear to you as a—how you say—Chevrolet?"

"No," Owens admitted that she did not resemble a Chevrolet.

"Then, what sort of trade?" she persisted.

"A very important one." Owens would say no more. At his signal, a pair of marines appeared and marched the lady at a brisk pace inside the building and upstairs to the third floor. There, she would remain under the guard of armed marines until arrangements with the GRU could be completed.

At the front door, as Spencer Morgan was preparing to depart, he said to Owens in a low tone, "I hope to hell Edmondson's report is worth all this trouble."

"It is. Believe me, it is."

Spencer Morgan could not have known that Edmondson's report would change his life forever.

CHAPTER EIGHT

Reynolds was not a religious person. Raised a Lutheran, he had broken away from the church quietly in his late teens, having become convinced that, out of a need to explain his own existence, man had created God rather than the other way around. But Reynolds respected the rights of others to believe or worship as they saw fit, or not at all.

Setting down the Sunday edition of the *Bangkok Post*, one of the city's two English-language newspapers, Reynolds took a few minutes to wonder which members of the detachment did hold religious beliefs and might be attending a religious service somewhere at—he glanced at his watch—this very moment.

He knew that Colonel Morgan was a staunchly religious man, as was the First Sergeant—a pair of zealous Catholics. Reynolds had it on good authority that Morgan was involved in an affair with a married woman. He wondered how that played out in the colonel's weekly confessions.

Don Cooper, on the other hand, was a nonpracticing Methodist. He continued to hold beliefs but didn't follow up on them. Marilyn Dunn, Ed discovered, developed during her college years what seemed to be her own personal, stylized religion. She believed in a Supreme Being, but it was not the God of Christianity or the Bible. It was an all-encompassing, universal consciousness that just kind of kept an eye on things.

"Well, how does that work exactly?" Ed had asked.

"This is not a jealous God or a punitive God," she had explained patiently. "This is simply a power greater than we are that guides us and shapes our destinies. If we simply learn to tap into that power through meditation and similar activities, it will guide us in wise and positive directions."

On a hunch he had asked her, "Do you believe in reincarnation?"

"Of course. Doesn't everyone?" she'd asked with a sly smile.

"Well, naturally." He'd laughed.

"And by the way, I prefer the term 'multiple lives.'"

Reynolds once had asked Cooper if he knew what religion Major Harris might belong to.

"*Religion?*" Cooper had exclaimed, sipping from a bottle of Coca-Cola. "I'm not even sure what *species* he belongs to." This response was followed immediately by a subtle belch.

But what of the others? What of Doug Wilson and Irv Bonner, for example? What of Captain Scharfenberg? What of Al Finsky?

Despite his own lack of beliefs, Ed Reynolds took considerable pleasure in learning about the religion of his host country—Buddhism. He enjoyed wandering through the various temples of Bangkok, especially in the company of Kanlaya Chanyangam. She made an excellent guide.

Once, she even brought along her father. Tawan Chanyangam, professor of foreign languages at Chulalongkorn University, had just returned from one of his frequent lecture visits to campuses and cultural centers in various parts of the country. Ed enjoyed meeting the professor and having him along on their tour of the temples, fascinated by his scholarly and historical insights.

Wat Po and the Temple of the Emerald Buddha were Ed's favorites. He was impressed by the bright colors. Oranges, greens, whites, and golds were particularly prominent. He was fascinated by the gilded spires that were shaped to resemble serpents and, on the inside, by the smell of burning incense and the dozens of golden statues of Buddha. Standing, sitting, reclining, they were everywhere. Some were surprisingly large. All showed a fine craftsmanship that made Ed marvel.

Buddhism—a peaceful, quiet, nonintrusive, congenial, beautiful religion. Ed Reynolds liked that.

❧

Passing through the courtyard of Wat Pratart at Doi Sutep, a slightly stooped, middle-aged tall man from Dayton, Ohio, who had just removed his shoes, began following a continuous mural painting that depicted the life of Prince Siddhatta, better known as the Lord Buddha. Wat Pratart, located in Chiang Mai and thought by many to be the most impressive temple in the northern sector, was situated on the side of a mountain, requiring a long uphill drive and, after that, an uphill climb almost as long. The American was still working at catching his breath as he studied the mural's individual panels.

About halfway along, he came upon a picture of a seven-headed snake hovering over the prince. The American puzzled for a time over its meaning.

"This picture depicts the Lord Buddha in a violent storm. But he is protected by a serpent with seven heads, all hooding together above him."

These words came from behind the American on an Asian voice that was old and quaking but confident. It was a voice that handled the English language unusually well for a native Thai, meting out clear, concise phrases as though regulated by a metronome.

With eyebrows raised, the man from Dayton turned, half expecting to find at his back some distinguished professor in a three-piece suit from nearby Chiang Mai University. Instead, his gaze fell on a bent, wizened old man, an orange, religious robe draped over the left shoulder and from there encircling a tiny body.

A shining dome of a head sat squarely atop this slight frame, and the smooth, hairless surface swept downward to where the eyebrows should have been but were not. Shaved off or lost through disease or because of roots that were too old or tired to hold on anymore, they were gone. Below the ridge, deep-set brown eyes appeared as buttons enveloped in folds and wrinkles. Between the buttons was a nose that was short and thin-bridged. Lips curled back over barren gums, creating tiny, vertical lines everywhere.

"*Sawa dii*," said the man from Dayton, bowing with hands together, as he knew was the custom.

The Buddhist monk bowed in greeting, then went on, "We believe that during the storm the serpent—a cobra—hooded, arching its seven heads above the Lord Buddha to form a roof, a perfect shelter. That is why Buddhist temples incorporate serpent heads into their roof structure. It is to acknowledge Buddha's debt to the serpent."

"I've been wondering about that."

Moving with him to another scene, the monk pointed a wavering finger at it. "This panel shows Buddha's son, Rahula. It depicts him *buad pen pra*—becoming a novice monk. He is going through the lengthy ceremony."

"Do all Thai boys go through that?"

"They do, indeed. For a three-month period, they lead a life of study and meditation. In Thailand that is the custom."

The man from Dayton listened intently.

A few scenes later, they came to the end of the story. "At the age of eighty, after a life of dedicated teaching and good works, the Lord Buddha died and was cremated. But his disciples carried on the work, spreading his philosophy of peace and brotherly love throughout all of Southeast Asia, and many parts of China and Japan as well."

The man from Dayton thanked the orange-robed monk for his narration and for his concern over a Westerner's understanding of the Buddhist religion.

"*Mai pen rai,*" the old man responded, bowing. "I must depart now. My students await my return. Always they are impatient for learning."

Pressing his palms together, the man from Dayton bowed also. Then he left the temple, regaining his shoes at the entrance.

At about that same time, another man approached the monk. He was a stout man wearing glasses and with a face that was distinctly Chinese. Bowing at the waist, he said, "*Sawa dii, taan* Koekong. *Sabai dii ryy?*"

"*Sabai.*"

Continuing to speak in Thai, the man stated, "I bring you sad news, *Taan* Koekong. The Soviets have this morning abducted Somtob Tajarunsak from his very home."

"Somtob Tajarunsak? That is alarming news, indeed. He is one of our most valued agents. Why would our allies, the Soviets, do a thing such as this?"

"Tacked to Somtob's door was a note offering to trade him back to us for the American, Harold Edmondson."

"Hmm." The old man stroked his leathery cheek. "Why do you suppose they want Harold Edmondson?"

"I do not know. But they must want him quite badly to take such a drastic step against the Communist Party of Thailand, a supposed friend."

The old monk continued to stroke his cheek. "I wonder if they want him badly enough to—the Americans have an expression for it—sweeten the pot."

His associate was puzzled by this. "I do not see—"

"Would they, for example, be willing to include in the bargain such items as automatic rifles? Ammunition? Plastic explosives?"

The face of the Chinese man brightened. "Ahh, a most intriguing thought."

"How are arrangements to be made for the exchange?"

"The note stated that we are to contact Andreyev Ivanovich at the Soviet Consulate here in Chiang Mai this afternoon and arrange to deliver the American."

As the monk nodded, a strange smile came to his lips, and he rocked back and forth on the balls of his bare feet.

At three o'clock, the Chinese man was seated in the office of Andreyev Ivanovich, a hulking bear of a man with hair whiter than aspirin. "That is correct," the Chinese man was saying. "In addition to the return of Somtob Tajarunsak, we must have forty automatic rifles, ten thousand rounds of ammunition, seventy-five pounds of plastic explosives, and one copy machine."

"But that is preposterous!" the Russian blustered. How had the CPT suddenly grown so bold, he wondered, as to make such demands?

"Those are our terms."

The Russian fumbled nervously with some papers on his desk, stapling a handful of them together in no particular order. "You will have to excuse me, then, while I place a telephone call to the Soviet embassy in Bangkok. I myself do not have the authority to enter into such an agreement. I'll need to obtain that from my superior."

"Very well." The Chinese man left the room, and he sat in a chair in the hallway with arms folded, preparing to wait. He closed his eyes and recalled pleasant memories from his youth in Peking. He skipped over the less-pleasant ones.

Then he recalled his relocation to Thailand, a move that had worked out very well for him in many ways—the warmer climate, for example.

Ten minutes later the door opened, and he was beckoned to reenter. He did so and sat down. Ivanovich, a severe frown on his face, said, "We accept your terms."

"Excellent."

"We will require some time to transport everything you have asked for. It should be here by tomorrow at noon." In truth, Ivanovich expected it to arrive considerably earlier.

"Shall we say one o'clock, to be on the safe side?"

"Yes. One o'clock," Ivanovich said.

"Shall we say Wat Pratart at Doi Sutep?"

"But that is so public. All right, but it will have to be handled very discreetly," Ivanovich commented.

"Of course. And shall we say—no tricks?"

"No tricks," Ivanovich lied.

"Until tomorrow then." The Chinese man rose from his chair.

"Until tomorrow."

At twelve-thirty the following day, two GRU agents and three agents of the KGB arrived at Wat Pratart. An old monk watched them from a balcony as they stationed themselves at various locations around the temple and the courtyard, evidently trying to be inconspicuous. It seemed the Soviets were up to something.

One by one, during the next fifteen minutes, two GRU agents and the three agents of the KGB vanished. Their disappearance came about quietly and without fanfare. It was as though they had never been there.

When the last was taken care of, dragged into a storeroom and tied up, the old monk laughed. It was for just such emergencies that he kept a container of chloroform in his quarters. Ah, he thought, the wisdom of the Lord Buddha is miraculous indeed, but modern medicine also has much to offer.

At twelve fifty-eight, Harold Edmondson arrived in the company of two CPT escorts. At three minutes past one, Somtob Tajarunsak showed up in the company of a pair of GRU agents.

One of the CPT people asked, "Where are the weapons, the ammunition, the explosives, and the copy machine?"

The taller of the GRU men, a lanky individual by the name of Josef Podgorny, dressed in a dark suit so large he seemed to be swimming in it, rolled his eyes about furtively. It was as though he was expecting some sort of help.

With an edge to his voice, Podgorny answered, "It is all down at the bottom of the stairway in the parking lot inside a blue panel truck." While he swallowed hard, he fished something from his pocket. "Here are the keys."

The Asian accepted the keys and gave Edmondson a push in the direction of the Russians. Podgorny, in turn, gave Somtob Tajarunsak a push, still using the corners of his eyes to survey his surroundings. He never had intended for the trade to go this far. He had expected they would have it all by now.

But at least they did have Harold Edmondson. At least they would be able to complete the exchange with the Americans. At least they would be able to get Tania Kolovich back. Podgorny hoped his superiors would agree that this was good enough.

CHAPTER NINE

"Move aside, motherfucker."

Ed Reynolds, waiting at the crosswalk in front of the Erawan Hotel, turned to find an elderly woman in loose-fitting, blue silk clothes and a straw hat, coming up behind him. She was carrying two large pots of steaming vegetables suspended from either end of a five-foot pole, which was supported in the middle by one scrawny shoulder.

"*Khawtod na khrop,*" Reynolds said, excusing himself politely for being in the way. "*Sabai dii, ryy?*"

"*Sabai dii,* cocksucker," the old woman replied somewhat less politely as she elbowed her way past him and out into the crosswalk.

Not for the first time, Reynolds was reminded of the contrasts presented here in Bangkok by the simultaneous existence of the old world and the new. The people themselves exhibited this dichotomy, as did surroundings that offered continual contradictions.

Tall, modern office buildings looked down at clogged streets and bustling sidewalks. Sprawling department stores, magnificent gourmet restaurants, architecturally superb movie theaters, and elegant hotels such as the Erawan, shared time and space with dilapidated shanties, muddy canals, rickety food stands, and wildly decorated trucks hauling produce to market.

And there were temples—ornate Buddhist temples with soaring spires and gilded roofs, resplendent with gold, orange, and green hues, filled with statues and incense and tourists and orange-robed monks with shaved heads. It was at the Temple of the Emerald Buddha during his second week in Thailand where Ed Reynolds had met Kanlaya Chanyangam, who, after two dinner invitations and one movie, was to become his girlfriend.

On the new-world side of the ledger, Reynolds was astounded and often frustrated by the traffic congestion. It was severe and it was constant. He'd heard it said, and could easily believe, that in all the world, only Tokyo and Rome were worse than Bangkok.

As in Rome, all the major intersections in the city were characterized by traffic circles—sometimes called roundabouts—with multiple lanes of automobiles spinning around a hub of concrete, grass, and an occasional statue, each driver searching for the proper exit point, lane by lane. Traffic circles, like giant centrifuges spinning perpetually, made even the shortest of drives a thrill-producing adventure.

He was amazed too by the intricate system of canals—called *klongs* by the Thais—connecting all parts of the city. Boats used the waterways in much the same way as cars used the roads, only more efficiently and more in keeping with traditional Thai ways.

"They call Bangkok the Venice of the East," Doug Wilson had remarked to him a while back.

"I can see why," Reynolds had agreed. "But you know, there are times when it reminds me of some American city."

"Yeah, me too."

"It's very Westernized." Reynolds hadn't meant that as a compliment or a criticism, but simply an observation.

"I know what you mean. Sometimes I get the feeling I'm back in Kansas City. But then I hear someone say *sawa dii*, and I suddenly remember I'm clear on the other side of the planet. It jars me back to reality."

The style of dress ran the old-world/new-world gamut as well. Miniskirts had burst onto the Bangkok fashion scene recently and in a very big way, and those women who chose to shun the traditional garb of silk smock and pantaloons usually wore cotton blouses and miniskirts made of lightweight wool.

Likewise, the men either dressed traditionally, or they wore business suits. On warmer days, the business suits were likely to give way to dark slacks, short-sleeved white shirts, and narrow neckties, not unlike the attire of the special agents of the 187th Military Intelligence Detachment.

That was Bangkok. With only a few exceptions, such as Coca-Cola, which was virtually everywhere, most of the other regions of Thailand showed little evidence of Western influence. To Ed's way of thinking, that was good. Western ideas were fine for the Western world, but he hated to see them corrupting Eastern people, as had happened to a great extent in Bangkok. He liked Eastern people just fine the way they were, thank you very much. And he enjoyed getting out of the city as often as possible so he could meet and learn about people that he considered real Thais.

Reynolds envied Irv Bonner. On his way to Korat in one of the unit's Land Rovers, Bonner was to conduct a surprise security inspection of the US Army facility at that location. He'd be there for several days. Reynolds gladly would have gone in his place if he'd been given the opportunity, which he hadn't, thanks to Colonel Morgan's biases.

He had a strong hunch that Bonner, who commented outside Major Harris's office after learning of the assignment, "I know that road, and there's a snake every three and a half meters of it," would have been agreeable to stepping aside.

Reynolds was far from disappointed to learn that he was to be left out of the Kolovich-Edmondson exchange. For one thing, he was busy with several other projects. For another, Major Harris was to be in on it, which in and of itself was reason enough for anyone in his right mind to want to be left out of it. Still, Reynolds did wonder about the information in Edmondson's report. He hoped it was worth all this trouble.

And so it was that, at 1300 hours on December 5th, Major Harris and Captain Scharfenberg of the 187th MI Detachment; Ralph Owens of the Central Intelligence Agency; and Tania Kolovich, recently apprehended Soviet spy, climbed into a Land Rover and headed for Sattahip. Harris carried with him a salami sandwich and a six-pack of beer. Owens brought a deck of cards. Each of the men wore charcoal-colored slacks, short-sleeved white shirts, and narrow neckties with diagonal stripes of varying hues. But for the varying hues, one might have thought they'd coordinated their attire in advance by telephone. Although his attire was consistent with the others, it was obvious to everyone that Orville Harris had neglected to shower. For her part, Tania was dressed in a navy skirt and a pale-yellow blouse. The Americans were armed, just in case, each with a .38 caliber Smith & Wesson Detective Special.

Colonel Morgan would have gone along in place of the captain but for the fact that this was Thursday and his availability was always limited on Thursdays. It was widely rumored that every Thursday after lunch, Morgan rendezvoused with Maureen Meadows, wife of Major Carl Meadows of OSI, for an afternoon of unbridled passion.

Sattahip, approximately eighty kilometers southeast of Bangkok, had been selected as the exchange site because of its remoteness. The exchange was to take place at 1415 hours at a spot three hundred meters past the Songkran turnoff, making it just outside the city limits.

The Americans were on time, but the Soviets were late. While they waited, the Americans had ample opportunity to survey their surroundings. On their side of the road was an extensive rice paddy stretching off into the distance. On the opposite side of the road was a six-foot stone wall, serving as the edge of what appeared to be a carefully landscaped lot, with a number of attractive tall trees and shrubs visible above the stones. Splayed across the wall from one end of it to the other was a massive amount of bougainvillea, spilling its scarlet blooms in every conceivable direction. Back in the direction of the town of Sattahip, the cobalt sky was punctuated by an occasional palm tree with fronds rustling in the warm but gentle breeze.

The Americans were aware that the wall constituted the eastern boundary of the huge estate of Ling Wansoo, the wealthiest banker, businessman, and land baron in this part of the country. They also were aware that Ling Wansoo and his entire family were in the middle of a four-week vacation in Switzerland, leaving the estate deserted except for two East Indian guards posted at the main gate more than a kilometer away, and one overworked gardener.

Ralph Owens and Quincy Scharfenberg whiled away the minutes by playing gin rummy in the front seat. Orville Harris whiled away the minutes by drinking beer and making passes at Tania Kolovich in the back seat. Tania, however, was too quick for him, dodging here and squirming there, barely escaping his lustful fingers.

Harris scowled in frustration. "Hold still, dammit," he told her.

"Huh-uh," she said. "You have a peculiar—how you say—odor. You stink, cowboy."

A dark-gray Chaika with USSR embassy license plates pulled up behind them. The driver switched off the engine, but no one got out. Three of the occupants, all wearing dark business suits, seemed to be huddled in conference, while the fourth, a slender man with thinning hair and wearing a purple Hawaiian shirt, remained seated upright, eyes focused straight ahead, evidently surveying the Land Rover and the prospect of freedom.

Inside the Land Rover, Captain Scharfenberg asked of no one in particular, "Do you suppose we should get out first?"

"Hell, no!" Owens thundered. "Let *them* get out first."

Ten minutes passed and Scharfenberg asked again, "Don't you think we should—"

"We wait," Owens interrupted.

Another fifteen minutes went by. Inside the Chaika, speaking in Russian, Vasili Federova said to Nikolai Menevich, "It does not appear that they are going to get out of their vehicle. Perhaps we should make the first move."

Menevich, stocky but trimmer than either of his associates, replied, "Do not be absurd, comrade. To do as you propose would be quite foolish. There is every possibility that the Americans have some trick planned. We will be safer here in our automobile." He reached inside his coat pocket and nervously fingered the butt of an automatic pistol. This act made him feel infinitely more secure.

"You are most probably correct, comrade," his colleague agreed. He returned his attention to the vehicle parked in front of them.

In the Land Rover, Major Harris was fumbling with the .38 revolver tucked inside his belt and mumbling, "Well, *I'm* ready for the sons o' bitches, whatever they're up to." Of Owens, he asked, "What do you suppose they're up to, anyway?"

"Damned if I can figure it out. I thought they'd be over here by now. Or at least meet us halfway."

Scharfenberg ventured, "Maybe we should—"

"No," Owens interjected, "we can't take the chance. We'd be defenseless out there. We'd be at their mercy. Sitting ducks. They could pick us off like clay pigeons."

"But maybe one of us could just walk up to their window and talk to the bastards and see—"

"Forget it," Owens said tersely. "That's a good way to get an ass full of lead. You just can't trust those goddamned Russians."

"Well, maybe one of them will come over here and talk to us," Scharfenberg offered, a note of optimism in his voice.

"I hope one of them does," Major Harris remarked. "I'll blow the motherfucker's head off."

Another twenty minutes passed. Inside the Chaika, Vasili Federova commented to anyone who would listen, "It does not appear they are going to get out of their vehicle."

"That does seem to be the case," someone else conceded.

The slender American fidgeted, mumbled something, and was promptly told to keep quiet because the whole thing was none of his business, anyway.

"What shall we do, comrade?" Federova asked of Menevich.

"We must think out and plan our next move very carefully. We cannot afford to be hasty. One miscalculation, and our families could be mourning each of us tomorrow."

A half hour later in the Land Rover, Orville Harris once more began making passes at Tania Kolovich. He had her half out of her blouse when Ralph Owens reached back and smacked him on the ear with an open hand.

"Ow!" Harris yelped. "What was that for?"

"For being an idiot. We've got more important things to be thinking about."

"Oh."

"Say, I have an idea that might work," Scharfenberg volunteered.

"Yeah? What?" This from Harris, now testy.

"We could hold up a sign in the rear window instructing them to push Edmondson out of their car on our signal—a honk of the horn—and we'd push Kolovich out at the same time, and they could just change places on their own. Or even better yet, they could each stay put and the vehicles could circle around and change places. The beauty of it is none of *us* has to get out."

Everyone agreed this was a good idea.

"Does anybody have a sheet of paper or anything to write with?"

"No," replied Ralph Owens.

"No," replied Orville Harris.

"No," replied Tania Kolovich.

"Shit," sighed Quincy Scharfenberg.

Inside the Chaika, someone had come up with a similar idea. A search for writing materials turned up two inkless ballpoint pens and one used envelope. The GRU agents were disgruntled. Their prisoner was exasperated.

"Look, fellas," Edmondson said earnestly, "why don't I just get out and walk over to them? I'll open the door on the lady's side and let her out. She'll walk over here and get in, and we'll be all set. Whattaya say, guys?"

All three of his escorts told him to keep quiet because it was none of his business, anyway.

Another hour and fifteen minutes went by. Inside the Land Rover, Orville Harris said, "I gotta piss."

Owens responded, "Well, then, get out and do it."

"I can't. It could be dangerous out there. And besides"—he gave a sideways nod in Tania's direction—"she'll see me."

"Oh for Chrissake! You'll just have to hold it then."

"But I can't," Harris wailed. The six-pack of beer had caught up with him.

Scharfenberg had an idea. "Maybe I can sneak out and pry off one of the hubcaps. You could piss into that, sir."

Owens interjected a question. "Are you sure Land Rovers have hubcaps?" He was growing weary of Scharfenberg's ideas.

"Hmm." Scharfenberg craned his neck, pressing his forehead against the window, peering outside and downward.

A half hour later, suggestions and decisions became academic as Orville Harris's face contorted and reddened and his bladder gave way. He proceeded to wet his pants in a most unmilitary manner.

"Oh!" Tania Kolovich shrieked. "Get me away from this—how you say—asshole!" She clambered into the front seat, tumbling head-first into the lap of Ralph Owens.

"You're wet," Owens complained to her.

"It is not my fault. Blame your friend, the pig back there!" She pointed an accusing finger over her shoulder at the major.

Two hours more went by. The Chaika occupants had found an effective method for relieving themselves—a vodka bottle, which among them they twice filled and emptied into a ditch outside the window. They all agreed that a vodka bottle was an appropriate receptacle for Russian urine.

"It does not appear that they are going to get out of their vehicle," Vasili Federova commented, scratching his head through fuzzy short black hair, unaware that this was the sixteenth time he had shared this particular observation. With the nail of a chubby index finger, Federova picked something from between his teeth—a bit of poached egg that his slimy, beefy tongue had missed at breakfast, was Nikolai Menevich's guess.

"Indeed it does not," Menevich replied, thinking what an incredible dolt he had for a subordinate.

For that matter, Tito Bularin, the third member of the Soviet group, was not exactly a mental giant. Bularin had once been described by his wife at an embassy party as a lame-brained lummox. She was highly intoxicated at the time, but even so, Menevich could scarcely disagree. Bularin was napping now, fat chin tucked securely into his chest and the white shirt and hideous green necktie that covered it, a subdued snore emanating from wide nostrils. Somehow, Menevich found him less revolting asleep than awake and so chose not to disturb him. All in all, Bularin's greatest strength was his tendency to spend long periods of time in silence or slumber.

"Perhaps we should consider making the first move," Federova offered.

"An absurd suggestion, comrade."

Inside the Land Rover nearly 150 minutes later. Tania Kolovich had cautiously returned to the back seat, and Captain Quincy Scharfenberg had piled up points playing gin rummy with Ralph Owens. Owens was down ninety-six dollars and wasn't being the least of a good sport about it.

"Are you sure you've been dealing those cards from the top of the deck?" Owens challenged, directing a malevolent stare at the young captain.

"Why, yes, of course. I wouldn't know how to deal any other way." Scharfenberg was dismayed over the insinuation.

"Bullshit."

"But sir—"

"Bullshit."

"But—"

"I said *bullshit.* Now shut up and give me the deck. It's my deal." Owens's necktie had been loosened, and perspiration was soiling his collar.

"Yes, sir."

The sun went down in as beautiful a fashion as Tania Kolovich had ever seen, becoming a splash of orange and vermillion in the western sky. A sense of drowsiness was replaced for her by a sense of wonder, as she took a few moments to appreciate the splendor of it.

Darkness made it difficult for the card players to read their hands. Finally, Owens threw his to the floor in disgust. "Dammit! Can't see a damned thing, dammit!"

Inside the Chaika, Vasili Federova said, "It does not appear they are going to get out of their vehicle."

"Indeed it does not," Nikolai Menevich mumbled.

"Does anyone have any ideas?"

"I have one."

"Yes?" Federova was excited. An idea, at last.

"Start the engine."

"The engine?"

"Yes, we are departing."

Twelve seconds later, one of the Land Rover people shouted, "Look!"

Everyone looked. "They're leaving!"

The Chaika was out of sight in less than a minute.

"I knew it," snorted Ralph Owens, the color draining from his face. "You just can't trust those goddamned Russians."

"Yeah," Harris agreed. "The commie bastards."

Colonel Morgan was furious the next day in his office when he heard the details of the Sattahip debacle and the pitiful performance of his men. "You shitheads!" he roared. "You goddamn stupid shitheads! How could you be such idiots?" The colonel vented his anger on Captain Scharfenberg and Major Harris, in that Ralph Owens was not present, and of course Morgan would not have had the nerve to talk like that to the agency station chief, anyway.

"We're sorry, sir," Scharfenberg said.

Morgan's brow puckered, and he muttered something under his breath about the good old days and strict discipline and firing squads. "Well," he said finally, his tone turning philosophical. "I guess there's no use crying over spilled milk."

"I've always felt that way, sir. I'm a firm believer in that principle."

"Shut up, Captain." Morgan scratched his nose and began to think. "What we need is a new plan."

"Yes, sir. We do, sir. That's an excellent strategy, sir."

Colonel Morgan removed a cigar from his humidor, backed his swivel chair away from the desk, and did a slow but complete rotation, deep into the thinking process. "How about this?" he said at last.

"Sir?"

"How about if we arrange at an agreed-upon time to handcuff Tania Kolovich to a telephone pole on some deserted street. We'll make it late at night so there won't be any bystanders."

To Scharfenberg, it sounded pretty silly so far.

"The Russkies handcuff Harold Edmondson to a telephone pole about a block away," Morgan continued, "but close enough that both sides are in full view of each other. Then one person from each group walks to a central point where they exchange handcuff keys, and then they go back to where they came from."

"And then, sir?"

"Then each group gets into their own car and drives around the block in opposite directions, ending up with their positions reversed. The Russkies uncuff Kolovich, and we uncuff Edmondson... And that's it. Exchange completed." He leaned back in his chair and crossed his legs. "Naturally, I'll want to bounce this off Lieutenant Wilson first to get his astrological take on it. But assuming he gives me a green light, what do you two think?"

"I don't know, sir." Captain Quincy Scharfenberg was dubious. By the expression on Major Orville Harris's face, however, he could tell that the major was crazy about the idea.

In truth, Scharfenberg thought it was the dumbest idea he'd ever heard in his entire life and would have said as much had he not been so thoroughly outranked by the room's other two occupants. "Do you think we can persuade Owens?" he asked instead.

Morgan sighed. "You just never know with that bastard, but I'll give it a try. I'll call him as soon as I finish talking with Lieutenant Wilson."

"Good," said Harris. "And if you can convince him, he can go to work convincing the Russians."

"I just hope Edmondson and his information are worth all this trouble," Morgan mumbled as Harris and Scharfenberg were leaving his office.

To Quincy Scharfenberg's surprise, Owens was persuaded, as were the Soviets. To Quincy Scharfenberg's *amazement*, the plan actually worked!

CHAPTER TEN

"I had a dream about us last night."

"Really? Was it erotic?" Ed Reynolds caught the fragrance of her perfume. Chanel No. 5, if memory served him correctly.

"No, it was an athletic dream," Kanlaya explained. "We were playing tennis."

"No kidding? How was my backhand?"

"Actually, it could use some work."

Recently, Ed found himself considering the possibility that it might be time to take the training wheels off his relationship with Kanlaya. He wasn't quite ready to make that decision, but he found himself thinking those thoughts more than ever before.

The bright-yellow, motorized *samlor* careened around the corner, nearly tipping over and throwing its passenger into the street. Righting itself uncertainly, it sped onward, darting from one lane to another, picking a path determined by gaps between cars.

The passenger's right hand, clammy with perspiration, went to his chest in an attempt to corral a runaway heartbeat. Harold Edmondson never had trusted these three-wheeled taxi contraptions peculiar to this part of the world. Behind schedule, he had selected this method of transportation only out of desperation. Ralph Owens was expecting him in the third-floor conference room of the US embassy for a debriefing at nine o'clock.

It was already a couple of minutes past that. Owens didn't like to be kept waiting, especially for important information. About three weeks previous, Edmondson had put the awaited information into a written report and had attempted to submit it to Owens as a classified communiqué. He had encoded it as an additional precaution because of its importance. Evidently it had gotten misdirected or lost.

Still being jostled from one side of the seat to the other, Edmondson leaned forward and shouted to the driver, "Slow down, please!" Edmondson was a gentle and sensitive man, unaccustomed to this kind of pounding. While it was true he was running late, he was now focused on arriving in one piece.

The driver, evidently ignoring him, launched the *samlor* into the rapid stream of cars surrounding the traffic circle at the intersection of Satorn and Rajadamnern roads. Soon, the driver had wedged his vehicle into the third orbit from the outside of the circle and was bouncing along at a speed compatible with everyone else, and then he increased it. Obviously pleased with himself, he turned and tipped his cap to his not-so-grateful passenger.

Edmondson tried again, cranking up the volume of his voice. "Slow down!"

It did no good. Perhaps the driver hadn't heard him. Just then, Edmondson noticed a turquoise-colored car pulling up alongside.

At the sound of a loud pop a few moments later, two Americans, a middle-aged couple from Minneapolis inside a rented tan Toyota several spaces back, exchanged questioning glances. "Backfire?" the wife suggested.

"I dunno," the husband responded. "Maybe."

The husband craned his neck, searching for some clue of what had happened. "Jesus," he whispered a moment later as the door of the *samlor* up ahead swung open and its passenger spilled out onto the pavement, one hand still grasping the handle. Then his momentum and that of the *samlor* caused him to release the handle and roll. Blood was spurting from his temple. "Jesus," the husband said once more.

The *samlor* kept moving forward at a rapid pace. In the next instant, the American couple were out of their car and kneeling beside the victim. One tried to stop the bleeding while the other felt for a pulse. "Nothing," the latter announced. There was no pulse, and it was clear there never would be again.

Of the dozens of automobiles all around them, few even slackened their pace. Over the ruckus, it was impossible to determine where the shot had come from. The husband stood and waved his arms, attempting to flag down one of the many motorists for help, but none paid him any heed.

"We've got to call someone," the wife said.

"You're right. *The police*, I guess." They dragged the victim to the nearest curb, and then made their way back to the Toyota so they could begin their search for a telephone.

When Ralph Owens was informed an hour later at the US embassy of Harold Edmondson's untimely demise, he threw a temper tantrum the likes of which his secretary, mother of five and grandmother of twelve, had never seen before.

Chapter Eleven

A week had passed since Harold Edmondson's dramatic exit from the land of the living. Ralph Owens and Spencer Morgan had spent the better part of that time frame pointing accusing fingers at each other, competing vigorously for the distinction of most creative blame scenario.

"You jackass!" the agency man shouted into the telephone the day after the funeral.

"Now, wait a minute," Colonel Morgan countered. *"I'm* not the one who let him go off on his own and spend the night in a hotel. *I'm* not the one who let him furnish his own transportation to the embassy the next morning, unescorted and unprotected, so some CPT sharpshooter could pick him off."

"We're short-staffed. I didn't have a choice."

"Of course you had a choice. You could have asked *us* for help, dammit!" Morgan had grown uncustomarily bold in the last few days. It was not typical for him to swear at people from the CIA.

"Yeah? Well, you can just take a flying leap, you second-class spook. You junior G-man."

That one hit Spencer Morgan where he lived. He hit back. "I'm *also* not the one who screwed up the communication in the *first* place. You should have had a *backup* plan for information *that* important."

"We did. Edmondson routinely encoded important information and put it into a written report for transmittal to us in Bangkok. He'd make a carbon copy to be filed in a double-locked cabinet in his office, and then he'd arrange for the original to be transported to us by courier."

"So then, what went wrong on *this* one? Where's the backup document? Where's the *original,* for that matter?"

"We don't know. The courier, an Asian national we've worked with for a long time—he disappeared. We assume the CPT got him. The copy is an even bigger mystery. We've been through his office, including the file cabinet, and his house, with a fine-tooth comb. Nothing."

"Could the CPT have broken into the file cabinet and stolen the copy?"

"It didn't look like it had been broken into. In fact, there was no sign that the office itself had been violated. The only signs of breaking and entering were at Edmondson's house, and undoubtedly that occurred when they kidnapped him." Owens paused for a moment, then said, "That copy is missing...but goddamn it, it *has* to be someplace... And *we* have to find it."

PART THREE

THE MISSIONARY

CHAPTER TWELVE

First Lieutenant Irving P. Bonner knew the jungle. He knew it extremely well. It was not by choice that he had acquired this familiarity. Bonner was one of a pair of Thai linguists in the outfit, Ed Reynolds being the other. Each had been trained in the language during a fifty-one-week stint at the Defense Language Institute in Monterey, California. In fact, their tours of duty there had overlapped—with Bonner's class being twelve weeks ahead of Reynolds's—and they'd developed a friendship in Monterey, which continued here.

For Bonner, the role of linguist was at first a distinction in which he took a great deal of pride. A few months in Thailand had taught him that it also was a liability that could get him killed. For in most of the upcountry clandestine missions that arose with the 187th, it was Irv Bonner who was given the job. Sometimes he had help, but it seemed he was always in the picture. And always in danger! After all, he spoke the language.

Ed Reynolds spoke the language too, but Colonel Morgan had never had much confidence in Reynolds, a fact that Bonner tried continually, desperately, to change. No product on the market ever received a more vigorous and enthusiastic advertising campaign than that which Bonner gave Reynolds. If he'd thought billboards and jingles might have made a difference, he would have used those as well.

"Now, *there's* a guy with a good head on his shoulders," Irv would say to the colonel whenever the opportunity presented itself. "Bright. Good judgment. A crackerjack of a special agent. They just don't come any better, sir."

"Humph," Morgan invariably would reply.

"And what a linguist, sir! He was tops in his class, you know. Won some sort of outstanding student award, I believe. Big plaque and everything. Speaks Thai like a native."

"Humph."

"When he and I get going in a conversation, he completely leaves me in the dust. I just can't keep up. It's really kind of embarrassing."

But nothing worked. The colonel was not impressed.

Irv Bonner, slender and with neatly trimmed blond hair, used a cover identity whenever he was on an assignment. Generally, he assumed the role of a civilian employed by the US Army Corps of Engineers as an advisor to the Thai government. This gave him a bit of authenticity as he traveled about the country, supposedly lending his road- and bridge-building expertise to various local agencies.

He had all the appropriate identification. The MI supply officer, Captain Scharfenberg, had seen to that. Irv Bonner, a shy person with more than his share of insecurity, welcomed the opportunity to be someone else now and then.

And so Lieutenant Irving P. Bonner had become the detachment's "jungle expert." Circumstances had forced the title upon him. In truth, Bonner despised the jungle. The jungle. With its mysteries. And its dangers. And its snakes.

"Thailand has a hundred different kinds of snakes," someone had told him just after his arrival here. "Ninety-nine of them are poisonous."

"And the other one?" Irv had asked with great trepidation.

"The other one *eats* you."

Even as a child, Irv had been terrified of snakes. And growing up on a farm just outside of Grand Rapids, Michigan, the most fearsome thing he ever encountered was a garter snake. And that didn't happen very often. Southeast Asia, however, didn't bother with garter snakes. A waste of time. Strictly minor league stuff. Southeast Asia was the *big leagues*! Pythons, cobras, blue kraits, hornheads, sand vipers—major leaguers all!

But it was the king cobra that made the biggest impression on Irv Bonner. It was the king cobra he feared the most. Rearing, hooding, hissing, spitting, striking, deadly, the king cobra was everywhere.

Or at least it seemed so to Irv.

Back in May, Bonner had flown to Chiang Rai, a small town near Thailand's northern border. He met with one of his contacts, an American zoologist by the name of Frank Newton. Newton, a ruddy-complexioned big man with a huge shock of gray hair, liked to chew gum, talk loudly, and laugh often.

After obtaining the information Newton had for him—information about insurgency activities in the area—Bonner allowed himself to be talked into a jeep ride.

"You haven't had a chance to see much of the territory up here yet," the zoologist stated.

"Well, I'm really not all that curious."

"Come on. It'll be great fun. My jeep's right outside."

"I wouldn't want to put you to any trouble."

"Hah! No trouble at all. If you weren't here, I'd probably go on my own, anyway."

"Uhh, well, okay."

They donned their sunglasses, and within minutes they were in the very heart of the jungle, an occasional Coca-Cola stand the only reminder of civilization's existence. Varying shades of gray marbled the sky undoubtedly adding to the humidity. The terrain reminded Irv of scenes from *The Rains of Ranchipur*. A fan of movies in general but not that one in particular, Irv tended to relate to life in cinematic terms. That trait often brought him a measure of comfort, but not quite so much in this case.

At a bend in the road, they spotted a large gray object in the tall grass to their left. Closer inspection revealed that it was a bull elephant. It was dead. Hundreds of flies buzzed around it. The unpleasant smell was overwhelming! Three hundred meters farther along the road, they came upon another elephant. And then a bit farther, yet another. All dead.

"King cobras," Newton explained nonchalantly, between smacks on a stick of Juicy Fruit gum. "They can wipe out half a herd of bull elephants in no time flat. Some of those sleazy mothers can get to be over twenty feet long. When they hood, they raise up about one-third of their body length and—"

"Jesus," Bonner breathed. He was quick with his arithmetic.

"Yep. They can lift up and zap a poor old bull right about here." Newton thumped himself on the chest with two fingertips, emphasizing the point he'd just made.

Bonner had always thought of bull elephants as stalwart creatures. Unstoppable. Immovable. Sturdy. Strong. Immortal—a thousand times more immortal than he. Somehow, Irv hadn't been the same since May.

Lieutenant Irving P. Bonner had no way of knowing that in December things would get much worse!

CHAPTER THIRTEEN

In the middle of the second Thursday afternoon in December, Spencer G. Morgan awoke from a nap with one of those armor-piercing erections that for most men come along about once every three years. Morgan, however, had been getting them more often of late. Fortunately, Maureen Meadows, a woman of considerable compassion and understanding, was nearby.

In the latter part of the second Friday morning in December, Spencer G. Morgan met with his operations officer, Major Harris, to finalize plans for Operation Hornswaggle. The major was eager to complete their discussion so he could go out to the parking lot and apply a fresh coat of polish to his Mercedes. Harris frequently disdained food during the middle part of the day, preferring instead the pleasures that came from simonizing his most precious possession.

Operation Hornswaggle would require someone to make an upcountry journey to Tradit, a tiny town in the northeast corner of the northern sector, and attempt to recruit a missionary by the name of Bernice Wiggins. Morgan and Harris had concluded that they needed to establish an ongoing supply of intelligence from that region because of a recent increase in insurgency activities. Various sources had indicated that the missionary lady was in an excellent position to provide it because of her many contacts with local villagers and hill tribesmen.

"We need to stay one step ahead of the agency," Morgan pointed out, recalling Ralph Owens's stinging remarks about the Edmondson mess and second-class spooks and junior G-men.

"I agree."

"This has got to pan out for us. Let's give this our best shot."

"Who shall we send, sir?"

"Our jungle expert, of course."

"Good choice."

"He'll have to go through Chiang Mai to get to Tradit. While he's there, I want him to take a thorough look through Harold Edmondson's office and his house too. It couldn't hurt for one more set of eyes to take another crack at finding that report." Morgan bit off the tip of a cigar, spitting the tip into an ashtray on his desk about three feet away. Pleased by his accuracy, he leaned back in his chair and lit up. "I'll clear it with Ralph Owens at the embassy, so he can give Lieutenant Bonner the access he'll need. I'm sure even *Owens* will agree it's a good idea."

And so it was that on Monday morning, Irving P. Bonner found himself on a Thai Airways DC-7 bound for Chiang Mai, first stop on his journey to Tradit. His .38 revolver, checked out from Captain Scharfenberg shortly before, was tucked securely inside his belt, disguised by a red Hawaiian shirt that hung loosely over beige cotton trousers. Carrying of a government-issued .38 was standard procedure for special agents on upcountry assignments.

In his mind, Irv went over his cover identity—Earl Sommers, civilian working for the US Army Corps of Engineers. Rehearsal was important in such matters.

As they neared the Chiang Mai airport, Irv looked out the window to see countless farms and rice paddies separated by irrigation ditches, creating a checkerboard landscape, an effect similar to magazine pictures he'd seen of Vietnam.

His eardrums approached the bursting threshold as the airplane continued its descent. Thai pilots, Irv often noted, had never mastered the art of changing elevation gradually, probably most easily explained by the fact that this was a society that had progressed from the oxcart to air travel in less than one generation.

Once the plane had landed, Irv was mildly embarrassed by a wink from one of the flight attendants as he moved toward the exit door.

"Thank you for flying Thai Airways," she said and winked again.

"Goodbye," he said with an uncomfortable smile.

Irv Bonner was the owner of an inferiority complex that dated back to the sixth grade when, running for class president, he was advised matter-of-factly by his campaign manager that he would be voting for the opposition. "I can't help it," the boy had said, "Billy is a better candidate, and I have to vote my conscience."

Irv had made some strides in recent months battling his complex. Ed Reynolds, in particular, had been very supportive in helping him build his ego. He'd encouraged him to focus on his strengths. "You're a good guy, Irv," he'd pointed out. "And you're good looking. And you're *smart*. People *like* you. Just give them a chance to get to know you."

Irv very much appreciated Ed's support and considered him a good friend.

In Chiang Mai, Irv made his way to the American consulate and checked in with the ranking CIA official there. A tall, slender man with jet-black hair and sunken cheeks, the CIA agent arranged for Irv to spend an hour scouring Harold Edmondson's office. Then he gave Irv a ride to Edmondson's home, where he spent another two hours in a stem-to-stern search. Nada. Nothing even remotely resembling the report in question. It had to be somewhere else.

From Chiang Mai, Irv Bonner caught the eastbound train and headed for Boonalok, his next stop. Warm sun, high humidity, wooden seats, slow speeds, and frequent stops to pick up any combination of men, women, children, and animals made him wish that Booanlok had an airport. For six hours he used a handkerchief to mop up perspiration. Brow. Eyes. Throat. Back of the neck. He barely could move the handkerchief fast enough to keep up.

At Boonalok, Irv spent the night in a hotel that reminded him of the house on the hill in *Psycho*. Tony Perkins was in the next room—Irv was sure of it—sharpening his knife on a grinding wheel and mumbling something about not hurting a fly.

"Are you over there, Tony?" Irv said to the wall.

There was no answer, thank God. Irv slept fitfully and dreamed at least once of little old skeleton ladies with gray wigs and sharp knives.

Irv would need to rent a taxi the next morning to complete the journey to the town of Tradit, another hundred-and-fifty kilometers to the north, a hundred-and-fifty kilometers of bad roads if the map was any indication. After a light breakfast, he made the short walk back to the train station, knowing it would be surrounded by Datsun and Toyota taxis as it had been the evening before. Dozens of cab drivers were there, fighting eagerly over prospective customers.

"Taxi, sir?" one shouted in Irv Bonner's direction.

"Over here, sir. Please, sir, my taxi is the best in all of Thailand," another claimed.

"No, no, sir. I will take you wherever you are going for the lowest price."

Bonner, he of the charitable heart, picked out an older man who appeared most in need of the money. Slightly built with wilted features, the man had the bright red lips and jagged tooth stumps of a regular chewer of betel nut, a popular hallucinogen found in many parts of Southeast Asia. When the man walked, it was with a pronounced forward lean.

"My name is Piboon," the man volunteered in a raspy voice. "Tell me where you want to go."

"Tradit. Do you know the way?"

Piboon assured him that he was very familiar with the road to Tradit, knew it like the back of his hand, in fact, although he'd never actually driven it before.

In Thailand, Bonner knew, it was customary to bargain for everything. Whether it was the price of a pineapple or the cost of a prostitute, foreigners who did not *taw rakaa* were held in very low esteem by the Thais.

"I will give you five hundred baht," Bonner stated, "for a round trip."

"Eight hundred," Piboon countered. "My children need new shoes."

"Six hundred. My mother needs an operation." This was fun.

"Seven hundred fifty. Gasoline prices are going up."

"Six hundred twenty-five. My parents just disinherited me."

"Seven hundred. Taxes went up this year."

They eventually agreed on six hundred seventy-five baht.

Piboon tossed Bonner's suitcase into the trunk of the car while Bonner himself climbed into the back seat. On their way out of town, they passed a group of youngsters playing *takra* with a wicker ball in a nearby field. Bonner envied their athletic skills and, most particularly, their coordination.

Piboon and Irv Bonner began a rough ride through the jungle over narrow, heavily rutted dirt roads. Then it started to rain, and the dirt turned quickly to mud. It rained heavily, a hot, smoldering rain, Thailand's version of a monsoon.

"Will we be able to get through?" Irv asked of Piboon.

"Sure thing. You bet."

A glance to his left just then disclosed what Irv took to be a green-horned viper draped from the branch of a large tree beside the road. He shuddered.

A short time later, the latch on the trunk broke. Piboon jumped out and sloshed back to make a try at fixing it. Unsuccessful, he hopped back into the car moments later and, with a shrugging of shoulders, said simply, "*Mai pen rai*." It doesn't matter.

He drove on, the trunk lid flapping in a tempo established by the pattern of ruts in the road. He drove on past trees and past chained elephants pulling logs for their owners and past water buffaloes with small children on their backs, despite the rain. The Asian water buffalo, Irv knew, was much tamer and calmer than the variety found in Africa.

In the back seat, Irv found his thoughts drifting in many directions. He thought about his past. He thought about his future. He thought about his favorite films, ranking them in several categories and along several dimensions. Movies had always been an important part of his life.

He thought too about Harold Edmondson, wondering about the unfortunate man's murder, wondering about the information he'd collected and attempted to communicate, information that continued to elude the agency and MI.

As the miles went by, the road narrowed, and the vegetation turned even thicker. This was the jungle at its deepest and purest. "Are you sure we'll be able to get through?" Irv asked, concerned over the steadily declining quality of the road.

"Sure thing. You bet."

Piboon enjoyed talking. He switched from English to Thai and back again on several occasions. Even though Irv had some difficulty understanding this particular brand of the northern dialect, he soon learned that his driver had five daughters and two sons—the latter were a great disappointment to him—that he loved Americans, that he hated communists, that his favorite food was something called *khowpot sii daeng*, that the male members of his family including himself had a history of heart problems, and that if the rain didn't stop soon his price was going up.

"That's highway robbery," Bonner protested in English with unintended accuracy.

"No, it is only good business," Piboon insisted. "And besides, my children need a college education."

"To match their new shoes?"

Four and a half hours into the journey, the rain finally halted. Bonner could see that they were approaching a river, and as they drew closer, he came to realize there was no bridge. The road ended abruptly at the water's edge, then picked up again on the other side.

Irv rolled down the window and surveyed their surroundings. Amid the trees and other lush surroundings, the area was dotted with several small shanties supported by wooden stilts, protection from flooding, Irv assumed. And probably from snakes too.

As if on some sort of signal, dozens of people appeared all around the taxi, laughing and pointing. A man dressed in loose-fitting, khaki pants and black shirt and smelling of sweat came up to Bonner's window. His clothes were rumpled, as though his entire family had slept in them on alternate nights for a month. In Thai that was barely better than Irv's and a couple of notches below that of the taxi driver, the man said, "I am sorry, but we have no bridge here. Cars do not travel this road. Sometimes bicycles or motorcycles, but no cars." He laughed again at the foolishness of these visitors.

"How do the bicycles and motorcycles get across?" Bonner asked him.

"We ferry them across on a raft."

"Would the raft support a car? As you can see, this car is small and not very heavy."

"No, the raft is not strong enough," the man guffawed. "You will have to turn back."

"I've come too far to do that." Irv recalled the movie *Red River*. He knew that John Wayne wouldn't turn back if he were in this situation. "If you could manage to get the taxi across on your raft, I'd pay you well."

The man scratched his head, then held a hurried conference with some of his colleagues. "We will try it," he announced at last, "if the price is fair."

"Wonderful."

"But we are afraid the raft might break or sink," the man added. "If it does, you will have to pay for us to build a new one."

"In addition to the cost of the ferry ride?"

"Yes."

"Very well. I'll agree to that. How much do you want for the ferry ride?" He reached for his wallet.

"Three hundred baht," the man said.

"Two hundred," Bonner suggested with mounting enthusiasm. "My mother needs an operation and I can't spare the extra money."

"Three hundred baht. All our mothers have just died, and we need money for funeral expenses."

"Two hundred twenty baht," Bonner ventured. "My children need shoes."

"Three hundred baht. Wrap their feet in newspapers."

"Two hundred forty," Bonner attempted. "I promised my sister a new dress."

"Three hundred baht. Mend the old one."

"Two hundred sixty," Bonner pleaded. "My dog needs flea treatments, or he may scratch himself to death."

"Three hundred baht. When the dog dies, turn the fleas into pets."

"Two hundred eighty," Bonner implored. "Or I'll have no money for food."

"Three hundred baht. Eat your dog."

They eventually agreed on three hundred baht.

The Thai signaled his friends to begin work, and instantly, eighteen men whose mothers had just died leaped into the water from various positions along the bank. Two of them waded downriver. When the pair returned moments later, they brought with them the raft, towing it by a rope tied to one corner. Made of branches and twigs laced together with rawhide, it didn't inspire much confidence in Bonner.

Nor in Piboon, it appeared. Bonner could tell by the expression on his taxi driver's face that he was beginning to have second thoughts about this arrangement. Bonner hoped the men would hurry and complete their assignment before Piboon had a chance to change his mind.

With everyone working together, it took twelve minutes to load the automobile onto the raft. "Be careful! Be careful!" the man in charge shouted minutes later as the crew pulled raft and taxi out into the river.

"Be careful! Be careful!" Piboon echoed, wading along behind them. Irv Bonner waded across behind his driver, working hard to keep his head above water.

About two-thirds of the way across what turned out to be a fairly shallow river, a strong current nearly wrenched the raft loose. Grips tightened and muscles tensed as adrenaline surged. Recovery brought a collective sigh of relief.

And then they were across. Several of the Thais helped Bonner push the taxi up the steep, muddy incline to a point where the road leveled off. Here, money changed hands, bringing smiles to the faces of eighteen motherless Thais, and the travelers resumed their journey.

A short time later, a king cobra slithered across the road about ten meters in front of them. Irv Bonner experienced a shudder as Piboon braked to a stop. Then, cautiously, the driver started up again. Thirty-eight kilometers of more bad road, mostly muddy, brought them to the town of Tradit. Irv studied the town as they drove into it, craning his neck to the left and then to the right.

Tradit didn't amount to much—a post office, a general store that looked like it belonged in a US Civil War movie, a school, a small temple, and a half-dozen houses, none of them on stilts. *Population 27* proclaimed a sign next to the post office. Irv could see most of the twenty-seven from the back seat of the taxi.

Piboon parked in front of the general store, and Irv leaned out the window to ask a passerby, "*Baan khong khun* Bernice Wiggins *yuu tii nai?*"

"*Yuu tii nan.*" Over there.

"*Khobkhun, khrop.*" Thank you.

"*Mai pen rai.*" Not a problem.

Irv got out of the taxi, taking care as to where he placed his feet. The sun was out, but It was still muddy, and the road was punctuated with water buffalo feces. "I will be gone for two, maybe three, hours," he explained to Piboon. "Please wait for me." His driver hadn't been paid yet, so Irv was sure he would be patient.

"All right," Piboon replied, he of the gravelly voice. "But that is a long time to wait. I will have to charge you one hundred baht extra."

Irv was tired and no longer in any mood to argue or complain, or even to bargain. "Okay," he mumbled as he walked away, thrusting his hands into his pockets. "Okay. Okay."

Chapter Fourteen

Stepping carefully, Irv Bonner made his way around behind the post office to the home of Bernice Wiggins. It was a house very much like all the others in the area—wooden, unsteady, unpainted.

Irv had never met the missionary before and knew that she was not expecting him, but he was confident that his cover story would help him get into her good graces. Irv liked pretending to be someone else. It made him feel like Cary Grant in *To Catch a Thief.* Irv knocked on the door.

"*Cheun si!*" a woman's voice called from inside.

He entered. All the blinds were drawn, and despite a bright sun outdoors, the living room was dark. Irv guessed that electricity had not yet reached this little town. He already knew that telephones had not. It was a large room, sparsely furnished. The most noticeable items it contained were two waist-high ceramic elephants, each with a potted fern sitting squarely on its back.

Irv caught the scent of inexpensive perfume and could barely make out the stoutish form of a woman kneeling beside the couch on the far side of the room, her back to him. Evidently, she had been praying or meditating.

"*Sawa dii, kha,*" she said without turning.

"*Sawa dii, khrop.*"

Apparently detecting a Western accent in his Thai, she spun her head around. "My god! You're a *farang*. Haven't seen a *farang* around here for weeks. Except for a Peace Corps worker or two, and I usually don't count them. You're not Peace Corps, are you?"

Irv shook his head.

"Didn't think so. You don't look Peace Corps." She lit an oil lamp, bringing a flood of light to the room, revealing her appearance to Irv. It was a plain appearance marked by brown hair tied into a bun. She wore khaki slacks and a plaid shirt. A pink comb in her hair seemed to Irv to be her only concession to comeliness.

"No, you don't look Peace Corps at all," she went on. "Not a bit. Much too healthy. Peace Corps workers usually thin and anemic. Nice people, good people, but sickly looking. You know, now that you mention it, there *was* a *farang* up here just last week. Short fellow. Red hair. Big nose. Said he was with the Army Corps of Engineers. Turned out he was nothing of the kind. A *khemoi* is what he was. Stole me *blind*. Took all my silver, my best tablecloth, two candelabras, and a bottle of wine. Say, you're not here to rob me, are you?"

Irv shook his head.

"You don't seem the type. Clean-cut. Good-looking. Blond hair. Well-combed. Clear complexion. Robbers usually sinister and shifty eyed. Not at all like you. Say, you're not with the Army Corps of Engineers, are you?"

Irv shook his head and immediately put his brain to work manufacturing a new cover story.

"Good. Can't stand those engineer types. Think they know everything. Won't even *listen* to anyone else's ideas about how to build roads and bridges and things. Even though, heaven knows, that other person's ideas might be just as good or even a whole lot better than theirs. Say, have you given any thought to your soul lately?"

Irv shook his head.

"You really should, you know. Each of us has only one, and we can't afford to trifle with it. That could mean eternal damnation. And *that's* forever, any way you slice it. Jesus loves you, you know. He wants to take care of you. And he will if you just give him the chance and open up your heart to him. Say, you're not Catholic, are you?"

Irv shook his head.

"That's good. Can't stand Catholics. Devious people. Never know what they're thinking. You don't look Catholic. Not with those sincere blue eyes. And I'm glad you're not, because I like you and I'm hoping you'll make it to heaven someday. And you can, you know, if you'll just give your heart to Jesus. So are you CIA, OSI, or MI?"

"Uhh, MI."

"Good. I can tolerate MI and OSI. But those CIA jerks really tear me up. Big shots, all of them. *Superspies.* And can you imagine wearing trench coats in this climate? They're good in bed, though, every last one of them. Got to admit that. Say, you don't have VD, do you?"

Irv shook his head.

"Glad to hear that. It's a big problem in these parts, you know. Nasty business. Okay, here's my deal: if you'll accept the Lord Jesus Christ as your personal savior and ask his forgiveness for all your sins and come up here once a month to screw the bejabbers out of me, I'll agree to provide you with whatever information I can on a regular basis about communist insurgency activities in this region. I'll be your informant, and you can be my case officer. Sound all right? Say, you don't chew betel nut, do you?"

Irv shook his head.

"That's good. Terrible stuff. Does dreadful things to your mouth and gums. But your mouth looks fine. Good lips. Excellent teeth. Very sexy. It's a hallucinogen, I understand. Does strange things to you. Plays tricks on your mind. Makes you see things that aren't there. Yes, sir, I've seen many a marriage ruined by it. Worse than alcohol. Say, you're not one of those astrology people, are you?"

Irv shook his head.

"Well, I'm glad of that. They're all weirdos, you know. What difference does it make when someone was born, anyway? I mean, am I a better person than you are just because I'm a Capricorn, like Jesus was? Say, you're not a faggot, are you?"

Irv shook his head.

"Good. Faggots give me the creeps. Faggoting around all over the place. Unnatural. The whole business. The Bible itself condemns it. I had a cousin turned out that way. Brought disgrace to the whole family. They finally had to move to another country—Luxembourg, I think it was—but they'll never escape the taint of it. You can be sure of that. Say, you don't have any doubts about the power of prayer, do you?"

Irv shook his head.

It took them thirty-seven minutes to pray, beg forgiveness for their sins, copulate, and make arrangements for their next meeting.

The experience gave Irv a greater appreciation for the concept of the missionary position.

On the way to the door, Bernice said, "I'm so happy you're not Catholic. They're such idolaters, you know. I mean, really, statues and beads and holy water. All that stuff gets in the way of meaningful worship. The Lord can't hear what you're saying when you're rattling those beads. Say, you're not Buddhist, are you?"

Irv shook his head. Standing on the front porch, he smiled and told her, "My name's Irv Bonner. Goodbye."

Piboon was not in the taxi when Irv returned to it. In fact, he was nowhere to be seen. He was probably inside the general store, Irv concluded, getting a bite to eat.

But then he noticed a cluster of children and a water buffalo gathered around a spot a couple hundred meters to his left. The youngsters seemed to be upset about something. Irv hurried over. There, he found Piboon lying in the tall grass. Kneeling, Irv touched the driver's forehead and then checked his pulse, finding none at all. The man was dead. And even in the warmth of the sun, his skin was cold.

Irv managed to put the pieces of the puzzle together by talking with the young bystanders. Approximately forty-five minutes earlier, Piboon had wandered across the field to this spot, probably to relieve himself, and had accidentally stepped on a cobra. The snake, reacting in a very natural and predictable way, had bitten its perceived assailant on the leg. And that…had been that. The children had chased the snake away with rocks and taunting noises, but poor Piboon, they'd discovered, was beyond help. He died quickly.

Irv recalled Piboon's comment early in their journey about family heart problems. That probably had contributed to his rapid death.

Holding his emotions in check, Irv Bonner negotiated with the children. Giving them four hundred baht to cover funeral expenses, he extracted from them a commitment that they would arrange a proper ceremony and burial, preferably via their missionary neighbor.

Then Irv fished the car keys from Piboon's pocket. He returned to the taxi, started the engine, and headed back toward Boonalok, forcing himself to think happy thoughts. Under the circumstances, he found that to be quite a challenge. Finally, recollection of a few scenes from Abbot and Costello's *Buck Privates* brought a grin to his lips.

In recrossing the river, with the current even stronger than before, the raft broke and the taxi sank, as eighteen frantic Thais attempted to save the raft and one even-more-frantic American tried to save the taxi. Frustrated, Irv swam, then waded, to safety. As agreed, he gave the locals money to build a new raft—seven hundred baht.

Irv set out on foot, darkness settling, the deepest of snake-infested jungles on either side of him. The moon was nearly full. Strange sounds and slithery shadows were everywhere.

It was the better part of two nights and two days before he was able to reach Boonalok and the train station. It was the better part of two *weeks* before he was able to stop babbling.

CHAPTER FIFTEEN

The army would be a pretty decent organization, Irv Bonner had been convinced for some time now, if not for people like Orville Harris, a man he considered offensive and dangerous.

"We oughta nuke the sons o' bitches," Irv had once heard the major growl mightily through clenched teeth. Harris, seated at a small table in the break room, was drinking a cup of coffee and reading that morning's edition of The *Bangkok Post*, an English-language newspaper. He folded the paper and slammed it onto the table.

"Sir?" Irv had said, seeking clarification. Irv was standing beside the detachment's newly acquired Xerox machine, making a file copy of a multiple-page agent report he'd just completed. He was amazed at this new technology. Until a better location could be found for it, the machine was positioned on a counter in the break room just a few feet from where Major Harris was sitting. While making his copies, he had been gazing out the window and across the street at the little hardware store owned by an elderly Chinese couple. The store was doing a good business today. Mostly Americans or Europeans, it seemed. Probably a great place to Christmas-shop for the family handyman, Irv mused.

"Nuclear weapons." This from the major. "I say we oughta put 'em to good use. That's what they're *for*, for Chrissake! Let's *nuke* those bastards!"

"North Vietnam, sir?"

"Berkeley."

"Oh."

"One well-aimed missile would do the job. Right down the old smokestack."

"I see."

"The rotten little Bolsheviks deserve it." Harris gave Bonner a look that chilled him.

"If you'll excuse me, sir, I'm late for an appointment." Bonner finished the last of his copies and gathered them up, along with the original document.

The major continued to grumble as Bonner departed. "Just give *me* that button and see how long it takes me to push it."

That conversation had given Irv Bonner new insights into the thought processes of Orville Harris. It had also scared the hell out of him. A short time later, he'd shared the gist of this conversation with Colonel Morgan. "Yep, he's a wild one" had been the colonel's reaction. "But let me tell you this: I'd give my left nut for ten more just like him."

Upon his recent return from Tradit, Irv Bonner had explained excitedly to anyone who would listen the circumstances of his trip and of his return. He talked in rapid-fire manner of trains, of taxis, of a missionary with information to provide, of tall grass, of jungles, and of snakes.

"Ah hell, Lieutenant," Major Harris interjected from the edge of the group of listeners, "don't be such a baby. *I* walk through tall grass and jungles all the time, and *I've* never been bitten. Hell, I've never even *seen* a goddamned snake. I guess they know enough to leave *me* alone."

It was then that Irv Bonner realized with some surprise and a certain fascination that even snakes have standards.

Irv recalled a time some weeks ago when Ed Reynolds related one of his experiences with the major. As Ed was approaching the Chairanee Building from a distance, he saw a half-dozen Thai young-sters, eight to nine years of age, playing a game of *takra* on the side-walk. The object of *takra*, a cooperative sport played with a hollow wicker ball about the size of a grapefruit, is to keep the ball airborne, not allowing it to touch the ground for as long as possible, making use of only feet, knees, and heads. Everyone works together toward that end.

Then Major Harris had happened upon the scene, having just parked his bright-red Mercedes Benz in its reserved space next to the building. Apparently, Harris was annoyed that the game was impeding his progress along the sidewalk. Making use of his height and his reach, the major intercepted the *takra* ball. With a gleam in his eye, he pivoted and heaved the ball mightily into the always-busy intersection of Sukhumvit and Rajadamnern Roads. Almost instantly, the ball disintegrated beneath one of the tires of an old blue pickup truck heaped high with some sort of leafy green vegetable.

Harris turned back to the youngsters, clearly unconcerned about the tears that had begun to form in the eyes of some of them, and snorted, "*Sawa dii*, ya little sons o' bitches." With that, he spun around and marched into the Chairanee Building.

Reynolds, having just witnessed this event from across the street, entered the building a few steps behind. The two of them found themselves on the elevator together, heading up to the eighth floor, home of the 187th. Reynolds, pretending to focus on the changing lights and numbers as they moved from one floor to the next, mumbled in a voice that was barely audible, "You asshole."

"What was that, Sergeant?"

Reynolds's head snapped around innocently, as though he'd just been startled out of a deep and focused concentration. "Uh, I don't quite recall. I was thinking about something that happened last weekend. But I believe I forgot to say 'sir.' I certainly won't let that happen again, sir."

"See that you don't." The elevator doors opened, and the major stomped out.

When Irv Bonner heard this story later from Reynolds, he'd found it interesting and revealing. There was a time when Irv had toyed with the idea of a military career. And perhaps he would again someday when Orville Harris moved on to his next assignment in the coming year.

For in many ways this was a fine life. The salary and benefits were good, especially for officers. The retirement plan was downright unbeatable—half pay after twenty years, three-quarters pay after thirty, medical benefits for life.

And there was much about the role of an MI special agent that Bonner found appealing. For one thing, it was not so dangerous as being assigned to the infantry or the artillery, or most other army outfits for that matter. For another, MI special agents generally lived off-post in accommodations of their own choosing, and that arrangement was supported by a housing allowance.

And MI special agents dressed in civilian clothes. MI special agents got to meet a lot of interesting people through interviews and investigations. MI special agents carried official government credentials that brought them instantaneous esteem from practically everyone they dealt with.

Esteem had been a relative newcomer to Irv Bonner's life. All through high school in Grand Rapids, he'd gone without it. A beanpole of a boy with size twelve feet, a slouching of the shoulders that he could not tame despite the fact that he fought it daily, and a case of acne that defied medical explanation, he'd rated low on the popularity scale.

Irv hadn't dated in high school, although it surely was not for lack of effort on his part. His list of rejections ran the gamut from Rosemary Allen, class president and prom queen, to Ann Styles whose vocabulary supposedly didn't include the word *no*. It seemed she'd added it just before he got to her.

Irv's first date happened during his sophomore year of college. His first 'all the way' date occurred in his junior year, and that turned into a disaster when he set what may have been a world's record for hasty ejaculation. Betsy Winston had been her name. "Get lost" had been her farewell remark to him.

During his high school and college years, Irv acquired what would become a lifelong love for films. He was not bothered by the realization that films were for him an escape from the harshness of reality. Nor was he bothered by the fact that he was nearly always alone when he went to watch them.

Things began to change for the better during Irv's senior year of college. He had filled out some the summer before. His feet had stopped growing. The last trace of acne had left his face. And he had managed to correct his slouch. His popularity went up a few notches. It was wonderful!

And women—suddenly, they weren't running away from him anymore, not all of them anyway. Many stopped long enough to talk with him and get to know him. Some even went out with him, and a few of those went to bed with him.

Having conquered his early-ejaculation problem of the previous year—thank God for the multiplication tables—Irv became a relatively good lover. At least, so he was told. By his reckoning, this was the result of a combination of traits: patience, sensitivity, creativity, and enthusiasm, enhanced by an interest in learning about and understanding a woman's body. He read all the anatomy-type books and sex manuals he could find.

"You knock my socks off, baby," one partner had told him.

"Why, thank you," he'd responded, ever the modest one.

"Come around again tomorrow, honey. I can always go to the store for more socks."

"Tell me your size and the color you'd like. I'll pick some up and bring them with me," he'd responded, ever the polite one.

Although Irv's self-confidence lagged behind these other changes, it too came around eventually, at least part of the way. By the time he completed his university's ROTC program and gained an army commission as a second lieutenant, a feat of which he was immensely proud, he was ready to meet the world head-on, to tackle any challenge.

He then proceeded to sail through sixteen weeks of intelligence training at Fort Holabird and fifty-one weeks of Thai instruction at the Defense Language Institute. Now, here in Bangkok with the 187th, he had met with a good deal of success also. And a promotion.

First Lieutenant Irving P. Bonner. He rather liked the sound of that. Special Agent Irving P. Bonner. That had a ring to it that he liked even better. Now that he'd had a taste of this kind of success, he was reluctant to give it up. Maybe he would turn it into a career after all. *Colonel* Irving P. Bonner. Now *that* had a ring to it.

Irv Bonner was fond of recalling his days at the Defense Language Institute in Monterey, California. Not only was the Monterey

Peninsula an incredibly beautiful setting for spending a year of his life, with four charming little towns about seven miles apart surrounded by trees and ocean, but the Defense Language Institute was a military installation with its own very fine movie theater.

The theater featured mostly first-run movies, a quartet of different films each week, at a cost of thirty-five cents for military personnel. A true bargain! Irv most often had attended three of these films every week, operating under the viewpoint that one out of any four movies was likely to be a dud.

Typically, he would stock up on popcorn and Pepsi and haul it all down to the center of the front row. Here, he would make himself comfortable, setting up his home for the evening. He would lean back and stretch out his legs, crossed at the ankles, and begin to watch and munch and sip. Irv didn't mind that this location forced him to look up at the screen. That minor disadvantage was more than offset by the sense of privacy it created, the sense that the movie was being run for his benefit alone.

He'd seen some great films in this manner at this location. It was here that the hills came alive with *The Sound of Music*. It was here that he'd learned much about life and about women from a film called *The Group*, based on a novel by Mary McCarthy. It was here that he learned some of the pitfalls of marriage from *Who's Afraid of Virginia Wolf?* It was here that he learned about the Old West from cinematic masterpieces like *Cat Ballou* and *El Dorado*. And it was here that he came to fully appreciate the James Bond films. This was where he first viewed *Goldfinger* and *Thunderball*.

Irv Bonner had come to mark time by specific films and when and where he'd seen them. His memories of Carmel, Pacific Grove, Pebble Beach, and Monterey all hinged around a string of more than a hundred movies. And rich, warm, wonderful memories they were.

On December 20, 1967, during the wee small hours of the morning, Irv Bonner was jarred awake by the sound of his telephone ringing. He picked up the receiver and spoke into it. "Hello."

"Apricot marmalade," chortled Al Finsky.

Irv's responsibility was the countersign. "English apples and muffin jelly," he said, still groggy. He knew that wasn't quite right but figured it was probably close enough.

CHAPTER SIXTEEN

It was January 4, 1968. Christmas and New Year's had come and gone in Thailand without much ado. Over here, these were minor holidays at best, and ninety-degree temperatures seemed to push them even further into the background. But Irv Bonner felt an unusually strong ache for Grand Rapids, a homesickness, a vision of snow and sleighs and family and Christmas decorations and turkey dinners.

First Sergeant Barnett had invited all the members of the 187th to a New Year's Eve party in his tent. Barnett had become an immediate convert at Colonel Morgan's very first "might have to take to the jungle" speech. By the end of that week, he'd moved out of his house on Soi 73 of the Bangkapi district and erected a tent in the approximate center of Lumpini Park. Not only would this make the transition to jungle life easier, but it would save him all those thousands of baht in rent he otherwise would have wasted. He'd dug a well and somehow struck water. More miraculously yet, he'd managed to get a telephone and electricity installed.

Of course, there was a problem at first in getting the authorities to accept the presence of a tent, with a twelve-by-fourteen canvas overhang to serve as a carport, in the middle of a public park in the middle of the city. As it turned out, though, the challenge was merely one of discovering the proper officials to bribe.

"See in the New Year from the middle of Lumpini Park," his invitation had read, followed by, "Be the first to see the First with the First Sergeant." Unable to think of a more undesirable way to spend the final hours of 1967, Irv Bonner didn't attend. Nor did anyone else, as it turned out.

It was now time for Irv Bonner's next trip to Tradit. After a relaxed breakfast at the Montien restaurant with Ed Reynolds and his girlfriend Kanlaya Chanyangam, Irv was off for Chiang Mai, the first leg of the journey. The flight left right on schedule.

During the flight, he reflected over the good fortune of his friend Reynolds. Kanlaya, he'd decided, was delightful, and Ed was fortunate to have found her. A bank teller and management trainee, with a college professor for a father, she was bright and she was ambitious. She had a seemingly boundless energy for her career and for life in general, and Irv suspected that she would be president of the bank someday. She was also charming, pretty, and just witty enough to hold her own with Ed. And it was obvious that she was head over heels in love with the guy. That Ed Reynolds was one lucky son of a gun, all right. And he deserved to be. Irv wanted the very best for both of them.

From Chiang Mai, it was across to Boonalok by train for Bonner, in steaming, tropical heat. The taxi ride that followed turned up something new at the river—a bridge. God bless those engineers! Bonner remembered the previous trip and was incredibly grateful for the new structure. But two kilometers outside of Tradit, a cobra slithered across the dirt road just in front of the taxi. The driver barely managed to slow the taxi enough to avoid running over it. Thoughts of gratitude were long forgotten as Bonner's entire body went numb.

Bernice Wiggins was happy to see him. "*Sawa dii, kha,*" she said with obvious joy in her voice. She was sporting a new pageboy hairstyle and a bright yellow dress that appeared to be new.

"*Sawa dii, khrop,*" he responded.

"*Cheun si.*" Please enter.

Bernice had had a number of visitors since Irv was here last, and she told him about them. Two Peace Corps workers had stopped by on their way to Laos and stayed a week. A police officer had dropped in one afternoon to inquire about a local villager who had been reported missing by his wife and fourteen children. Following closely on the officer's heels were a group of college students up from Bangkok, hoping to learn something about the life of a missionary,

Despite all this company, it was obvious that Bernice was delighted by Irv's visit. "Sit over there on the couch. Make yourself comfortable." She adjusted the blinds to cut down on the glare from outside. "You don't have to leave right away, do you?"

Irv shook his head.

"Good. I'll get you some coffee. I've got a pot on. Always keep a pot on for just such occasions. Never know when a friend or a stranger might drop in, and there's just nothing like coffee for social situations. Except maybe rum. You really can't beat rum for loosening people up and getting them to relax."

She was in the kitchen now, carrying on her end of the conversation from there. "Of course with rum you always run the risk of overdoing it. And oh boy, do I know how *that* can be. I could tell you stories you just wouldn't believe. So," she said, returning with a cup of coffee for each of them and seating herself next to her guest, "how was your trip? That ride up from Boonalok can be so tedious sometimes, as I'm sure I don't need to tell *you*, no matter whether it's by bicycle or by taxi. A pain in the butt either way. Sure is good to see you again. Say, you're not sick or anything, are you? You look a little pale."

Irv shook his head.

"Good. Can't think of anything worse than being sick. Except maybe being pregnant. Oh boy, I could tell you stories you just wouldn't believe." She saw the puzzled look on his face. "Not *me*, silly. Say, you know, I've gotta tell you, the Lord has been very good to me while you were away. He's blessed my testimony and I've made dozens of new converts, and they've already begun witnessing to their friends."

She used her hands as she talked, and there was energy in her voice. "It's so exciting and rewarding to watch God's love spread like that. These people are like children, you know, once they're turned on to Jesus. They get so worked up they just have to run right out and tell everyone they know. Oh, I tell you, it's absolutely inspiring! How are *you* and the Lord getting along these days, by the way?"

"Just fine," Irv replied, settling into the couch. That had been part of the deal—information in exchange for acceptance of salvation. Irv did his best to convey to the missionary that he had kept his part of the bargain.

"That's good!" She seemed highly pleased. "I can tell that Christ has been good for you. That kind of thing shows. It's a sort of radiance that comes upon a person. And you definitely have it. Why it's all *over* you. And it makes me feel warm just to see it."

Irv gave her an embarrassed smile. He didn't feel any radiance. But he concluded, he could fake that too. He set his mind to it.

Bernice Wiggins talked religion to him for about forty-five minutes, presenting a softer, sexier version of Billy Graham. Irv noticed that her face seemed more tanned than the last time he'd seen her. He liked that. He couldn't decide if he liked her new hairstyle, though. He did his best to radiate as he listened.

Finally, Irv decided it was time to get down to business. With care and finesse, he entered the conversational stream, managing to steer it in the direction of recent guerrilla activities in the area. "I heard from my taxi driver that the house of the mayor of Boonalok was bombed and burned down a couple of days ago," Irv said. "My driver thinks it may be the work of communist terrorists."

"Uh-huh. It was the CTs, all right. Plastic explosives. The Boonalok mayor is well-known in these parts for being a strong anti-communist. The terrorists have threatened him many times before, and I'm sure this was just one more attempt to get his attention, and maybe to get him to change his mind, or at least to keep quiet about his opinions."

"Do you think that will happen?"

"About the same time hell freezes over." She laughed. "And temperatures there have been in the high six hundreds lately, from what I hear. I know the mayor pretty well, and he's a tough cookie, he is."

"What other information do you have for me?" Irv asked, trying to keep her moving in the right direction.

"Weapons and equipment. More and more in this area all the time. It appears they're coming in from China. By way of Laos. Looks like a steady supply. The Border Patrol Police recently raided a CT camp site just east of here, up in the mountains. All the terrorists escaped, but they left behind a cache of weapons and explosives the likes of which you just wouldn't believe. Pretty advanced stuff, my sources tell me. I didn't get all the details. Some Russian stuff, it seems, but mostly Chinese."

A low whistle forced its way between Irv's teeth. He found this news surprising. "This is the first I've heard of Chinese or Soviet weapons making their way into Thailand. Vietnam, sure. But Thailand?"

"No kidding?" It was Bernice's turn to be surprised. "Been going on for a long time, at least that's what my sources tell me. And they're generally very reliable. Told my other case officer about it… oh three or four months back. Don't you intelligence guys ever talk to each other?"

Irv shot her a questioning look. "Other case officer?"

She laughed again and said, "Well now, you didn't really think you were the first. Did you?"

Irv gave a sheepish shrug, then asked. "Which organization was he with?"

"CIA. 'The Company' is what he usually called it. Thought it was such a big deal working for 'The Company.' Talked about it all the time. Hardly even gave anyone else a chance to get a word in edgeways. Just couldn't shut up about how wonderful 'The Company' was. He once said to me it was America's best weapon against the forces of evil. Naturally, I had to correct him. 'My friend,' I told him, 'that distinction belongs to Jesus.' Can you imagine anyone saying something as blasphemous as that?"

Irv shook his head.

"Always wore a trench coat too. Even in the hottest weather you can imagine." She brightened. "Didn't always wear anything *under* it, though."

Irv prodded her. "Do you think you might be able to get more specific information about the weapons and explosives found at the terrorist site?" This could be important, he realized.

"Sure. I'm friends with some of the local BPP officers. I'll go to work on it right away and see what I can come up with. I think I've just about won them over to the Lord. Maybe I can kill two birds with one stone next time I see them. Say, you're not a vegetarian, are you?"

Irv shook his head.

"Good. Vegetarians give me the creeps. It's not natural, you know. Jesus ate meat. So did the apostles. But Cain—you know, the guy in Genesis—he was a vegetable grower, and he up and killed his brother. Ever since then, God's been big on beef and down on veggies. Say, you're not going to have to leave before dinner, are you?"

Irv shook his head.

"Wonderful! We're having beef."

Irv enjoyed the dinner of steak, mashed potatoes and gravy, buttermilk biscuits, and the apple pie that followed. The smells alone were captivating. And the taste was magnificent! Bernice was a fine cook although her repertoire was, by her own admission, limited. "Always liked the idea of focusing on just a few dishes and learning to make them very well," she stated. "I'll take quality over quantity any day." She cupped her face in her hands, elbows resting on the edge of a table that was covered by a red and white checkered tablecloth.

"There is a lot to be said for quality," Irv agreed.

As they were clearing away the dishes, Bernice simultaneously stated and asked, "You're staying the night, of course?"

"I guess I could, if you'd like me to. I'll have to find my cab driver and make sure he's willing to wait." At times like these, Irv felt like Clark Gable in *It Happened One Night*, one of Irv's all-time favorite films. He wished Bernice looked a bit more like Claudette Colbert.

"Hurry back."

Irv nodded his head.

Upon his return, they made their way to Bernice's cool, shadowy bedroom, where they copulated for hours beneath her blue down comforter, an upright fan working overtime. Bernice was as skillful at lovemaking as she was at cooking. She put a lot into it.

Her only flaw, from Irv's perspective, was her insistence at praising the Lord at the peak of every climax, with a "hallelujah" or two thrown in for good measure. Irv found this habit to be a severe distraction. French kissing helped quiet her, he discovered. But eventually he had to come up for air, and then he was met with a slightly off-key rendition of "Rock of Ages, Cleft for Me."

Breakfast was excellent—bacon, eggs, hash browns, lightly browned toast with raspberry jelly, and strong black coffee. Irv was on his way at nine o'clock that morning with a goodbye kiss at the front door and a promise to return soon. "Thanks for the information. I'm sure it'll turn out to be useful."

"You're welcome." She smiled beneath her new pageboy hairstyle.

Irv Bonner was on a Thai Airways jet that was beginning its descent into Bangkok before it struck him that he ought to have asked Bernice the name of the CIA case officer she'd mentioned.

Could it have been, he wondered at this late moment, Harold Edmondson?

CHAPTER SEVENTEEN

It was the third time Irv Bonner had seen this particular movie. As with all the other Bond films, it was a winner. Titled *You Only Live Twice*, it was jam-packed with action and excitement. Although it didn't have quite the story line of *Goldfinger*, nor the technical gadgetry of *Thunderball*, it seemed to offer just enough of each to capture the fancy of the audience.

Although Irv spoke and understood Thai, he appreciated the fact that in Bangkok the American movies shown were not dubbed. The original soundtrack was left intact, with the simple addition of Thai subtitles for the benefit of the local citizenry. That way, the nuances and the tones of voice of the performers were not lost.

Irv Bonner moved up his monthly visit to Tradit by two and a half weeks, eager to pursue the thought he'd experienced on his return flight from the last trip. He was armed with some new and very important questions for Bernice Wiggins. If only she had a telephone, he could have called.

It was raining when Irv arrived in Tradit, a downpour complete with thunder and lightning. He knocked on Bernice's door, and while he waited for her to answer, a particularly loud clap of thunder sounded. He pulled his lightweight jacket up over his ears and began to work diligently at cleaning his shoes on the mat.

When Bernice invited him into the house with a broad smile and a comment about his early arrival, Irv wasted no time. "The CIA case officer you worked with a while back—what was his name?"

"Harold Edmondson. Why?"

Just as Irv had suspected. "I hate to have to tell you this, but he's dead. Killed by the communists."

"Harry? Oh dear god!" Alarm turned to despondency.

"I'm sorry. I know that's a shock."

Bernice fell uncharacteristically silent, staring vacantly at the floor. She sat down and seemed to melt into the frayed, floral-designed fabric of the couch.

Irv went on, "We think he was killed because of some information he'd obtained and was about to transmit to the CIA station chief in Bangkok—Ralph Owens. Do you have any idea what that information might have been?"

She thought for a moment, sighing deeply. "No, we never talked about anything like that."

"That doesn't ring any bells? Trigger any memories?"

She shook her head. "I'm sorry."

Irv had hoped for better luck. He was disappointed. "Well, it was worth a try," he said, shaking his head.

"Say, you don't suppose the papers Harry left behind would give us a clue?"

Bonner could scarcely believe his ears. "Papers? Where are they? Take me to them, please."

"Of course. He seemed to feel this was a safe place to leave them. He mentioned that the Thai Communists knew where he lived and worked."

She led him to the guest bedroom, a room with inexpensive landscapes framed in teak hanging on three of the four walls. She went to the closet. A number of shirts and several pairs of slacks—all made for a man—were hung there. A leather briefcase sat on the floor, next to a dark brown umbrella that leaned into the corner.

Bonner went for the briefcase. In an instant, he had it open and began riffling through the papers inside. Routine reports mostly, write-ups of security interviews and inspections, surveillances, that sort of thing.

And then, there it was! A two-page communiqué addressed to Ralph Owens and dated November 1967. That *had* to be it. However, elation quickly gave way to dismay as his eyes dropped to the body of the report. "Damnation," Irv muttered. He rarely swore.

"What's wrong?" Bernice asked, peering over his shoulder.

"It's in code."

"Do you know the code?"

"No."

"I guess you'll have to take it to this Ralph Owens guy."

He sighed. "I guess so." He'd hoped MI would get the first crack at the information. What was it all about anyway? He could scarcely contain his curiosity.

Irving P. Bonner went to sleep that night without the slightest awareness that the Edmondson transmittal would change his life forever.

PART FOUR

THE LOPBURI INCIDENT

CHAPTER EIGHTEEN

The Green Bay Packers beat the crap out of the Oakland Raiders in the second Super Bowl, by a score of thirty-three to fourteen. Bart Starr, Jim Taylor, and a half dozen others attained fame that seemed likely to be eternal. And Vince Lombardi became an instantaneous legend, widely recognized as a genius and an outstanding motivator, the greatest thing since Knute Rockne. Talk was widespread that this might be the greatest football team ever, especially on the heels of a similar achievement in the first Super Bowl a year earlier.

Unable to watch the game while it happened, because of geographical constraints, Ed Reynolds and several of his colleagues managed to view highlights of it the following Friday evening in a Chavalit Hotel conference room with punch and cookies in the back, courtesy of NFL Films Inc. Reynolds was not pleased with the game's outcome. In viewing sporting contests, he was typically one to pull for the underdog, in this case Oakland.

But those Packers, he had to admit, they were really something!

J. Edgar Reynolds awoke the next morning with the worst hangover in the history of the world. And he deserved it. Too much bourbon and water at the Hollywood Bar the night before, following the Super Bowl highlight film. Too many tequila chasers—bourbon and tequila, not a good mix. Too much trying to cheer up Doug Wilson, who hated the Packers for having humiliated his Kansas City Chiefs in January of the previous year. Too much listening to Don Cooper describing his latest medical symptoms and speculating about their meaning.

"Oh god," Reynolds groaned as he stumbled across the tan tiled floor of his bedroom and on into the bathroom. He swung open the medicine cabinet and grabbed the aspirin bottle by the throat. "Gimme."

He popped three tablets into his mouth and swallowed. "Shit!"

Remembering too late that aspirin is meant to be accompanied by water, he reached for a glass. He coughed spasmodically while he filled and emptied the glass twice. Looking in the mirror, he saw clearly the haggard face and bloodshot eyes of a guy with a hangover.

His stomach, already queasy, grew queasier when the aspirin hit, triggering memories of a half dozen different episodes of negative reactions to the bacteria count in this part of the world. "Bangkok belly" was the term most Americans used to describe that condition. Projectile vomiting. Projectile diarrhea. Much pain and discomfort. The mere memory of it made Reynolds shudder. The hangover was bad enough, thank you very much.

To make matters worse, the day was a scorcher, much hotter than usual, it seemed. He was wet and sticky. He smelled rotten. His head hurt. His throat was on fire. His stomach was doing the twist. And he was still almost two hundred days away from separation.

A shower helped him cool off, but it was only temporary. Living in Thailand, if you didn't have air-conditioning, you damn well better have a couple of good fans. Reynolds had one *bad* fan and an air-conditioner that had been out of order for six days and which the apartment manager had been promising to repair for five and a half.

"We will fix tomorrow afternoon," the manager had told him Thursday evening, sipping a mai tai through a straw and then taking a bite from a slice of pineapple.

"Yesterday you told me I was third on the list," Reynolds had reminded him. "What happened?"

"Third? No, no, you misunderstand," the manager had laughed. "Not third. *Thirteenth.* Maybe you cool off in swimming pool."

"Yeah. Right. I suppose I should *sleep* there too." Reynolds noticed that the manager had a galloping hairline that seemed to recede even as he watched it.

Without air-conditioning, the nights were the worst. It was then that the mosquito invasions occurred. Mosquitoes appreciate warm temperatures. If it's warmer indoors than out, they tend to come indoors. In platoons. Ed, lying in bed with the covers thrown back, must have seemed to them a picnic. A national holiday. Cause to celebrate. "Hey, guys, we eat!" he could almost hear their platoon leader proclaim.

Having been viciously attacked and chomped on the night before, Reynolds vowed that he would eat poison just before bedtime. He'd fix *their* wagon, by god!

But it was still daytime. The poison could wait. Ed was expecting Kanlaya Chanyangam—he looked at his Timex watch with the silver stretch band—any minute now. He scurried about the apartment, straightening up. Dishes became stacked neatly in the sink; dirty clothes were thrown into the yellow wicker hamper in the closet. The bed got made, mosquitoes and all.

It was a small third-floor apartment, modestly furnished and decorated. A white faux-leather couch with matching chair, along with a small teak coffee table, provided the focal point of the room. A few teak-framed prints, mostly with scenes in varying shades of blue, and a large framed photograph of Edward R. Murrow, were all that stood between the walls and total nudity.

The Murrow photograph was intended to serve as a constant reminder to Ed of his ultimate goal—to become a respected journalist and, through a constant determination to find the truth, to help protect the world from evil. Corny? Oh well.

From a dust-and-dirt perspective, the apartment was kept clean by a reasonably priced maid who came in to scrub and such on Mondays and Thursdays. The same maid worked on Tuesdays and Fridays for Ed's English neighbors—the Hucklebys, a couple so British they persisted in referring to the US as "the colonies."

Connie had passed along many suggestions to Ed for sprucing up the apartment. More wall hangings, plants, more and better lamps, wicker baskets. He was sincere in his promises to consider these suggestions. In fact, he'd already made two changes as a result of her advice. The first, an ornate kelly-green Persian rug (that had put quite a dent in his savings account) was spread under the teak coffee table, making the place look brighter and more comfortable. The second, a Fisher stereo component system with high-resolution speakers, made the place *sound* brighter and more comfortable. Ed was proud of his Fisher, and listening to it made him happy. It also made him think of Connie, and that made him even happier.

He put on a Simon and Garfunkel album now, poured himself a Coca-Cola, and settled into the couch, thinking that this was the way life was meant to be lived. He heard the strains of "The Sound of Silence" filling the room. Great song! Irv Bonner had recently seen *The Graduate* at a Bangkok theater and had raved to Ed about the film and the song.

When Ed answered the knock at the door, Kanlaya Chanyangam walked into the room looking for all the world like a goddess. She was wearing a blue silk blouse and a white cotton skirt. Her high-heeled shoes were dark blue. It never failed that each time he saw her, it took him a few minutes to get his breath back.

"Hi, baby," she said, her steady gaze, meeting his.

"Hi, baby." Ed felt his heart quicken.

An hour later, they were lying in bed, blankets thrown on the floor in disarray, perspiration everywhere, the result of vigorous love-making on a warm day. The one bad fan cranked furiously in a feeble attempt to keep things cool.

Smiling mischievously, Kanlaya and Ed decided it was time to indulge in one of their favorite pastimes—exchanging fantasies.

"You tell me one of yours, and I'll tell you one of mine" was the way it usually began.

There were two men in Kanlaya's fantasy. One of them was a matador. The other, thank God, was Ed. "No bull?" he asked.

"No bull."

"I have to admit I'm glad to hear that. Well, there are no animals in mine either. Just a few whips and chains…and some bikers… and thou." In truth, his fantasy had to do with Connie sitting in a red velvet swing suspended from the ceiling. And black lingerie. And whipped cream.

"It sounds messy," she teased him when he'd finished describing it.

As always, their discussion of fantasies led to more lovemaking. When it was over, they collapsed in a heap, happy but exhausted. Ed lifted his face from the pillow and propped himself up on one elbow to say, "Lady, you've got style."

"Thank you, kind sir."

"And the way you make love, Connie. My goodness."

In a Mae West impersonation that Ed found remarkably realistic, Kanlaya told him, "Goodness had nothing to do with it."

Sometime later, after a nap or two, Ed turned to her and asked a potentially dangerous question. "Connie, have you ever thought about living in the States?"

"Yes...but I am certain I could never do it."

"Oh?" This reply surprised him, somehow. "Why not?"

She smiled. "I would miss Bangkok too much. Thailand is my home. I really am a very traditional Thai. I love my country, and I know that my future is here." Then she added, "It may not be obvious, but the Thai way of life is ingrained very deeply within me. I am much like my father in that way."

"Your father?"

"Yes. In spite of all his education and knowledge, and his mastery of five languages—three of them Western—he is steeped in the culture and customs of the East. Sometimes he surprises even me. No, I could never leave Thailand. Any more than my father could."

Ed sighed. "Well, just thought I'd ask." From strong emotions came such awkward and ill-advised questions.

The two of them snuggled together, getting comfortable, kissed, and then fell asleep in each other's arms.

※

At two thirty that night, the telephone rang. Ed picked up the receiver on the second ring and handed it to Kanlaya with a wink and a nod.

She spoke into it, "Hello, goddammit, Finsky, you prick!"

"Uh, well, uhh, apricot marmalade," Al Finsky said without his customary chortle. It seemed he was not expecting to hear a woman's voice.

"English muffins and apple goddamn jelly, you goddamned son of a bitch!" said Kanlaya Chanyangam, and then she handed the phone back to Ed. The pair convulsed in laughter.

Chapter Nineteen

"Like hell I will!" Colonel Spencer G. Morgan boomed. "It's mine and I'm not giving it away!"

"But sir, it's addressed to Ralph Owens. It's agency business. It was prepared by a CIA operative to be delivered to the CIA station chief."

"I'm well aware of that, Captain. But there's been a lot of water under the bridge since then. And besides, it was one of *our* people who found it. As far as I'm concerned, all bets are off."

Quincy Scharfenberg nodded. "Right, sir." He knew better than to tangle with his commanding officer once the man had his mind made up, and clearly that was now the case. Major Harris was there as well, grinning in obvious agreement with the CO. The Edmondson transmittal, suddenly produced by Lieutenant Bonner, had left them with a decision to make.

"Well then, let's get to work on that code. Major, put our best people on it. Let's crack that mother." He rubbed his hands together. "Let's find out what old Harry Edmondson had to say."

"Yes, sir." The grin on Harris's face widened.

Morgan leaned back in his chair, steepling his fingers and furrowing his brow. With the tips of his index fingers, he rubbed his upper lip. "You know, gentlemen, when Lieutenant Wilson gave me my astrological update this morning, he told me this was going to be a good week to venture into new areas, to test new waters. This Edmondson transmittal business could be exactly the sort of thing he was getting at."

"Maybe so, sir." In truth, Major Harris didn't put much stock in astrology. From his point of view, if you couldn't see it, touch it, smell it, drive it, polish it, put gas in it, or smash it with your fist, it simply didn't exist.

Morgan was beaming when he unsteepled his fingers and said, "Let's get on with it. Gentlemen, you're dismissed."

"Yes, sir." Harris and Scharfenberg left the room.

Major Harris doubled up on the decoding assignment, giving it simultaneously to Lieutenant Wilson and Lieutenant Bonner. He made a Xerox copy for each and kept the original for himself. "Get to work on it," he instructed. "The CO wants answers. Pronto."

Bonner took a careful look at his copy, noting the slick texture of the paper that came from the detachment's new Xerox machine, and studied the intricate series of symbols on it. "It'll take a while," he told the major. "Two or three weeks, maybe. This looks like a tough one."

"Just do it. We don't want excuses, just results. Got that?"

"Yes, sir." Irv pulled back slightly, as the major had invaded his space. "I'll let you know as soon as I come up with something."

"And it better be *soon*." The major departed then through the main door of the suite. Irv assumed he was off to polish his red Mercedes. It was nearly lunchtime.

Over a cup of coffee a few minutes past 1500 hours, Irv mentioned to Ed Reynolds that Colonel Morgan intended to hold onto the Edmondson transmittal, rather than passing it along to the CIA, and that he wanted it decoded.

"No kidding?"

"And he wants it done fast. He's got the major riding herd on a couple of us trying to get it finished in record time."

"Oh, *that* should be great fun. Working hand in hand with good old Orville Harris."

"Uh-huh," Irv grimaced. "I can't tell you how much I'm looking forward to it."

"I wonder what it's all about, anyway. Why does Owens think this is so important?" J. Edgar Reynolds mumbled only half aloud and with a philosophical tone, completely unaware that the Edmondson transmittal was to change his life forever.

Chapter Twenty

Spencer G. Morgan grasped the black leather humidor that his love interest of six years, Maureen, had sent him for Christmas two holiday seasons previous. He'd been stationed in Okinawa then, despising every minute of it. The rock. The lousy, stinking, boring rock! Too far away from the action—that was the problem. Fresh from a tour of duty in Vietnam then, he had missed the thrill of battle.

Thailand, on the other hand, was closer to the war and a definite improvement over the rock. And hell, Thailand even had some action of its own—guerrilla activity of varying degrees in three of the outlying sectors. The north. The northeast. The south. And of course, the Nakorn Phanom Royal Thai Air Base in the northeast was a key launching point for US aircraft destined for missions over Vietnam.

All that was exciting! Stimulating. In fact, this assignment would be damn near perfect if it weren't for the likes of that troublemaking smart-ass, Sergeant Ed Reynolds.

Morgan reached inside the humidor to grasp a costly Havana cigar, rolling it lovingly between thumb and forefinger. Then he leaned back in his swivel chair and bit off the tip of the cigar, spitting it unerringly, as if his mouth were a rocket launcher, into the white, porcelain ashtray on the front corner of his new desk. It was a huge walnut desk that had taken weeks to procure from the States. Everything in *Thailand* was *teak*. Damn, how he hated teak!

Momentarily buoyed by the accuracy of his cigar-tip launch, he fumbled through his pockets for a match. Shit, he scolded himself, spend a fortune on cigars and can't even remember to pick up a free book of matches. He was reminded of an earlier time when he could scarcely afford one *bad* cigar, let alone a dozen *good* ones. Ah, but the army had changed all that. The army had been good to him. It had given him the chance to attain status and respect and a good salary and, yes, a few extra pounds around the middle. It had also given him the chance to become a part of Military Intelligence.

Military Intelligence (MI), identified by the title Counterintelligence Corps (CIC) until 1965, had always lacked the fame of the Federal Bureau of Investigation (FBI) and the glamour of the Central Intelligence Agency (CIA), formerly known as the Office of Strategic Services (OSS). It was true that MI generally was considered to be on a par with the Office of Naval Intelligence (ONI), the Office of Special Investigations (OSI), the National Security Agency (NSA) and the Defense Intelligence Agency (DIA). But was it really good enough to be on the same level as these sister organizations? And was it acceptable to operate in the shadow of the FBI and the CIA? Some thought not.

Lieutenant Colonel (LTC) Spencer G. Morgan was one of these. Morgan had commenced his army career in the Artillery branch. Then in 1961 he'd made the switch to the CIC (later MI), stumbling with a difficulty that surprised him through the sixteen-week curriculum in intelligence training at Fort Holabird, Maryland. From that time forward, Morgan had focused all his energies on the task of bettering the CIC (later MI) image.

He was aware, of course, that there were other people in other organizations with similar ideas. He'd even met some of them. There was Commander (COM) Steven Kearn of ONI, a former neighbor from St. Paul. They had kept in touch over the years. There was Major (MAJ) Carl Meadows of OSI, the air force's intelligence service. Carl had been a good friend since college days, a fellow Minnesota Gopher. He had entered the air force on the same day Morgan had enlisted in the army.

"The skies are the place to be, Spence," Meadows had proclaimed proudly. "The wild blue yonder."

"I damn well like to see who the hell I'm fighting, look 'em in the eyes. So I'll take the GI route," Morgan had countered confidently. "And besides, it's manlier."

"How about strafing an enemy stronghold or dropping a few bombs on a munitions plant? Now what could be manlier than that?"

As luck would have it, Meadows was now in Bangkok, serving as the operations officer of the OSI detachment, a mere four blocks away from where Morgan worked. Small world, eh? Morgan carried the competition one step further by having an affair with Carl's wife, Maureen. Now, what could be manlier than *that*?

Actually, the affair had begun six years and two duty stations ago, continuing throughout that time frame with only a few brief interruptions, despite the geographical challenges presented. Now they were in the same city, and things were much easier. Thursday afternoons had taken on a special significance. God bless Thursday afternoons!

And then there were the other intelligence organizations to contend with. CIA people, a bunch of intellectual hotshots for the most part, were so in love with themselves it made Morgan want to puke. It seemed like they were all graduates of one Ivy League school or another. And talk about working on an image, those CIA assholes were at it constantly. By carefully screening information to be released to the press concerning their activities, they were in an excellent position to manipulate situations and mold public perception.

They were, in fact, nearly as adept at this strategy as their Soviet counterparts, the GRU, not to mention the KGB, formerly known as the NKVD. There were times when Morgan would swear the resemblance didn't end there.

Many of Morgan's colleagues in MI made it a habit to refer to the CIA as "the Agency" or "the Company" or "big brother." The first two of these nicknames Morgan could abide, but the third he could not. Never! It implied a superior-inferior relationship, and that was entirely unacceptable.

MI, he'd concluded one morning as he stepped into his BVDs and raised himself up to his full five feet nine inches of height, must not be thought of as inferior in any way to any organization on earth. MI, he'd concluded with fierce determination, was the finest organization in the entire intelligence community. Or at least it damn well *could* be with the right people at the helm. Was he, LTC Spencer G. Morgan, one of the right people? You bet your MFA!

Colonel Morgan sometimes made mistakes. Actually, Ed Reynolds had noticed over a period of time that Morgan took a back seat to no one when it came to mistakes. With experiences ranging from forgetting to tie his shoelaces to rear-ending the limousine of Thailand's King and Queen, Morgan was the master of the miscue. The earl of the error. The baron of the boo-boo.

According to reliable sources, many months ago while Reynolds was still in language school in Monterey, Colonel Morgan had taken it upon himself to conduct a surveillance of Nadja Romanov, special assistant to the Soviet ambassador. Waiting for several hours in a parked car across from her residence, Morgan had become drowsy and finally slumped over the steering wheel as sleep overtook him. Later, he was awakened by the sound of an engine starting, and he looked over in time to see his quarry behind the wheel of her blue Chaika, pulling out into the gentle flow of traffic.

Hurriedly, Morgan turned the key in his ignition, started the engine, and stomped on the accelerator. With a violent snap, the rear tires hurled the car forward and off two wooden blocks that had been supporting the front end without the knowledge of the colonel. The front end then landed on the pavement with a resounding smack, jarring his insides and causing his heart to pound.

Morgan leaped out of the car, bellowing curses and breathing fire. "Somebody's gonna pay for this, goddammit!"

The front tires and rims, he discovered, were missing. Also missing were the rear hubcaps, the headlights, the antenna, and every inch of chrome.

CHAPTER TWENTY-ONE

On the morning of the second Thursday in February 1968, a day that would turn out to be a full one for Spencer G. Morgan, he received a telephone call. On the other end of the line was Captain Craig Benson, commanding officer of the 212th US Army Storage Facility, typically referred to simply as "the warehouse at the end of Ploenchit Road."

"I need your help," Craig Benson said. Despite their difference in rank, Benson and Morgan were friends. They'd worked in adjacent buildings in Okinawa a couple of years back, and they'd frequently gotten together to share a drink or a cup of coffee and to commiserate about "the rock" and what a lousy duty station it was.

"What is it, Craig? You know I'll help if I can."

"I've got a concern about a guy who's been dating a woman in my unit—Judy Nicholls. She's a supply sergeant. Been with me about six months. This fellow she's been seeing is a Special Forces guy, assigned to the detachment up in Lopburi. She tells me he's been acting kind of strange lately. I'm worried he might be a security risk."

"How do you mean?"

"Why don't you come out, Colonel, and I'll tell you more about it."

"Okay, I'll be there in thirty minutes."

At 0945 hours Morgan pulled his Ford Falcon into the parking lot of the 212th. He walked across the expanse of dark-gray tarmac that stretched between the parking area and the building. At one end of the tarmac were a basketball hoop and a set of painted boundaries. Three small, tractor-type jitneys were parked at the other end.

Morgan entered the massive warehouse through a huge bay door that stood open in the center of the front of the building. A musty smell presented itself to his nostrils. Countless rows of tall shelves

153

laden with helmet liners, canteens, web belts, and other assorted army equipment items seemed to stretch on forever. And everything, it seemed, was the same color. A sea of olive drab, a color that always had been one of Spencer Morgan's personal favorites.

Morgan made his way between two rows of shelves that were on his right, eventually finding himself at the door to an office. The door was open, so he entered. "Good morning, Captain," he said when he saw the man seated behind the desk.

In his early thirties, Craig Benson had a roundish face and curly black hair. Dressed in army fatigues with crisp, prominent creases, he was carrying a few extra pounds around the middle, more than Morgan recalled from the last time they'd seen each other. Benson stood, acknowledging the presence of a senior officer. Then he reached out to shake the hand of an old friend. "How are you, Colonel?"

"Fine, Craig. Just fine. How about yourself?" Morgan sat in one of the two chairs in front of the dark metal desk. Captain Benson sat down also.

"Well, I've been better." Benson got up again, this time ambling across to a coffee pot on a small table next to the wall on his left, "Coffee?" he asked.

That wall featured four framed eight-by-ten photographs, two above and two below. Each photo was a group shot, the same group in each case: Craig; his wife, Bonnie; and their two preteen youngsters, Jennie and Neal. The only variation from one photograph to the next was the situation: picnic, all dressed up outside a church, fans at a softball game, eating cotton candy at a carnival. All the family members in the pictures seemed to share the same wholesome smile. Morgan had never met Benson's family, but he'd heard plenty about them from Craig. He was pleased *not* to meet them, actually, as he was pretty sure he wouldn't be able to stand all that sweetness in one dose.

"Yeah, coffee'd be great."

"You take it black, if memory serves correctly."

"Uh-huh." A moment later, Colonel Morgan accepted the steaming Styrofoam cup. "Thanks. Now, why don't you tell me what this is all about?"

"I have a better idea." Captain Benson eased into his chair and took a sip of coffee. "I want you to hear this straight from the horse's mouth."

Benson picked up the phone and punched two buttons. "Sergeant," he said into the receiver, "can you come in here for a few minutes?" A moment later, "Good."

An attractive young woman with short blond hair and a dark tan came to the still-open door. She too was wearing freshly pressed fatigues. The captain ushered her inside and then closed the door in a quiet, conspiratorial way. "Colonel, this is Sergeant Judy Nicholls."

Morgan rose. "Sergeant Nicholls."

"Colonel." They shook hands.

They all sat down. Judy Nicholls turned down Benson's offer of coffee, stating that she'd already had her quota for the day.

"Sergeant," said the captain. "I'd like you to tell Colonel Morgan what you told me earlier this morning."

"Yes, sir." She took a breath. It's about my boyfriend, Mason. Mason McElroy. He and I have been seeing each other for about two-and-a-half months. It's been getting pretty serious. We've even talked about marriage."

Morgan nodded encouragement for her to continue.

She did. "He's in Special Forces. Jumps out of airplanes, and he teaches the Thais to do the same thing up in Lopburi." She smiled. "Heck of a way to make a living, huh? Anyway, he has this gambling problem. I think he may be addicted to it. He keeps saying he's only one win away from making a killing. He hasn't been very specific, but I get the feeling he's pretty deeply in debt."

"I see."

"He's been getting a lot of pressure to pay up. I don't know who it is that's putting the pressure on, but I can tell it's really starting to get to him. He seems to be getting desperate. He needs money badly, and he's started to hint that he's figured out a way to get some. I think it may involve this warehouse."

"Really?" Morgan steepled his fingers. "In what way?"

"Four days ago, we received a shipment of infrared, telescopic rifle sights from the States. Twenty crates. They came in by ship to the Port of Sattahip, but we're just providing temporary holding space for them. They're due to be transported to Saigon tomorrow, to be issued to our troops."

Captain Benson interjected, "Arrangements have been made for a small convoy of eight army trucks to come by here at 0830 hours tomorrow. We'll load up the trucks with the scopes, and a lot of other GI stuff—helmet liners, boots, fatigues, web belts, canteens, you name it—for use in Vietnam."

"Since the scopes arrived," the sergeant added, "we've had them sealed up in what we call 'the cage.' That's way back in the corner of the warehouse. It's our most secure area. Heavy door. Two incredibly sturdy padlocks. One combination lock. In fact, we'd like to have you take a look at it in a few minutes to see if you can recommend any ways to improve our security."

"I'd be glad to."

"My boyfriend, he's been asking all sorts of questions about the scopes. What do they look like? What are their capabilities? Where are they stored? Yesterday, he even asked to take a look at the cage. I made up an excuse and told him 'no' politely. He seemed very disappointed."

"You think he's up to something?"

"I hate to say it, but yes I do. He met some bad folks up there in Lopburi. He first told me about it more than a month ago. Thai communists. They offered him money for information. He turned them down flat. Said he wasn't interested. I guess he got pretty indignant about it."

"But you think things may have changed since then?" Morgan offered.

"Yes, sir. The comments he makes, the things he asks me about—I think he's got his eye on those rifle sights. And some quick cash from the Thai communists."

"Interesting."

"And he knows tonight is the last night they'll be here."

Benson said, "Colonel, we'd like you to help us keep an eye on the warehouse tonight. We won't be able to breathe easy until we get those scopes safely loaded onto the convoy. We need your help."

Morgan was flattered but asked, "Why me? Why not CID?" The Criminal Investigation Division of the Military Police.

"No crime's been committed. At least not yet. We see this more as a counterespionage assignment. And I'd say that's right up your alley, sir."

"Well, yes, I guess it is at that," Morgan admitted with some attempt at modesty. "Okay, I'll help."

"Terrific. A seasoned intelligence professional is exactly what we need. Now, here's what we have in mind, sir. Let's divide the night into two shifts. You take one shift, and Sergeant Nicholls and I will take the other. We'll stake the place out, stationing our vehicle at the edge of the parking lot. That location provides an excellent view of the only entrance to the warehouse."

"That sounds like a good plan, Captain. I'll be happy to take the first shift."

"Fine. That would run from 1700 to 2400 hours. We'll come in to relieve you at midnight. And one more thing, Colonel, I'd suggest you bring a weapon, just in case."

"Of course."

As they stood and shook hands all around, Judy Nicholls volunteered, "If you'll follow me, sir, I'll show you the cage."

"I'd appreciate that," Spencer Morgan replied, falling into step with the captain a couple of steps behind Nicholls.

Approximately twenty-five feet square, the cage was located at the rear corner of the warehouse, directly diagonal to Captain Benson's office. The walls were made of thick concrete, and they extended all the way to the ceiling, a height that Morgan judged to be about twenty feet. The door was constructed of heavy wrought iron, a large frame with vertical bars, such that one could see inside. As Morgan peered in, he was able to distinguish the outline of twenty large, wooden crates containing, no doubt, infrared, telescopic rifle sights.

On the outside of the door, Morgan noted, were three sturdy locks, two of them padlocks and the other a heavy-duty combination lock. "It looks very secure to me, Sergeant. I don't think I can suggest anything to improve on it."

"Thank you, Colonel. We do our best."

"I'll see you back here at 1700 hours," Morgan affirmed. "And we'll set up our stationary surveillance."

"Yes, sir. Thanks again for helping us out. We sure wouldn't want those rifle sights to fall into the wrong hands."

"Glad to do it." Morgan turned and made his way back to his car, climbed in, and headed back to the offices of the 187th MI Detachment.

At 1300 hours, Lieutenant Colonel Spencer G. Morgan disappeared from the 187th. It was, after all, Thursday. At 1325 hours, he pulled into the driveway of his yellow, one-story house on Soi 38 in the Bangkapi district. Already in the driveway was the familiar white Saab. He knew that Maureen Meadows, who had her own key, was in the house waiting for him.

She greeted him at the door with a scotch and water and an even wetter kiss. "Hi there," she said.

"Hello." Morgan wiped his mouth with the back of his hand. He hated sloppy kisses. They reminded him of Saint Bernards and other creatures with saliva problems.

"I'm sorry, Spence. I guess I forgot." She ushered him into his own very-familiar living room. They stopped in the middle of a teal-blue area rug with intricate floral designs and white fringe.

"S'okay." After all this time, how could she forget something as basic as that? He took a sip of scotch and water.

Maureen reached out and clasped her hands behind his neck, giving him a coy look. "Forgive me?"

"Sure." It was difficult for him to stay angry with her for long. She was too damned beautiful and too damned sexy. An auburn-haired lovely with a peaches-and-cream complexion and a body that Venus de Milo would surrender her goddess credentials for, Maureen Meadows was a knockout! Today, a pink skirt and a lightweight white sweater accentuated her curves even more than usual.

"I'm glad," she cooed. She picked up a vodka tonic from the coffee table, one that she had prepared for herself earlier.

They polished off their drinks in a hurry, not even bothering to sit down. Passion became more important that alcohol. And then they were in the kitchen, her bare back on the counter next to the sink, he between her legs in a standing position. She was naked, while he wore only a pair of olive drab boxer shorts, making effective use of the slit in front.

Spencer Morgan climaxed almost immediately. As he did so, he pictured himself gloating to Major Carl Meadows of OSI, Maureen's husband, "Now what could be manlier than *that*?"

It was a frantic, explosive, wonderful thing. For Spencer Morgan, that is. For Maureen, on the other hand, it was a major disappointment. It seemed that month by month, his lasting power waned.

"Spence, you promised me that this time you'd do the multiplication tables in your head to try to slow things down," she said as she slid off the counter, found her clothes, and began to dress.

"I did." He laughed. "But it's the damnedest thing. I always get stuck on the times-sixes."

Maureen, not seeing much humor in that quip, slipped into her skirt and sweater and began looking for her shoes. She was solemn about it.

"Hey look, baby," he said, seeking an olive branch to extend, "why don't you stick around a while longer? Maybe we can do it again. And I'll do better this time. Honest."

"I don't think so, Spence. I'll see you again next week, but that's all for today."

And then she was gone, leaving him to wonder about many things.

Later that afternoon, after a stop at MI headquarters to pick up his Smith & Wesson revolver, Spencer G. Morgan piloted his car to the warehouse at the end of Ploenchit Road. He pulled into the parking lot at 1657 hours.

Sergeant Nicholls and Captain Benson were at the bay door, securing it when Morgan approached. They saluted, and he did likewise.

"Colonel," Benson said, "you're right on time. Good to see you."

"Everything locked up tight?"

"Yes, sir. Tight as a drum."

"Okay. I'll just make myself comfortable in my car and keep an eye on things."

"Great, sir. Judy and I will relieve you at 2400 hours."

"Sounds good."

Morgan returned to the Falcon and got in. From the glove compartment, he pulled a cigar, unwrapped it, and bit off the tip. He found a book of matches, tore one off, and lit the cigar. Also from the glove compartment, he removed a paperback, an Agatha Christie novel, *Murder in Retrospect*, and set it on the passenger seat. He would save that for later. Maureen had recommended it to him a couple of weeks before. Rolling down the window, he took three puffs of the cigar and then settled back, preparing for a long stay.

Morgan entertained a number of thoughts as he sat there. He thought of his affair with Maureen Meadows, wishing he could find some way to spark it up again. Maybe he should send her some roses. But of course that would be difficult for her to explain to her husband.

He thought of that smart-ass, Sergeant Reynolds, wishing he could find some explainable and defensible way to get the bastard transferred to another unit. One in Greenland, maybe, or Antarctica. Or even better, to have him shot. Without breaking any army regulations, of course. This idea brought a smile to his face.

He thought too of the Edmondson transmittal. It bothered him, not knowing what it contained. His men hadn't managed to break the code yet, but he was sure they would succeed soon, and he was immensely eager for that moment to occur.

Morgan reached over for the book and began to read it from the beginning. "Damn," he muttered softly when he realized it was one of those Hercule Poirot mysteries. There was no way he could identify with a character whose name he couldn't even pronounce. Disgusted, he threw the book onto the floor in front of the passenger seat.

As darkness descended a few hours later, Morgan fired up another cigar, more to fight off a trace of drowsiness than out of a desire for a good smoke. It did the trick, bringing him fully alert once again. Just to confirm that, he breathed deeply and shook his head back and forth a few times. The cobwebs had been cleared. Morgan spent the next 120 minutes with his gaze focused on the entrance to the warehouse, barely visible in the glow of floodlights affixed to the eaves of the building in a half dozen locations. The floodlights were on a timer switch and had come on automatically at 2100 hours. He hadn't been briefed in advance about the lights, but he appreciated their presence. Spencer Morgan was determined to prevent any unauthorized intrusions on his watch, by god!

Three times during the next hour, though, he had to slap himself to stay awake. He wished he'd brought along a different book. Something racy. With lots of sex. And beautiful babes. And macho guys. Something by Mickey Spillane, maybe. A book like that sure would have helped him stay alert. No question about it. It also occurred to him that a thermos full of coffee might have been a good idea.

During the half hour that followed those thoughts, it was as though he'd gotten his second wind of wakefulness. He was alert. He was watchful. He was nimble. His senses were sharp. He was ready for anything. Confident that the worst was over, he experienced a sense of relief.

But then, almost without warning and from out of nowhere, a wave of somnolence came over him. It was coma-like in its intensity. It was so powerful he knew it would be useless to resist. So he didn't.

A tapping at the window awakened him sometime later. His head snapped upright. A glance at his wristwatch told him the time was 2358 hours. A glance outside told him that Captain Benson and Sergeant Nicholls had arrived to relieve him. He rolled down his window.

"If you'll excuse me for saying so, sir, it looked like you were sleeping," Benson remarked.

Morgan stepped out of the car. "Sleeping? No, huh-uh, not at all. Resting my eyes, maybe. Just for a couple of minutes."

Morgan noticed that Sergeant Nicholls was surveying the front of the warehouse. "I think something's wrong," she said.

The three of them began moving in that direction out across the tarmac. Captain Benson had a flashlight with him. He switched it on, lighting the way. As they drew closer, all three of them instinctively broke into a sprint.

Once they reached the bay door, it was immediately apparent there was a problem. The door was ajar, and the huge lock lay opened on the tarmac, picked or sprung, a reminder that security is a relative, even fleeting, concept.

"Oh shit," Benson moaned.

Benson opened the door, turned on some overhead lights, and led the way through the warehouse to the cage. Here, Benson, Nicholls, and Morgan discovered a wide-open door and three opened locks on the floor. These locks appeared to have been battered, physically abused, probably subjected to repeated blows from a sledgehammer.

Craig Benson directed the beam of the flashlight into the cage. There were no crates. He turned toward the colonel, a look of profound disappointment on his face, and said simply, "They're gone."

Spencer G. Morgan peered into the cage, then looked at the captain who'd put his trust in a friend and seasoned intelligence professional. Morgan turned back to the cage. "Oops," he said.

CHAPTER TWENTY-TWO

Donald M. Cooper Jr., a mild-mannered but hyperactive, stocky, dark-haired cherub of a sergeant with rosy cheeks, was by his own admission a hypochondriac. This condition had surfaced at the age of four when he'd managed to convince his parents, themselves hypochondriacs, that he was suffering from rheumatoid arthritis. During the twenty years that followed, he'd contracted everything from diphtheria to cancer of the gall bladder, or at least all the proper symptoms as described in the family's home health library. When it came to disease symptoms, it seemed he was a magnet.

Don Cooper had earned a bachelor's degree in psychology a couple of years back from San Diego State University, his ultimate aim to become a clinical counseling psychologist, a goal he still clung to fiercely. He found the field of psychology fascinating and rewarding. It was that dream that kept him afloat during his challenging days in the army.

In his senior year at SDSU before the army entered his life, one of Don's research projects had consisted of training two rats to play basketball inside a wooden crate with an empty metal, adhesive-tape sleeve secured to each end, about four inches above the wire floor, serving as opposing hoops. The "basketball" actually had been a Ping-Pong ball painted bright orange.

Through the selective use of water as a reinforcer, training one rat at a time, the plan was to shape behavior by rewarding any movement in the desired direction until finally the proper movements were strung together smoothly and each rat had only one thing on its mind—to get the ball and slam-dunk the sucker!

Dribbling had been out of the question, of course. Once the rats were properly trained, the plan was to schedule "the big game"

163

for the two of them to compete in a formal, one-hour contest in front of the entire class. A member of the class had volunteered to sew little uniforms for the contestants, one green and one white. Another class member had suggested names for them, which Don liked and had made official. One was to be called "Flash," because he was extremely quick. The other, the lankier of the two, was to be known as "Wilt the Stilt," the nickname of a famous professional athlete.

By all accounts, the big game was a success! Both participants played with heart and emotion, battling from the opening whistle to the delight and wild cheers of the class. Although not confirmed, Don suspected that a number of wagers had been placed. In the end, Wilt the Stilt was victorious by a lopsided score of twenty-three to twelve. The height advantage was simply too much for his opponent to overcome.

Later, when taking the contestants downstairs to the cage room, Don Cooper set the milk crate on a countertop. Gingerly, he reached in and removed the uniforms one at a time. Then he lifted Wilt the Stilt out of the crate and carried him over to his assigned cage—*Row B, Number 6*. He opened the door, inserted the victor of the recently concluded competition, closed the door, and latched it.

Don returned to the milk crate. As he reached in, the remaining rat lunged at his hand, biting him fiercely on the index finger. Taken aback, Don recoiled and then checked his finger. It was bleeding slightly, and already it hurt like crazy.

"Well, Flash," Don mumbled to the rat, "I guess you're what's known as a poor loser."

The rat looked up at him and bared his teeth, clicking them together a few times for effect. If Cooper was expecting some sort of apology, he was to be disappointed.

Taking no chances of a repeat performance, Cooper left the crate behind and went out the door and down the hall to locate the cage room attendant, a psych research assistant who received a small stipend for looking after the room. Cooper asked the attendant to put Flash back in his cage.

"And be careful with him," Cooper cautioned. "The little son of a gun just bit me."

"No kidding?" the attendant, he of light hair and sallow complexion, commented. "Say, are your shots up to date? You can get tetanus from a rat bite, you know. Happened to a friend of mine once."

"Thanks for the reminder. But yeah, they are." Donald M. Cooper Jr. was always timely with his immunizations. Where matters of health were concerned, he was not one to take foolish risks.

As he was walking away, the cage room attendant called after him, "By the way, rats sometimes carry rabies! Just thought you should know!"

Don froze in his tracks. Rabies? Rabies? Rabies was fatal, as he recalled, *always* fatal. *No exceptions.* He was pretty sure of that. Oh god. Rabies. Within the next few minutes, he found himself in the Student Health Center, a happy-looking place with colorful graphics painted on the walls. Don found the antiseptic smells of the hallways pleasing to the nostrils.

"I'm sorry," the nurse told him after a brief inspection of the bite area, "rabies is one of those diseases with a very lengthy incubation period." She had gray hair and a long, narrow face with what Don guessed was a perpetual sad expression. "It can be up to a hundred and eighty days."

"Wow, that's lengthy, all right."

"And we have no way of detecting it until the onset of secondary symptoms—convulsions and that sort of thing."

"And by then, it's—"

"Fatal."

"Always?"

"Always."

"Let me make sure I've got this right. You can't tell me I have it until it's too late to do anything about it."

"Exactly."

"And by then, I'm a goner?"

"Right."

"Isn't there a shot you could give me that would prevent the onset of secondary symptoms?" Don wasn't going to give up that easily. There must be some way to deal with this predicament, and he was determined to find it.

The nurse hesitated. "Yes, but it's pretty drastic. It's painful, and it tends to make people very sick. Our policy is not to administer it unless there's compelling evidence that the person has actually been exposed to rabies. That's pretty standard medical policy at most health care locations."

"What kind of evidence would you accept?"

"Well, why don't you bring in the rat? We'll test him to see if he has the disease."

Don brightened. "Great idea! I'll be right back."

He excused himself and sprinted out of the center and then back to the psychology building. Taking the stairs two at a time, he made his way to the basement and the cage room. Locating Flash's cage, he unlatched it hurriedly and opened the door.

Empty!

Oh god, where could he be? Flash. Flash, where are you? Seeing the attendant over at the counter washing some equipment, Don dashed over to him. "Excuse me," Don said, "that rat you handled for me a few minutes ago—where is he? He's not in his cage."

The attendant shook his head. "He got away from me. Just as I pulled him out of the cage, he squirted right through my hands. It was like he had grease or something on him, you know? And he was really fast. Darnedest thing."

"Well, did you look for him?"

"Yeah. Sure. No luck. But he can't have gone very far. Got to be in this room someplace, you know? Under one of these tables. Or behind the cages. I'll find him. Don't worry."

"I'll help you," Don volunteered. Frantically, with movements quicker than he knew he was capable of, he searched the room. He looked everywhere. Under things. Behind things. On top of things. Between things. No Flash.

Finally, Don returned to the attendant. Feeling weary, he handed the young man a slip of paper. "Here's my phone number. Call me when you find him. It's important."

"Okay."

From there, Don went to the campus library, a short walk to an impressive four-story brick building. He ran up the stairs to the second floor and the reference section. From a tall shelf, he pulled down a large volume of an encyclopedia. "Rabies…rabies…rabies," he mumbled as he flipped through the pages. "Rabies…yes, here it is." He began reading. "Hmmm. Yes. Invariably fatal. Secondary symptoms. Giving the appearance of foaming at the mouth." *Oh boy*, he thought, *I can hardly wait for* that. "Convulsions." Right. Terrific.

"Primary symptoms," he mumbled. "Yes, here. Primary symptoms include: pain at the site of the wound." *God, I've got that,* he thought. "Redness around the wound." He reexamined his finger even while he used it to skim the page as he read. Yeah, it's pretty red all right. "Nausea." *Yeah, I can barely keep down my lunch.* "Disoriented condition, confusion, and inability to concentrate." *Who was the twelfth president of the United States?* he asked himself. *Can't remember. Oh Christ, I've got* that *too.*

He left the library to discover that darkness had descended, so he decided to return to his room at the dormitory to wait for a phone call from the cage attendant. It was a call that never came. Finally, after what seemed to him a very long day, he fell asleep in an easy chair where he was to sleep the entire night, experiencing what were not the most pleasant of dreams.

At nine thirty the next morning, immediately after his physiological psychology class, Don anxiously made his way to the basement and the cage room. He found the attendant at the counter fiddling with something that had wires and switches attached.

"Well," Don said, "did you find him?"

"The rat?"

"Of course, the rat! Flash! Did you find him?!" Don's frustration was beginning to show, and he didn't have the energy to try to hide it.

"Yeah, hey, no problem. I found him. Yesterday evening. It was late, so I didn't call you. He was cowering over there in the corner behind those boxes. I knew he couldn't hide forever." This was followed by a soft chuckle.

Don let out a relieved sigh. "Good. Good. Where is he?"

The attendant flushed. "Well, you see…uh…it's like this. When I found him, he was acting really weird, you know? Kind of dizzy and disoriented."

"Disoriented?" Now, *there* was a familiar word.

"Yeah. And whenever I'd reach for him, he'd snap at me. Really weird, you know?"

Don wasn't liking the sound of this. "So where is he?"

"Well, I went upstairs and found Professor Lukamen and brought him back to take a look at the little guy." Professor Warren Lukamen was the faculty member in charge of all the psych labs and storage areas. He was a very busy man, frequently working late in attempting to keep up with that and his other faculty duties.

"And?" Don, normally a very mild-mannered individual, was growing more impatient by the minute.

"Well, the professor couldn't figure out what was wrong with the little tyke, but he felt like we shouldn't take any chances. Thought the little fellow might have something contagious, you know? So he decided we ought to—his words—employ the no-risk solution."

"The no-risk-solution? What the hell is that?"

The attendant's face had begun to perspire. "Well, it's like this. The professor gave the little guy a lethal injection. I'm not real sure what he injected him with, but it was definitely lethal."

Don gasped. "Oh god, no."

"And then he cremated him."

Don's jaw went slack. Tears sprang to eyes that suddenly lost focus. A moment later, shock turned to rage. "Goddamn it! How could you idiots be so stupid?"

The attendant gave a shrug and a nervous laugh. "Well, hey, don't take it so hard. I mean, it's not like it was your own personal rat. It was university property, you know? I'll be glad to sign you out another one, if that'll make you feel any better."

"You fools! You stupid fools! Did you at least perform some sort of autopsy before cremating him?"

The attendant cocked his head to one side, a smile playing with the corners of his mouth. "An autopsy? You mean like with a coroner? *That* kind of an autopsy?"

"An *autopsy*, goddamn it! To determine the cause of death! Tell me you at *least* did *that*."

"Well, we *know* the cause of death. You remember, the professor..." He made motions with his hand to simulate the workings of a hypodermic needle.

"I mean the *nature of the disease*, you jackass! What was wrong with him?" The usually calm and even introverted Don Cooper grabbed the attendant by the lapels and pulled him so close the two of them were nose to nose. "What led up to the lethal injection, you ignorant bastard? Did you run some tests?"

"Well, no. We're not exactly set up to do that sort of stuff here. It's not like we're the *Pathology Department*, you know?" Another nervous laugh.

Don Cooper had had enough. He released his grip, and the obviously terrified cage room attendant crumpled to the floor. Don Cooper turned on his heel and stomped out of the building.

During the next few days, Don came to accept his fate. With the help of an attorney, he made out a will and generally got his affairs in order, and then he began to wait for the inevitable. Mostly, he waited in his room. For a dorm room, it was pleasant enough—*small* but pleasant. It contained a small bed, a small oak dresser, a small oak desk, a small swivel chair, and a small television set resting on a small metal stand. One wall featured a window, and another held a framed print of the Hotel Del Coronado.

Don stopped attending classes. What was the point? He ate only when he absolutely had to. Occasionally, he permitted himself some entertainment—a TV program or two, a book now and again.

But clearly, his main assignment in life had become to wait for death. Of course, there first would be those wonderful secondary symptoms. Convulsions. That cute little thing with the mouth. Oh yes, how delightful.

He took some time to wonder who would be there. His funeral. How many people would show up? His mother and father, certainly. His grandparents on his mother's side. He'd always been their favorite grandchild. That recollection gave him a warm feeling. A half dozen aunts and uncles. His college friends. A couple of high school chums. Surely they would all attend.

The funeral should take place in Colorado Springs, where most of them lived and where he had grown up. There would be crying, of course, as Reverend Nunnelly (it would *have* to be Reverend Nunnelly—such an old friend of the family) spoke of the many virtues of the deceased in that soft, moving way of his. There would be tears, no question of that. Yes, tears would stain the hardwood floors of the Meadowdale Methodist Church on the eastern edge of Colorado Springs.

The days and weeks that followed these thoughts passed slowly and quietly, with death presumably just around the corner. On the 180th day, however, Don allowed himself to experience a glimmer of hope. On the 210th day, he decided he had won. He was still alive. There were no secondary symptoms. He had won! Yes, indeed! He had "licked the big R"!

Since his entrance into the army, Don Cooper had been forced to squeeze his health concerns into the military mold. In Bangkok, for example, that meant frequent trips to the 603rd Medical Dispensary, usually ending up in the examining room of Captain Doctor Swanson. In his early forties, Swanson was tall with a slender build and dark, thinning hair that seemed plastered to his head with some sort of gel.

On Cooper's most recent visit, Captain Doctor Swanson had greeted him with, "Well, Trooper Cooper, it's you again. What is it this time?"

"It's a sore throat, sir. I've had it for several days, and it won't go away. I think it may be serious." As always, Don was comforted by the antiseptic smells that resided in the dispensary.

"Hmm, I'll be the judge of that."

Captain Doctor Swanson proceeded to take his patient's temperature, to check his blood pressure, to listen to his heartbeat at multiple locations, to probe his abdomen, to pinch his neck all around, to measure his height and weight (a recommendation for decreasing chocolate intake here), to test his knee-jerk reflexes, and to explore the depths of his ears.

"Well, shoot," Swanson said with a shake of the head. "I don't mind telling you, Trooper Cooper, this thing's got me buffaloed. How about you? Any ideas?"

"Yes, sir, I do." The doctor had asked the right question. "I think I've pretty well got it narrowed down to hepatitis B or undulant fever."

"Yes, well, let's attack this problem of yours head-on, shall we? Let's have a look at that throat of yours. Open 'er up."

Cooper stretched open his mouth. The doctor held down his tongue with a tongue depressor and directed the beam of a pen light against the back of his patient's throat. "Now say 'ahh.'"

Cooper obliged. "Ahh." After another look, the doctor removed the tongue depressor.

"Interesting," he mumbled. "Very interesting indeed. Haven't seen a case like this in years."

"What is it, sir?"

Captain Doctor Swanson, renowned for his profound medical diagnoses, puffed himself up for the big moment, and then delivered. "Tobacco throat."

Cooper inclined his head. "Tobacco throat? But sir, I don't smoke."

"Do you chew?"

"No."

"Ever *consider* chewing?"

"Well, maybe once...when I was in my late teens, but—"

"Same thing."

"But—" Cooper fidgeted uneasily.

"It's what we call a psychosomatic etiology. At some level of consciousness, your brain got in touch with your throat and sent a message about tobacco. It's actually very common, although I'm surprised it took this many years in your case. Now, do you still have those tablets I prescribed for you last week?"

"For glaucoma? Yes, sir, I do."

"Good. Now, all you need to do is double your dosage of those tablets. As it happens, they work wonders on tobacco throat, as well."

"Are you sure? That seems—"

Captain Doctor Swanson had already buzzed for the receptionist to send in the next patient. Bewildered, Cooper went on his way. At noon he took a double dose of glaucoma tablets. And by one thirty his throat was fine.

In addition to concerns over his health, Don Cooper had battled feelings of insecurity for many years. When he first arrived in Bangkok a few months ago, he was extremely anxious about being in a new role and in a new and mysterious country halfway around the world.

It was Ed Reynolds who helped him through that phase. Ed, after his own arrival, had assured Don that he would be able to make the needed adjustments and handle this new stage of his life, that things would work out. Ed's calming manner, mixed with just a trace of cynicism, had done the trick. Don would always be grateful for Ed's support, occurring at a time when he needed it most.

CHAPTER TWENTY-THREE

On the 12th of February 1968, Ed Reynolds and Don Cooper found themselves on their way to Lopburi. Their assignment—to investigate the theft of twenty cases of infrared telescopic US Army rifle sights. Their fate—to watch Mason McElroy die because of a parachute that didn't open, to be pursued by a gang of communist cutthroats, to be shot at, to be captured, to be tortured, and one of them to be taken away and...God only knew.

CHAPTER TWENTY-FOUR

Cooper was driving them all crazy. Through an interpreter—the youngest of the four, who had only a marginal familiarity with English—Don conveyed his complaints of headaches, dizziness, nausea, heart palpitations, and thickness of the tongue.

More than once, they regretted their decision to bring him along after abducting him and the other American outside of Lopburi, their initial attempts at interrogation having failed. Speaking in his own tongue, Prachar Keopraseurt voiced this thought to one of his associates with a roll of the eyes. "We should have brought the other one instead," he remarked in conclusion. They'd only had room in the car for one.

"This one is more likely to talk," commented Khamon Pranii, although he too was beginning to have doubts about their choice. "He is weaker, although certainly annoying. We must do all we can to obtain information from him about enemy strength and plans—anything that will help our cause when it is time for the coup."

"You are correct, of course. Do you suppose this foreign devil asshole is really sick?"

Khamon glanced at their captive in the backseat and replied, "What does it matter if he *is* sick? We will undoubtedly have to kill the American bastard pig eventually anyway. After we get every possible bit of information from him."

"An appropriate fate, indeed, for the dog-pissing imperialist."

Cooper would have felt a good deal sicker if he had been able to translate these exchanges. Just to hold up his end of the conversation, he threw in another symptom. It was a mistake.

"Put a handkerchief in the capitalistic lackey's mouth and keep him quiet," Khamon instructed one of his colleagues.

This was accomplished in a matter of seconds. A crusty, much-used, little-washed handkerchief was jammed into Cooper's mouth. Cooper gagged to think of the broad range of bacteria and viruses it might be spawning, now barely an inch from the passageway to his throat. Hell must be something like this, he concluded, his wrists straining at the rope that bound them behind his back.

The man sitting next to him pushed Cooper's head forward into his own lap and held it there, perhaps to degrade him further, perhaps to prevent him from learning where they were going. The last time Cooper had been able to see outside, they'd been heading in a northerly direction. But they made numerous turns after that. He tried to keep track of them but found it impossible. What seemed like hours, but was probably only minutes, went by.

A short time after an especially sharp right turn, the car was brought to a stop in the gravel driveway—Don was allowed to look now—of an unsturdy-looking bamboo house. Don then was dragged like an errant schoolboy as they entered the structure. The strong smell of garlic made his nostrils quiver. The strains of "It's A Small World" ran through his mind.

Their hostess, a middle-aged Asian woman of slender build, unusual height, and a distinctly Chinese look to her, met them at the door. Her bearing and mannerisms suggested it was she who was in charge. She spoke what sounded to Don like orders, gesturing animatedly.

As he looked about him, Don could see a few pieces of rattan furniture scattered in no particular pattern across the gray tile floor. He could also see twenty wooden crates stacked against the room's far wall. They were marked "US Army," and they probably held infrared, telescopic rifle sights.

His escorts hauled him into the kitchen, hurling him into a corner. "Sit there, Yankee shithead," one of them barked in rough English, and then proceeded to tie his feet together.

The group returned to the living room, leaving Don in the kitchen, a cold, filthy room that he hated instantly. It was rude, and it was hostile. Typically, he found kitchens appealing, associating them with smells like cookies baking, but this one was an exception.

His captors talked for a long time, just loudly enough for Don to wish he could understand Thai. In all fairness, it should be Reynolds here instead of him. Reynolds was a really good guy, and Don liked him a lot, but after all he spoke the language and would have been better equipped to deal with something like this. There ain't no justice, he cursed silently, suddenly realizing he had a headache the size of Montana.

Eventually, Don Cooper fell asleep, sleeping through the night, dreaming frequently of diseases and plagues and unwashed handkerchiefs. The next morning, just as he was waking up, a brown-and-white mongrel dog appeared from nowhere and began prancing in circles around him to and fro, intent on having fun with his new playmate. Then the dog licked his face. Dogs had never liked him before. Why now, for Chrissake?

Don struggled to get away from the dog. In the process of moving body and limbs about, he noticed that the rope binding his wrists had loosened just enough to permit minor movement. With new hope, he strained against it, determined to work his hands free. Fifteen minutes of this effort produced a gap of a good three-eighths of an inch. It also produced a great deal of fatigue in his forearms.

He began to devise an escape plan. Once he freed his hands, he'd be able to untie his feet. But even before that, he'd yank this damned handkerchief out of his mouth. Then, by tiptoeing across the kitchen, he could reach the back door. It was locked, he could tell, but from the inside. A simple throw bolt. He'd make short work of that. And then he'd become the sprinter he'd dreamed of being in his high school days.

Freedom. It was so close he could taste it. Just a little more work on the ropes, and he would make his escape. He'd be well on his way before they even noticed he was gone.

But then they came for him—the two largest men. He resisted, but they were too strong. They checked the rope and tightened it. Don felt all hope evaporating.

He soon found himself on the floor of the living room on his back, hands pinned uncomfortably between back and floor. The handkerchief was removed from his mouth.

"Who are you? What your mission in Thailand?" someone demanded in bad English.

"My name is Elvin Bradley. I'm a political science student at Chulalongkorn University in Bangkok. My only mission is to study the structure of the Lopburi government for a paper I'm working on." Somehow, he didn't think they'd buy it.

They didn't. "Lies! All lies, fucking bastard!"

"You lie, damn shit imperialistic pig fucker!" someone else contributed.

Reflexively, Don Cooper's eyes went shut, and he grimaced in anticipation of the blow to the head or body he felt certain was coming. He'd learned recently to associate such words with pain. Severe and persistent pain.

Instead, he heard a soft, vaguely familiar sound coming from a place behind his line of vision. It was a noise he associated with hospitals, and that familiarity comforted him for a moment. Soon, he was able to identify the sound—a strip of adhesive tape being pulled from a roll of tape.

Suddenly the tape covered his mouth, a strip about six inches long and three inches wide. A hand smoothed it down, systematically working out the air bubbles. Two things went through Cooper's mind: either they didn't want him to say anything—which seemed unlikely under the circumstances—or they wanted to interfere with his breathing.

He didn't have to wonder for long. His nostrils were penetrated unexpectedly by soft cylindrical objects. Everything within him was telling him this was not a good thing. He began to long for the good old days of the crusty handkerchief.

By rolling his eyes downward until they seemed to be slipping into his cheekbones, he could see a pair of cigarettes protruding from his nose. Cigarettes! He thought. Why cigarettes? Hell, I don't even smoke. It's unhealthy.

The answer came swiftly. While someone held his head against the floor with firm pressure on his forehead, someone else applied a lit match to the free ends of the cigarettes. After a few seconds the cigarettes lit smoothly, each displaying a handsome, glowing ash.

Cooper's eyes grew wide as he came to fully realize his predicament. With some stored air in his lungs from a prior breath, he concentrated on exhaling slowly. To inhale, he knew, would bring agony. He wasn't sure how long a human being could survive breathing only smoke.

In short, tightly-controlled doses, he meted out his precious collection of air. The tone of the voices around him—one of which referred to him in English as a "motherfucking, capitalistic, lackey pig"—led him to believe that those who were observing were surprised at how well he was holding out. What a time for compliments!

The woman checked the tape carefully to make sure there were no air canals. Then she checked it again. She wagged her finger and said something in Thai, which Cooper took to be, "No cheating now."

Scant seconds later, he ran out of air, his lungs having nothing left to exhale. The lungs begged for more. What they got was smoke, smoke that scorched nostrils and mouth and bronchial passages, smoke that made Cooper cough and gag and sweat, smoke that made tears stream from his eyes. More and more smoke.

Cooper wanted to scream, but no sound came from his taped lips. Unconsciousness was nearing, he knew, maybe death. He certainly couldn't imagine how anyone could live through an experience like this.

A voice that sounded fuzzy and far away was asking if he had anything to say. It reminded him of his tonsillectomy surgery many years ago, with doctors and nurses standing around the operating table asking him questions he hadn't anywhere near enough strength to answer, while the ether dripped away on his mask, and he slipped steadily into a thick fog.

"Just blink four times, Yankee son of a bitch, and we will stop," he heard a voice saying patiently.

Why would the doctor call him a son of a bitch? He wondered.

"Then you be able to rest, imperialistic cocksucking dog."

Such language for a surgeon. What would his mother say?

"Then everything be all right, American pig bastard."

Blink four times, the voice had told him. Blink four times and we will stop. At this point it did seem like a good idea. Finally, he attempted such a movement, unsure as to whether he'd accomplished it. But he *was* sure of one thing. He was dying.

"It looks like the capitalistic motherfucker stopped breathing," someone said in Thai several minutes later. Someone else, feeling for a pulse and finding none, nodded.

"Try to revive him!" shouted the Chinese-ish woman. "Take the cigarettes out of his nose and the tape off his mouth. Untie him. Give him room to breathe. Quickly!" Her tone bordered on hysteria.

They did as they were told. One of them even made a feeble attempt at mouth-to-mouth resuscitation. It was all to no avail. Their patient refused to breathe.

The Chinese-ish woman cursed over this lost opportunity. Then she issued a new set of orders. "Get the foreign devil shithead out of here. Take him where he will not be found." She added after a moment, "There will be other ways to aid the revolution that is to come."

Two of the men jumped to their feet to comply, and they dragged Cooper to the car, loading him and themselves into it. The driver pulled the car out onto the road and raced through the countryside. Only a few minutes had passed when they found what they were looking for—a deserted, grassy area with considerable brush and many trees. Carrying him well out into it, they dropped him. Then they returned to the car, one of them whistling a Thai holiday tune.

Don Cooper had been wrong. His captors had been wrong. He was not dead. Of course, he was not exactly alive, either. His lungs ached, as did every set of muscles he owned. And no matter how hard he tried, he couldn't seem to get enough air. Several hours passed, maybe the better part of a day, before he was able to make any significant movements without causing him immeasurable pain that radiated through his entire body.

He hurt, but he was living. And he was grateful. At last, he was able to pull himself upright, and to stand, and begin moving his limbs. He made his way to the road, and as he began hitchhiking his way to Bangkok, he had time to reflect. He decided that he had the ability to survive anything, that he was indestructible! He vowed that he would never need to visit Captain Doctor Swanson again!

PART FIVE

THE INVESTIGATION

Chapter Twenty-Five

"He's going to run. I can *feel* it." Marilyn Dunn was excited over the momentum building for Robert F. Kennedy as a candidate for president of the United States. "And he can win too."

Ed Reynolds was equally optimistic. The two of them were drinking coffee in the break room. They were standing by a window, gazing out at those parts of the city that were visible from that vantage point, including the little hardware store owned and operated by the elderly Chinese couple who refused to sell to the burgeoning businesses on either side.

Dunn and Reynolds had just come from one of Colonel Morgan's semimonthly pep talks, during which he attempted to pump up the troops by highlighting such singularly American virtues as baseball, motherhood, and apple pie. Reynolds wondered if Soviet colonels likewise exhorted their troops to strive for greater heights by stressing such singularly Russian virtues as borscht, vodka, and ballet.

"Things look promising," Ed added regarding Kennedy. "He's got momentum. And you can bet he'll be an improvement over LBJ. He'll get the US out of the war, for one thing."

"No doubt about it." Marilyn Dunn reflected on her own political ambitions. Perhaps by Bobby's second term as president, she'd be qualified and available for some sort of political appointment. Helping Bobby Kennedy steer the ship for the greatest country on earth? She felt a smile come to her face.

"Well, I guess it's up to you and me to head up the Thailand contingent of the campaign."

"What with absentee ballots and a bunch of folks returning stateside in the next few months, there's a lot we can do here." She set down her coffee cup. "Let's get cracking!"

Campaign '68, the Thailand component, was underway.

Under the assumption that neither Don Cooper nor Ed Reynolds could be objective about the situation, Colonel Morgan assigned the investigation of the Cooper kidnapping and the stolen rifle scopes to Lieutenant Doug Wilson and Sergeant Marilyn Dunn, and they were determined to get to the bottom of it quickly. They had few leads, they realized, so the investigation would not be an easy one.

Their first step was to visit Lopburi, with Don Cooper in tow, and to drive the roads in the vicinity of his abduction. They hoped to jog his memory as to the location of the house in which he'd been held captive and nearly had died. They drove for hours over every road imaginable, including a few that weren't paved. No luck.

"Sorry, guys," Cooper said to them. "I just can't remember. I guess I had too many other things to think about."

They also stopped in at Chonchai's Bar and Grill to speak with the bartender and two waitresses, trying to get a lead on the establishment's troublesome patrons of a few days earlier. Once again, no luck. It seemed they were not regulars.

Next, they swung by the US Special Forces detachment. Leaving Don behind in the car, Marilyn and Doug went inside the headquarters building. They spoke with the duty officer and three other people who happened to be in the main office, asking them individually about Mason McElroy. Who were his closest friends? What were his habits? What did he like to do, and where did he like to go when he was off duty?

There was general agreement that he was pretty much a loner, keeping to himself most of the time. Had a girlfriend in Bangkok, first name of Judy. Liked to gamble. Liked it a lot. Would bet on anything. Absolutely *anything*. Never turned down an opportunity to put money on something, from sporting events to poker to the weather.

A particularly popular activity in this part of the world was cockfighting, where two trained roosters square off against each other, and the last one standing is declared the winner. Marilyn cringed as the Special Forces folks described this phenomenon. McElroy, it seemed, loved to bet on cockfights, and he *always* lost. Had the worst luck any of these people had ever seen or heard of.

Unfortunately, they had no names to provide of specific people he'd spent time with in connection with these gambling activities. Dunn and Wilson had hoped for a name or two that might point them in the right direction.

"Sorry we couldn't be more helpful," one of them said as the two agents prepared to depart.

"Thanks, anyway," Doug Wilson responded. "If you think of anything else, give us a call. "He handed a business card to the duty officer.

"We sure will. Something else we can do—we can spread the word around among the other guys in the detachment to see if any of them know of any particular locals that Sergeant McElroy liked to hang around with."

Marilyn Dunn said, "We'd sure appreciate that."

Dunn and Wilson returned to their car to find Cooper sitting on the trunk drinking a Coke. "Come up with anything?" Cooper asked.

"Afraid not," Wilson replied. "We'll have to try something else." But Doug Wilson and Marilyn Dunn were determined to succeed.

CHAPTER TWENTY-SIX

"We can't break the code, sir," Lieutenant Wilson said, fresh from his trip to Lopburi.

"That's right, sir," Lieutenant Bonner echoed. "It's just too tough. We can't even get a foothold on it. I'm afraid Colonel Morgan will have to turn it over to Ralph Owens and let the CIA handle it."

"You candy asses make me sick!" Major Harris snorted. Harris had just returned from applying a fresh coat of polish to his Mercedes in the parking lot. This wasn't the kind of news he'd expected to receive when he came back upstairs. "The CO isn't gonna like this. Not one damn bit!"

"We did our best, sir," Bonner offered by way of apology, visions filling his head of the major calling for a nuclear strike against the two lieutenants for their failure in this matter.

"Nuke 'em," he could almost hear Harris advise the colonel.

In intelligence circles, it's been a widely known and accepted fact that the GRU and KGB operate primarily out of Soviet embassies in their various locations around the world. Likewise, the CIA bases its operations primarily in US embassies. A key reason for that is that personnel attached to an embassy have diplomatic immunity. The situation in Thailand ran true to form, as Ed Reynolds was quick to discover on his arrival in the country several months ago.

GRU agents, KGB agents, and CIA agents were headquartered in their respective embassies, with cover identities running the gamut from accountant to personal secretary to the army attaché. In fact, the number-two GRU agent in all of Thailand, a rotund little man with thinning, wispy white hair, was officially listed as a chauffeur. No one was fooled by these charades, of course. Each agency had a complete dossier on every agent of the others, including photographs in many cases. It was all part of the game.

MI, not to be outdone by anyone, especially with Lieutenant Colonel Spencer G. Morgan at the controls, had dossiers on all GRU agents, on all KGB agents and, in addition, on all CIA agents. If the truth were to be known, Morgan valued the data collected concerning this latter group most highly of all. The agency. There was nothing like keeping tabs on the competition!

Not everyone agreed. Reynolds, for example, regarded this as a terrible waste of time and resources. "This is asinine, sir," he'd told the colonel more than once. "There must be better ways to spend the taxpayers' money."

"Why is it, Sergeant, that you keep trying to undermine our mission in Thailand?" had been the colonel's response each time. "And by the way, *I'll* be the one to decide how the taxpayers' money gets spent around here."

And it came to pass that Spencer G. Morgan decided it was necessary to bug the US embassy. In addition to the obvious, ongoing advantages of such a strategy, he saw it as a means of getting a handle on the Edmondson report. Once he'd become convinced that none of his people would ever be able to decipher it, he'd turned the document over to the CIA. But it was killing him not knowing what the damned thing contained!

"There's more than one way to skin a cat," he said aloud, for no one's benefit but his own, when he hit upon this plan. A microphone strategically placed in Ralph Owens's office should do the trick—a surefire way to eavesdrop on interesting conversations and to find out more about the transmittal.

Who should he select for such an assignment? Harris and Scharfenberg, two logical choices, had just left on a two-week furlough to the beach at Pattaya, hoping to meet women. Wilson and Dunn were in the midst of an investigation involving missing rifle sights. (Morgan was particularly eager for them to succeed, in hopes of redeeming himself with his friend, Captain Benson.) Bonner had just departed on his monthly visit to the missionary lady in Tradit. Reynolds and Cooper were available, but he just didn't quite trust them with something this sensitive.

Then the name of Ernest K. Barnett came to mind. At first, Morgan shook his head, but then he forced himself to consider that possibility a bit longer. Although the first sergeant's usual range of responsibilities didn't call for him to become involved directly in covert operations, there were certain advantages to this notion.

To begin with, Barnett was loyal. He could be trusted. Secondly, he was enthusiastic. He had been begging for some time now for just such an opportunity.

"I know I can handle anything, sir," the first sergeant would point out with a puppy-dog expression on his face. "All I need is a chance."

Persistence should be rewarded, Morgan felt. He gave a sharp nod. Barnett it would be. He only wished that Lieutenant Wilson were available for astrological confirmation of this plan.

Morgan walked over to the open door of his office and motioned for the first sergeant, seated in a nearby cubicle, to enter.

Entering with a bit of a waddle, Barnett plopped his beefy buns into a chair. "What can I do for you, sir?" Morgan noticed that there were bags under Barnett's eyes the size of satchels.

He experienced a moment of worry about the man's health but then moved forward. "How'd you like to bug the embassy, First Sergeant?"

A smile appeared on Barnett's face. "Ours or theirs, sir? US or USSR?"

"Ours. I'm *convinced* you're the right man for the job." He wasn't really, but beggars can't be choosers. Or, he mused, should that be *buggers* can't be choosers?

By this time, Barnett's smile had extended to his earlobes. "Can you tell me more about it?"

Morgan leaned forward and dropped his voice almost to a whisper. "How do you feel about air-conditioners, First Sergeant?"

"Air-conditioners, sir?"

"I have the strangest feeling that the window air-conditioning unit in Ralph Owens's office is going to break down sometime tonight."

"Really?" Barnett's face showed his bewilderment over the colonel's predictive powers.

"A slingshot and a half-dozen good-sized pebbles should do the job." The colonel leaned back in his chair. "I'll put Finsky on it. The slingshot he can pick up at that little hardware store across the street. They carry just about everything there."

"Where do I fit in, sir?"

"We discovered a few months ago that all the air-conditioner repair work for the embassy is contracted out to a local outfit called Miidhoi Repairs Ltd. It's a big company that employs Thais, Chinese, Europeans, and a few Americans."

"I see."

"The guy who takes all the phone calls is a Thai, but he's a sub-agent for us. He's been quietly on our payroll for a couple of years now. I'll arrange it so that when the call comes in tomorrow from the embassy, this guy will contact me but won't mention it to anybody there at Miidhoi."

"Sounds good so far."

"By then we'll have a Miidhoi uniform to fit you"—Morgan made a quick appraisal of the first sergeant's girth and realized that might be a challenge—"a Miidhoi panel truck, and some appropriate identification. Our subagent will get that and the panel truck. You'll drive over to the embassy and present yourself at the front desk. At that point, they will undoubtedly provide you with an escort to the broken air-conditioner. That's US embassy SOP."

"But sir, I don't know how to fix one of them damn things. I couldn't do it in a million years."

"No problem. Specialist Finsky is a whiz with mechanical gadgets. I'll have him give you a crash course on air-conditioners late this afternoon. He'll also get our best and most sensitive miniature microphone ready for you."

The first sergeant nodded, although it was obvious to Morgan that he still had doubts.

"Don't worry about a thing. You'll do fine," the colonel insisted. "Your biggest problem will be to distract your escort long enough to plant the bug."

"Mm-hmm. Where do you think I should plant it?"

"Somewhere inside Owens's desk, if possible. Or under it. If for some reason, you can't swing either of those, just use your own judgment. The mic is a new variety. Specialist Finsky just got it in. It's very small but very sensitive, so you could put it most anywhere and it would do the job."

"That's good to know," Barnett said, then belched.

Lieutenant Colonel Spencer G. Morgan turned an intense gaze on First Sergeant Ernest K. Barnett. "What do you think, First Sergeant, can you handle this assignment?"

"You bet your ass. I mean, yes sir."

"Good. I'll alert Finsky, and he'll make sure you're properly trained and equipped."

"Thank you, sir."

By the next morning, after intensive training from Al Finsky, Barnett had learned all he was capable of learning about air-conditioning units. In a tight-fitting, teal-blue uniform with *Miidhoi Repairs Ltd* emblazoned across the back, he felt comfortable that he looked the part.

At 0910 hours, the call came in from Morgan's contact at Miidhoi. Barnett was in the CO's office. A request had been made by the embassy for a repairman. It seemed that an air-conditioning unit on the third floor was malfunctioning. Surprise, surprise.

"Good luck, First Sergeant," Morgan said to Barnett, sending him on his way. "And Godspeed."

"Thank you, sir. I won't let you down." He beamed above a sweat-stained collar. On his way out of the colonel's office, Barnett passed the cubicle occupied by Marilyn Dunn, and he smiled and gave her a wink. Although she didn't return the wink or the smile, she did cock her head to one side. Barnett took that to be an encouraging sign. He'd long sensed an attraction there. He promised himself to explore that further at some point.

In the panel truck, Ernest K. Barnett made his way across town and then turned onto Wireless Road. He pulled up at the front door of the embassy at 0943 hours. He would have arrived sooner but for the uncharacteristically heavy traffic on Sukhumvit. He pulled a small green toolbox from the back of the truck.

At the main desk he was asked for identification, which he promptly produced, and a young man in a marine uniform was detailed to accompany him to Ralph Owens's office, the way the colonel had predicted. The marine then stationed himself just inside the office door, assuming the position known as "parade rest."

Barnett was hoping Owens would be away. He was. Unfortunately, a man whom Barnett recognized from photographs as the US ambassador to Thailand, was using the office. Maybe his own was being painted or was unusable for some other reason. At any rate, the man showed no indication of leaving anytime soon.

"Oh, excuse me, Your Highness," Barnett gurgled as he entered the gloomy room with its dark, heavy furnishings and an artificial scent of pine. Large, expensive paintings were hung on three of the walls. Two large windows took up the fourth. One of the windows was partially open and an air-conditioning unit was wedged into the open space. "I'm just here to fix your air-whatchamacallit," Barnett offered. He waddled up to the massive mahogany desk and made a slight bow from the waist.

"Oh yes, the air-conditioner repairman," the ambassador responded, obviously pleased. "We've been expecting you. It's already very hot today. Getting that air-conditioner working will be a welcome relief." With a white handkerchief, he wiped several drops of perspiration from his brow.

"That's for sure."

A slender man with an abundance of gray-black hair, dressed in a long-sleeved white shirt and blue necktie, the ambassador appeared warm indeed. "The air-conditioning unit is over there at the window." He gave a nod. "Let me know if I can be of any assistance."

"Well, thanks, Your Majesty. That's mighty nice of you, but I'm sure I can handle it on my own. And you know what—it could get kinda noisy in here. I usually make a lot of racket when I work. You might wanna think about movin' to another office till I finish." The fewer onlookers, the better. The marine at the door was bad enough.

"I appreciate the words of caution, but I'm quite comfortable here. I'm sure it will be fine." He returned to his work.

"Suit yourself, Your Lordship." Damn the bad luck!

As the ambassador thumbed through the pages of the packet of materials he'd been reviewing, Barnett strode across to the window, set down his toolbox, and went to work on the air-conditioning unit. With the marine looking on, Barnett lifted the window to have better access to the unit. Then he used a screwdriver to remove the top plate. Peering inside, he spotted four pebbles, which he surreptitiously pocketed.

Barnett realized that the ambassador's presence in the room made the desk as a possible site for the bug impossible. He fiddled with the inner workings of the machine, stalling, thinking. Finally, locating a screw with a friendly appearance, he alternately loosened and tightened it for about a half hour, until his wrist began to ache. Where could he put the damn bug?

Finally, out of desperation, he removed the miniature microphone from his pocket, set it inside the air-conditioning unit, and clapped a strip of adhesive tape over it, confident that his movements were smooth enough to escape detection by the young marine at the door and the ambassador.

Barnett still had the problem of completing the repairs, or at least appearing to do so. He decided that, in order to make the activity appear legitimate, he would need to remove the bottom plate and do some tinkering with the temperature control mechanism. It was important for this not to look too quick or easy. But to get to the bottom plate, he would need to lift the machine away from the window and turn it on its side.

"I'll need to get at the temperature thingamajig," he explained to the marine, taking care to keep his terminology from becoming too technical.

"Oh sure, the Freon-distribution regulator. Do you need any help?"

"Nah, I got it. Thanks, anyhow."

Barnett opened the window as far as it would go. Placing a hand carefully on either side of the unit, he spread his legs and bent his knees slightly, keeping his back vertical. Over the years, he'd learned the importance of good lifting technique.

He drew in a long breath and straightened his knees, then backed two paces away from the window with the machine. It was heavier than it looked.

Feeling wobbly, he took a quick step to the right in an attempt to regain his balance. His weight shifting faster than he'd expected, he slid his left foot forward.

It would have worked except for the smallest overcompensation. Which somehow caused him to turn a slow but complete circle, the momentum of which created another, followed by yet another. Then came one more.

Still gripping the air-conditioning unit with both hands, a look of befuddlement on his face, First Sergeant Ernest K. Barnett fell backward through the window.

Most of the shrubs below were instantly destroyed by the three-story fall. Miraculously, the first sergeant and the air-conditioning unit were not. The buoyancy of the thick shrubbery absorbed most of the first sergeant's impact. The buoyancy of the first sergeant absorbed most of the air-conditioning unit's impact.

The ambassador crossed over to the window quickly, arriving at the same time as the marine. The marine turned to him as though waiting for orders to be issued.

Ignoring the young man for the time being, the ambassador thrust his head out the window, surveying the scene. "Are you all right?" he called down to Barnett.

"I think I've just about got it fixed, Your Holiness!" Barnett called back. "Say, could ya toss me my screwdriver?"

The ambassador chewed on his lip for a moment, then turned to the marine and remarked, "MI would be my guess. The Soviets generally prefer wiretapping."

The young man nodded.

CHAPTER TWENTY-SEVEN

As part of their investigation involving missing infrared, telescopic rifle sights, and Cooper's abduction, Marilyn Dunn and Doug Wilson arranged to meet with Judy Nicholls, girlfriend of the late Mason McElroy. They drove out to the 212th US Army Storage Facility, better known as "the warehouse at the end of Ploenchit Road," for a midmorning meeting. Captain Benson, the commanding officer, was involved in inventory duties in the main part of the warehouse and suggested that the three of them use his office for their discussion.

Marilyn was dressed in a pale-yellow blouse with a Peter Pan collar, a navy-blue skirt, and black shoes with one-inch heels. She rarely wore jewelry, but today she sported a stylish stainless-steel bracelet on her right wrist, almost a match for the watch on her left. Doug wore a white shirt with a striped burgundy tie and black slacks. Judy was wearing her dress-green uniform.

Wilson began the interview with "We know this is a difficult time for you because of Mason's death, but we need to ask you a few questions to see if we can get some information that will put us on the right track. So far, we have absolutely no leads."

"I understand," said Judy Nicholls. "Ask away."

"How long had you and Mason been romantically involved?"

"Not long. A little less than three months."

"Where did you meet?" This from Marilyn Dunn.

"A nightclub on Petchburi Road one Saturday evening. I don't recall which nightclub, but we met out on the dance floor. He asked me to dance a couple of times, and then we found ourselves in a twist contest. We won, and we decided we should celebrate."

She smiled a shy smile, but there was a twinkle in her eye. "Eventually, we ended up at my place celebrating in bed."

"How well did you get to know him during the time that you were going together?"

"Pretty well. We saw each other as often as he could get down to Bangkok, or I could get up to Lopburi, probably two or three times a week as an average. We really did care for each oth—" The last word didn't make it all the way out, interrupted by a sob.

"We're sorry. We know how hard this is for you."

Doug Wilson waited a moment for Judy to compose herself, then asked, "Did you have a chance to meet any of his friends?"

"No. Every time we were together, we just focused on each other. We wanted to be alone. I didn't share him. He didn't share me."

"Sounds pretty normal," Doug said, "especially for a new relationship."

Marilyn interjected, "We understand that Mason had some gambling problems and that he was in debt. Did he ever mention any names in connection with that situation?"

"Yeah, there were a couple. But only first names. One was Mungchai. Another was Prachar. I've never met them, and I don't know anything about either of them. Except this Prachar guy—he sounds like one mean son of a gun."

"I see. Did you pick up on any hints about where they live or like to hang out?"

"I'm not even sure what city they're in. I get the feeling that some of Mason's conversations with them happened in Lopburi and some in Bangkok, but I'm not even sure of that."

Marilyn and Doug thanked Judy Nicholls for her time and moved toward the door. "If you think of anything else that might help, give us a call at this number." Marilyn handed her a business card.

"You bet I will. I want to see those bastards caught."

"Believe me, so do we," said Marilyn Dunn.

"Special Agent Dunn!"

"Yes, First Sergeant?" She made her way from her desk over to his. "What is it?"

"Two misspellings on this last agent report you submitted," the first sergeant said. "We just can't have that. Sloppy ARs make a bad impression on the brass at USARPAC and the Pentagon." Proofreading of agent reports was one of his responsibilities.

"Two? Really? Where?"

Barnett ran his finger across the second paragraph of the report. "Here's one," he announced, "*ensure* That's supposed to be *insure*. And here's the other one. *Impart*. That oughta be *import*."

"Afraid not, First Sergeant. The dictionary specifies that *insure* and *ensure* are both acceptable spellings of the same word. And *impart*, as I use it here, means to convey information."

"Impart means the same as convey? Are you sure? I thought you were talkin' about importing information, you know, like from another country."

"No, I definitely meant convey."

"Hold on a sec. Let me look that up." As Barnett reached over to a credenza for his dictionary, Marilyn noticed that his movements were cautious and awkward. Rumor had it that he'd recently experienced a fall from a three-story building.

Marilyn offered to get the dictionary for him.

"No, no, I've got it." He began leafing through the pages of the *Webster's*. "*Immunize, impact*. Here it is. *Impart*. To convey, transmit, or disclose."

She smiled.

"Humph," said Barnett, "let me try the other one. *Ensure*. Here it is—oh shit, you're right about that one too. Sonofabitch."

"Uh-huh."

Barnett sighed noticeably. "From now on, use words and spellings that everybody knows about. Okay?"

"All right, First Sergeant. Whatever you say."

"I can't be spendin' all my time lookin' up these damn words."

"Right." Marilyn Dunn returned to her cubicle, amazed at the depth of Barnett's ignorance. It was generally agreed among the members of the detachment that the first sergeant, who was expected to review and approve all written documents before they could be submitted to the CO for eventual transmittal to USARPAC or the Pentagon, couldn't spell for shit. Ed Reynolds often commented to Marilyn that First Sergeant Barnett's motto was "e" before "i" except after "y."

In truth, the problem was far worse than that, as Marilyn well knew. Barnett's greatest fault in the spelling arena was his tendency to transpose letters. Rumor had it that he had once written a memo to Colonel Morgan complaining about the "unmitilary and insub-rodintae additute of Sergeant Ed Reynolds." Her own experiences led Marilyn Dunn to believe this rumor was probably accurate.

Marilyn had found herself in a number of disagreements with the first sergeant over the matter of spelling in her reports, which he would read while mouthing the words. With the help of a dictio-nary, she invariably triumphed in these differences of opinion, to the ever-increasing consternation of the first sergeant.

"Sonofabitch," Barnett invariably would say, heaving his incred-ible chest in an incredible sigh.

Recently, however, Marilyn Dunn had begun to sense another facet of this man. She had begun to suspect that, in addition to his more obvious traits, First Sergeant Barnett was a lustful and lascivi-ous individual.

Mentioning this suspicion one day to Doug Wilson over lunch, she was told that she must be mistaken because the first sergeant's only thoughts were of food and finding new ways to make ready for the inevitable need for the 187th Military Intelligence Detachment to take to the jungle.

But on the afternoon of the 3rd of March, Marilyn found a letter in the mailbox at her apartment that confirmed her suspicions. The letter, typed neatly with perfectly even margins on military sta-tionery, read:

2 March 1968

Marilyn Dunn
148 Congkolnee Road
Bangkok, Thailand

My dearest Special Agent Dunn:

    I have been yurning to tel you of my faelings for low thes many months. Eahc tyme I sea you I shutter with delite. You aer a vioin of lovliness. Your eyes have the sparkl of diminds. Your lips set my por hsart afir. Althow you try to hyde them, your brests ignight a pashin in me that cannot be quelt. The courve of your hips drives me insane. And when I visualize the feminine charm that lies between your thighs, my masculinty springs to life. Say you wil be mine and I'l make your wildest dreems of asctasy come tru.

Sincerely,
Ernest K. Barnett
1SG, MI

P.S. I wont you to come and live with me in my tent and be my loev.

CHAPTER TWENTY-EIGHT

What Spencer G. Morgan needed was a new plan. First Sergeant Barnett's crash-and-burn experience at the embassy of the previous week had all but eliminated the possibility of ever getting a bug planted at that location. Fat chance—Morgan chuckled over the pun—of any success after that disaster. The embassy people would be on their guard even more than usual.

But what about Owens's house? The man was married, Morgan knew, and his wife was with him here in Bangkok. They lived in a huge house on Soi 15, number 83. Morgan had discovered this a while back as the result of a keeping-tabs-on-the-competition surveillance. Did *Mr.* Owens ever discuss work-related matters with *Mrs.* Owens at home. Over martinis, perhaps? A bit of pillow talk? Government employees with security clearances were prohibited, of course, from doing such things. But Morgan was aware that some gave in to temptation from time to time, as a means of release, or simply to boast about their level of importance.

Morgan had the agency man pegged as a braggart. Surely, Owens would not pass up an opportunity to regale his wife—Eunice was her name, as Morgan recalled—with tales of all sorts of derring-do regarding the acquisition of the Edmondson transmittal, even if he had to fabricate some of it. What was called for here was a tiny, well-placed microphone in the Owens household. That would do the trick!

But who was there to handle such an assignment? Spencer Morgan was confronted by the same limitations as those he'd met when selecting the first sergeant for the embassy caper. Everyone was either away or involved in something else. Everyone, that is, except Barnett—once burned, twice learned; Reynolds and Cooper—forget it; and Al Finsky.

Finsky? Why not? A whiz with gadgetry of various kinds, this would be right up his alley. In addition to being familiar with a wide range of microphones and other electronic equipment, Finsky was an accomplished practitioner in the fine art of lockpicking, a skill that had been acquired a few months ago through a correspondence course, a skill that might just come in handy on this particular assignment.

Specialist Fourth Class Alexander P. Finsky was overjoyed at the opportunity when Colonel Morgan described it to him. "I can handle it, sir," he said. "You won't regret this."

"I knew I could count on you, Specialist. Just pick out your most sensitive bug and plant it in a key room. The master bedroom is probably your best bet."

"I agree, sir."

As he studied Al Finsky, he took a moment to wonder if acne were ever a terminal condition. He hoped not. Intelligence coordinator slots were difficult to fill. "One more thing. Bring your Minox along. While you're in there, you might as well get photos of everything you can, especially financial records and such. You never know when something like that might come in handy."

"I'll get you enough pictures to fill a new photo album," Finsky promised with a laugh. "When shall I tackle it, sir?"

"There's an embassy party Sunday evening in honor of some visiting dignitary. I'm sure Mr. and Mrs. Owens will be there. I'm told they're regulars on the party circuit. That'll be a good time for you to make your move." Morgan opened one of his desk drawers and reached inside. "One of the detachment's Ford Falcons is currently unassigned. You can borrow that and return it on Monday." He tossed a set of keys, which Finsky failed to catch but then leaned over to pick up.

"Thanks, sir. I'll take good care of it."

As Finsky departed the CO's office, Morgan was reminded of the young man's lack of coordination and his awkward, uneven gait. When he walked, it seemed that knees and elbows and other unidentifiable joints were everywhere. Don't hurt yourself, son, Morgan was tempted to say.

At 2115 hours on Sunday evening, inside the Ford Falcon borrowed from the colonel, Al Finsky found number 83 on Soi 15 in the Bangkapi district, one of the nicest parts of Bangkok. The driveway was lined with colorful flower beds on each side and bright-red bougainvillea on a fence to the left of the house. Finsky bypassed the driveway, parking about a block away. Backtracking on foot, he made his way to the front door of number 83. Just in case they'd decided not to attend the embassy party, he knocked. While he waited, he invented a cover story. Encyclopedias. Working his way through college.

Yeah, that would do the job. No answer. No need for cover stories.

From his hip pocket, Finsky withdrew two slender metal implements, a pick and a rake, traditional tools of the breaking-and-entering trade. He went to work on the lock. With the rake, he applied a twisting motion to the lock mechanism, while he used the pick to massage the tumblers, springing them one at a time. When the lock itself popped open, he slipped the pair of tools back into his pocket.

Cautiously, Al Finsky swung open the door and stepped inside. It was an elegant home with large overstuffed furniture pieces and cream-colored wall-to-wall carpeting, a very unusual refinement for this part of the world. Finsky caught the scent of lavender as he moved forward, perhaps some sort of air freshener.

He lumbered over to the kitchen, located the refrigerator, and helped himself to a bottle of beer—Singha, his favorite. He found an opener in an adjacent drawer and popped the cap. He took a drink—very refreshing.

"Okay," he said aloud, "time to get started."

"Right," he replied to himself with a foamy grin.

Finsky produced a small device from his shirt pocket. About the same length as a cigarette lighter but slightly narrower, the Minox camera was remarkably portable. He'd always been enchanted by its simplicity and its usefulness.

He took several shots of each room, lay-of-the-land stuff. Then he located a room that had the look of a den and the smell of old books. Finding a file drawer on the lower, right-hand side of a roll-top desk, he pulled it open. It was filled with papers, neatly organized in manila file folders. Receipts, product guarantees, copies of income tax forms, budget worksheets—Al Finsky photographed them all, with a *click-click* here and a *click-click* there.

"Say 'cheese,'" he chortled in a loud whisper. "Smile real pretty for the camera."

He slid the drawer shut and then returned to the kitchen for another beer, making a mental note to dispose of both bottles once he'd finished his assignment. No sense leaving any evidence behind.

Then Finsky made his way through the other rooms of the house, giving the shutter of the Minox a frantic workout. After several shots of the master bedroom, he dropped the camera back into his shirt pocket.

From his left-front pants pocket, he pulled a precut strip of masking tape, and then the tiny microphone that was the main purpose for his visit, the electronic marvel that symbolized the continuing evolution of technology in the modern age. Ah, how he loved being part of it all!

Finsky immediately went to a painting hanging on the wall adjacent to the doorway—a pastoral scene with a heavy, dark, scrolled frame. With considerable care, he turned the painting over and positioned the microphone in the approximate center of the back. He secured it with the masking tape and restored the painting to its original posture. Satisfied with his work, he took a step backward with hands on hips to admire it.

Suddenly, Finsky heard the front door open, and he heard voices. A woman was saying, "And if I ever catch you flirting with that Anderson tramp again, I'll break your knees."

"We weren't flirting," a man's voice insisted. "She was telling me about her vacation in Hawaii, and I was just asking a few polite questions."

"Don't lie to me, you bastard. I can spot a flirtation a mile away."

In a panic, Al Finsky dove under the bed. It was a king-size bed, and he slid as quietly as he could toward the middle. Breathing hard from this flurry of activity, he worked at calming himself. He would have sworn that his heartbeat could be heard in the next province.

Lying here now, he felt a severe pain in his right knee, and he wondered if the dive might have shattered his kneecap.

The voices came closer. The woman said, "Everyone knows that Anderson bitch has the morals of an alley cat."

"Where did you hear that?"

"Oh come now, do you mean to tell me you haven't seen her name and phone number scrawled all over the walls of every men's room in the embassy?"

"And just how do you know that?"

"I've never been inside one, mind you, but it's a well-established fact."

"Well, *I've* been inside *all* of them, and *I've* never seen *any* names or telephone numbers on any walls." He switched from defense to offense. "And by the way, I don't think the ambassador appreciated the fact that we left the party so early."

"Who cares what that pompous windbag thinks? You didn't really expect me to stand idly by and watch you make time with Little Miss Hot Panties, did you?" They had moved into the bedroom without disrupting the flow of their verbal exchange.

"You didn't have to watch." An attempt at humor.

"Very funny, fart face. Do you see me laughing?"

"I was just trying to ease the tension, my dear."

"Well, it didn't work."

"I can see that, needle-nose."

"Shut your trap, shit-for-brains."

Under the bed, Al Finsky was growing restless. He hadn't expected them to return home so soon, and he was beginning to worry that his opportunities for escape might lie somewhere in the distant future. And his throbbing knee hurt like hell!

About two hours later, it looked like Finsky's chance had arrived. The Owenses were snoring in rhythms that seemed to complement each other. Finsky began to crawl out across the open floor. Slowly. Carefully. Keeping a low profile.

"That you, Ralphie?" Mrs. Owens mumbled in a voice thick with sleep.

"Uh-huh," Finsky grunted, frozen midcrawl.

"Don't be long, fart-face." A loud yawn.

"Okay, needle-nose." He scampered back under the bed so hastily that he banged his right knee once again and had to suppress a loud cry of pain.

Another yawn from above. "I swear, I'm so worn out I could stay in this bed for a week."

Specialist Fourth Class Alexander P. Finsky broke free from the clutches of the Owens household at about 0430 hours. At 0815 hours he reported for sick call at the 603rd medical dispensary to have his knee examined by Captain Doctor Swanson. Fortunately, it turned out to be a bruise and not a break.

Several days of listening in on the Owenses' conversations while sitting in a van parked two blocks away via the microphone Finsky had planted, produced little of substance for Lieutenant Colonel Spencer G. Morgan. A few dictionary-expanding terms surfaced, such as "buffalo-breath," "puke-face," and "rectum-lips," but that was about the extent of it.

The agents of the 187th, including Colonel Morgan, took rotational assignments at monitoring the listening equipment in the van. The colonel actually took the longest shifts of anyone, simply because he was eager to hear something useful.

It wasn't until ten days after the plant that he overheard Ralph Owens saying, "The guy must have been on drugs or something."

"What are you talking about?" Mrs. Owens asked.

"Harold Edmondson—you know, the guy I told you about—submitted his most recent report in a different code than the one we're used to. He's dead now, so *he* can't help us. We've been trying like crazy to decode it, but none of it makes any sense. It looks like hieroglyphics or something. Doesn't match up to any of our codebooks. We've tried them all. Edmondson had a close friend at OSI, so we even borrowed OSI's codebooks and tried them. Nothing. Nada. Nix. Bupkis."

"So what are you going to do?"

"My secretary swears it's a legitimate code but an old one, and she's been around for a while, so she ought to know. She points out that the agency hasn't used symbol substitution schemes since 1964, and that pretty well jibes with my own recollection."

"Really?"

"She thinks this particular one is about vintage 1961."

"Do you think it's possible this Edmondson fellow would have used a codebook that's seven years old?"

"Well, Edmondson always was a tad out of date and behind the times. A hell of an agent but a throwback to a different era. Hell, his wardrobe was right out of the forties, just to give you a clue. Looked like a balding Humphrey Bogart most of the time."

"He could have done worse. I've always liked Humphrey Bogart."

"It's a damned shame he picked this particular time to switch to an old code."

"This report must've been pretty important."

"Yeah, we think it was *very* important, as a matter of fact."

"You guys don't have codebooks going back to 1961?"

"We only go back as far as '65 at the station here in Bangkok. We contacted the CIA contingents in Laos and Burma to see if they might have something that old?"

"No luck?"

"Huh-uh. I sure thought we had a shot, though with old Brad Collins, the head guy in Laos. He never throws *anything* away. The man saves *tinfoil*, for Chrissake."

"What are you going to do next?"

"We'll keep trying other locations for a codebook. My secretary has some useful contacts in South America, so maybe something will work out there."

"Good."

"And of course, we've still got a couple of people trying to crack the code, symbol by symbol. But that could take forever."

Inside the van two blocks away, Colonel Morgan smiled. He was pleased to discover that the CIA was having similar problems to those MI had experienced. Still, he continued to wish he knew what was contained in the Edmondson transmittal.

CHAPTER TWENTY-NINE

Marilyn Dunn's deep affection for Robert Kennedy, and in fact her own political ambitions, actually had begun with Robert's older brother, the man generally credited with inspiring widespread use of the word "charisma." What a tragic loss to the world his death was. Marilyn hadn't quite recovered from it even yet. Now that Jack was gone, she bestowed all her hopes and all her admiration on Bobby. She knew, even while he was still attorney general, that he was destined someday to become president of the United States.

On March 31, 1968, Lyndon Johnson announced that he would not be seeking reelection. The door was now wide open!

Although Marilyn Dunn was opposed philosophically to the concept of marriage, she was a firm believer in the concept of sex. A victim of puritanical parents and a provincial upbringing, it had been entirely up to her to liberate herself, and she'd gone about it with fervor at the earliest opportunity. They had lied to her about sex, she proceeded to discover one delightful summer evening in her eighteenth year.

When it came to making a pitch for a man she liked, Marilyn was no longer impeded by the outmoded standards of her mother, having concluded that life is too short to waste time playing silly little games. One Friday she set her sights on Doug Wilson, her partner in the investigation of the Cooper abduction and the stolen rifle scopes. She liked him and found him appealing. He liked her also, she believed, and she would soon find out for sure.

"Let's go to my place after work," she suggested to him that afternoon. "We can celebrate the weekend."

"Great," Wilson agreed without hesitation. Clearly he already had given this possibility some consideration. "We can stop on the way and pick up some wine."

"Wonderful," she responded, thinking that his smile was much like that of Bobby Kennedy. Doug had a gentle quality, and yet managed to maintain his masculinity. And he did have that warm, winning smile.

Later, inside Marilyn's apartment, they downed a glass of Chardonnay apiece and, wasting little time, undressed each other. She led him into the bedroom, and they romanced one another thoroughly.

He was on top for a while. Then they reversed positions and started moving rhythmically, up and down, back and forth, to and fro, hitting just the right spots for both of them, aided by Doug's lubricated and strategically placed thumb. These movements were accompanied by deep sighs. At times it was difficult for Marilyn to tell if the sighs were hers or his.

The telephone rang.

"Going to answer it?" Doug asked.

"Ooooh no. Let it ring."

It rang several more times. "It might be important."

"Hmmm, maybe you're right," she relented still moving and moaning. "But don't stop. This feels awfully good."

Doug closed his eyes and clamped his free hand onto her hips.

Marilyn reached across and picked up the receiver to murmur, "Hello?"

"Apricot marmalade," chortled Al Finsky.

"Oh...ohh...ohhh my god!" replied Marilyn Dunn.

CHAPTER THIRTY

The stars rule the earth and all of its inhabitants. To First Lieutenant Douglas T. Wilson, this was as rudimentary as the fact that the sun rises in the morning.

"Yeah, sure, if you say so," his friends would humor him.

"It's the only explanation of life's events that makes any sense," he would reply.

"Right."

"Scoff if you will, but you're missing out on the true meaning of life."

"Huh-uh," Ed Reynolds had countered on one occasion. "I've got the true meaning of life all figured out. Life is a bowl of cherries. Except in Idaho, and there it's a bowl of potatoes."

Doug Wilson believed with all his heart that if one could fully understand the stars and the planets and the myriad of ways they were capable of relating to each other, one could predict earthly events, or at least patterns of events, with reasonable accuracy. In addition, one ought to be able to categorize the earth's inhabitants and their traits on the basis of the relationships between these creatures and the various celestial bodies. It was all so incredibly logical!

Born on May 27, Doug Wilson was a Gemini. At an early age, he had learned the importance of tuning into that identifier. "Douglas," his mother had said to him often, "you must always remember that the stars show the way. Look to the stars and they will guide you."

"I will," he'd promised, because he loved her more than life itself, and because he knew she was right.

Helen Wilson, a robust and flamboyant woman, widowed early, had raised her son alone in Kansas City. This rearing had spanned two decades of turbulent times—times of change, times of challenge, times of crisis. Juvenile delinquency. Gangs. Drugs. Racism. The Civil Rights movement and persecution of its activists. So many potential obstacles! But the two of them—mother and son—had come through it all.

Helen Wilson was proud of her efforts. More than that, she was proud of her son. He, in turn, loved her and respected her more than he could say.

Wilson had known for the past fifteen years that he ultimately would find himself in the army and somewhere in the Far East, just as he had known that he would make a four-year stop at Stanford along the way to earn a degree in philosophy. The stars had pointed the way.

"I'm precisely where I belong…for now."

He also knew that he was destined for a postmilitary career involving the written word. The life of an author awaited him. He already had begun making notes and preparing an outline for his first endeavor—a book on the subject of astrology, of course. It would be a primer, something to whet the appetite of the beginner or the faintly curious.

This would be followed by a novel or two, perhaps drawing from some of his own experiences. He envisioned at least one story emerging with a Kansas City flavor to it, probably with an early-fifties time frame. It would focus on the lives of people who worked hard, but who repeatedly were met with challenges but who managed to find occasional moments of joy along the way. He pictured this novel as having just the right blend of warmth and tragedy and happiness, with just a pinch of humor thrown in for good measure.

Doug Wilson never resented the fact that his life was guided by external forces, merely accepting it as inevitable and unalterable. On the other hand, he did resent Major Harris, a devious Scorpio. And he also resented the awkward situations Colonel Morgan often forced him into by attempting to plan the detachment's activities around Wilson's astrological advice. This sometimes resulted in Wilson shouldering the blame when the CO's ill-founded schemes went awry, which they often did.

On top of that, Wilson took a lot of good-natured guff from the other members of the unit. Ed Reynolds, in particular, took great delight in ribbing him. At the drop of a hat, Reynolds was likely to say something along the lines of, "I noticed the CO missed the urinal again this morning. Did you tell him to do it, Doug?"

"Hell no, I told him to use the sink."

"I guess Virgos just don't aim so good, huh?"

"Yeah, that must be it."

Wilson didn't mind that sort of thing, especially from Reynolds. Despite the fact that Reynolds was a Libra with mercury rising and a moon that was out of whack, Wilson liked him. In fact, there were few things he enjoyed more than sitting around a table at the Red Door Restaurant or the Yard of Ale or the Hollywood Bar with Reynolds, Marilyn Dunn, and Don Cooper, and sometimes Irv Bonner, exchanging jokes and commiserations over sandwiches and beer.

This group, astrologically compatible but for Reynolds, frequently got together for lunch or after-hours drinks. Even the newest addition to the group, Marilyn Dunn, fit in nicely. And of course, Doug had developed a soft spot for her for other reasons.

※

The infrared-scope investigation had nearly ground to a halt when Doug Wilson received a telephone call. He would not realize until later that this was precisely the break he and Marilyn had been waiting for.

The caller was a woman who identified herself as Rawi Tisiwad. Rawi was upset about something and needed to talk. She thought maybe MI could help. "Can you come to my house, please?" she asked.

"Yes, where do you live?"

"I live at 521 Rattan Lane. It is just off Soi 7."

"I'll be there in thirty minutes."

"Thank you."

"May I bring an associate?"

"That would be fine."

At the corner of Soi 7 and Rattan Lane, Special Agents Dunn and Wilson parked their car, a blue Ford Falcon. A glance down Rattan Lane had told them it was too narrow to drive into. Two Buddhist monks, orange-clad with shaved heads, emerged from the lane just then, probably speaking softly of philosophical and religious matters.

After a hike of a block and a half, Dunn and Wilson knocked at the door of Number 521, a pleasant, two-story dwelling, yellow with white trim and a mansard roof. The door was opened cautiously by a delicate-featured Thai woman in her mid-twenties.

"Rawi Tisiwad?" Wilson asked.

"Yes."

"I'm Doug Wilson of the 187th Military Intelligence Detachment. This is Marilyn Dunn."

"Oh yes, please come in."

As they stepped inside and then past the entryway into a sump-tuously furnished living room with a number of indoor plants, Wilson noticed that the house had a clean and comfortable smell to it. It reminded him of lilacs.

He took a moment to admire a pair of Cambodian temple rubbings hanging on the wall behind the white leather couch. "Very pretty," he commented, and meant it.

"Thank you. Please sit there on the sofa." As Doug and Marilyn did so, Rawi walked over to the window and, with a twist of a plastic wand, gave the Venetian blinds a downward slant to filter out some of the afternoon sunlight. "Would you care for some tea?" she asked.

The visitors shook their heads. "You go ahead, though, if you like." This from Marilyn Dunn.

Rawi poured herself a cup of tea and then sat in an armchair across from her guests. Crossing her legs, she rested the saucer on the top knee. The saucer rattled slightly, and her discomfort showed. It was obvious that something was weighing heavily on her mind.

Slowly, she began her story. "I'm afraid that my brother is a thief. He may be a communist as well." She paused as if to evaluate their reaction.

"Please go on" was Dunn's response. She scooted forward on the couch, folding her arms and resting them on her knees.

"His name is Mungchai—Mungchai Tisiwad. He is young, only twenty years. He lives with me here and has since our parents died in a fire three years ago." She drew in a breath. "During the past several months, Mungchai has been associating with bad companions." Her English was excellent.

Wilson and Dunn exchanged glances. The name "Mungchai" rang a bell with them.

"They lie," Rawi went on, "they steal—frequently from American servicemen—that is why I contacted *your* agency. They frequently discuss the CPT, and in quite positive terms. I think they may be members. This all causes me great concern, and I have spoken to Mungchai many times about it. He turns a deaf ear. He insists he is old enough to make his own decisions and to select his own friends. He is my brother and I love him. I don't want to get him into trouble, but I am very worried about how all this might end if something isn't done."

"Is there anything else that leads you to believe these young men might be communists?" Doug Wilson asked.

"They frequently quote sayings from Chairman Mao. In fact, I found a book of those sayings in my brother's room while cleaning it a couple of days ago. I also found a considerable amount of money. At least a hundred thousand baht. It must have been stolen."

"I see."

"It was all quite disturbing, as I am certain you can appreciate."

Dunn nodded her agreement. "Do you know the names of any of your brother's friends?"

Rawi thought for a moment. "One is called Rapang. I do not know his last name. Another is Prachar Keopraseurt. He is very tall. Also very slender."

Wilson's ears perked up. Dunn's eyes grew wide. Reynolds had told them of a man named Prachar whom he and Cooper had encountered at Chonchai's Bar and Grill in Lopburi.

"Are there any other names you can recall?" Dunn asked.

"No. I am sorry."

"Do you know where any of these people live?"

"Prachar lives somewhere near Lopburi. The others live here in Bangkok. I am not certain exactly where."

"Do you have a picture of Mungchai that we could see?" Wilson inquired.

Getting to her feet, Rawi moved across to a shelf unit on the wall and lifted away an eight-by-ten framed photograph. She returned and handed it to Doug Wilson. "This is a recent picture," she announced, "except he now has a mustache."

Wilson studied the photograph for a brief time, then handed it to Marilyn Dunn, while Rawi settled back into her chair and took another sip of tea.

"I have one just like that but wallet-sized. You may have it if you would care to."

"That would be helpful," Marilyn told her, continuing to study the photograph.

"He is a handsome young man, is he not? It is quite a pity that he has allowed himself to become involved in this bad situation."

"Yes, indeed," Marilyn agreed.

"What time do you expect him home?" asked Doug Wilson.

"Sometime this afternoon," Rawi sipped again from her tea cup. "Perhaps three o'clock."

Except for a closely cropped, freshly manicured lawn, the land-scaping was sparse. Two large hibiscus bushes stood at the west edge of the yard. The bushes had a full, healthy look to them, the one on the right slightly taller. Both appeared to have been shaped carefully and smoothly, as though at the hand of a professional gardener. All in all, they were fine-looking bushes. Viewing the bushes from her window, Rawi Tisiwad shrugged her shoulders and shook her head.

"Are you comfortable?" the taller bush asked the shorter one.

"What?"

"I asked if you were comfortable." More loudly this time.

"Hell, no."

"Neither am I. I itch all over."

"Well, don't scratch. It'd be the absolute worst thing you could do." Anyone knows hibiscus bushes don't scratch.

"I still don't see why we couldn't have handled this as a regular vehicular surveillance." The level of the taller bush's voice had risen a notch.

Impatiently, the shorter bush said, "Take a look around—just with your eyes, don't move your head—and tell me if you see any cars around here."

Wilson did as Dunn had suggested. "No," he agreed, "but there is a road in front of the house."

"Samlors and bicycles. No cars," Dunn pointed out in a whisper that was becoming raspy. "The road is too narrow. It was never intended for two-way automobile traffic. A car would stick out like a sore thumb."

"I suppose you're right."

"But I have to admit I hope we don't have to stay here much longer. My feet are getting tired."

Doug Wilson's eyes moved to the front door. "It doesn't look like we'll have to. There's our rabbit now. That's Mungchai on the front porch. Mustache and all."

Mungchai had returned home about forty minutes earlier. Now he was on his way out again.

The smaller bush said to the larger bush, "As soon as he's out of sight, radio Reynolds and Cooper and the other two teams, so they can watch for him and latch onto him as soon as he hits Soi 7."

Moments later, Doug Wilson spoke a few quiet words into a walkie-talkie. To Marilyn Dunn, he reported back in a whisper, "They're on it. They'll pick up the tail in a couple of minutes."

"Good. Now maybe we can get out of here and get all this green stuff off us."

"Sounds good to me. Let's change at your place."

She laughed. "Did your horoscope for today say anything about getting lucky?"

"It sure did. 'Gemini: Pay close attention to financial matters and, oh by the way, expect to get laid.'"

Inside the house immediately west of the Tisiwad home, George Thornton, a retired US foreign service officer who'd stayed on in Bangkok after his retirement, remarked to his wife as they looked out a side window, "God, what a beautiful day! Right, Margaret?"

She nodded. "Positively delightful. Hey, where did those two bushes come from?"

"Those?" George said. "Don't you remember? I planted those last year. They've just gotten bigger is all. Wait'll you see 'em in the summer. My gardening book says they get the brightest biggest pink flowers on 'em you ever saw."

"Hmm," Margaret responded, recalling her husband's sometimes unreliable memory.

"Just wait. They're gonna be gorgeous," George continued. "Or," he corrected a moment later, as he and Margaret watched the bushes slowly tiptoe away, "maybe not."

It was to be a three-vehicle surveillance, classic Holabird strategy, sometimes referred to as the "ABC surveillance method." Reynolds and Cooper were on one side of the street in the green Falcon. On the other side of the street and pointed in the opposite direction in Major Harris's red Mercedes, polished to a high gloss, were the major and Captain Scharfenberg. The direction selected by their "rabbit" upon his appearance would dictate which of these two cars would take the "a" position and which the "c" position. Once the surveillance began, the three cars would rotate as called for by changing circumstances and in such a way as to minimize the likelihood of detection.

Half a block behind Harris and Scharfenberg was a new, tan Datsun occupied by a pair of AFSC agents. Colonel Morgan had decided it would be wise to involve the Thai Government's intelligence arm, once Dunn and Wilson had reminded him they were dealing with a Thai national.

"Here he comes," Cooper said to Reynolds. He pointed in the direction of a young Asian man walking briskly from Rattan Lane. Cooper had been eating *khowpot sii daeng*. It had been purchased at a small café up the street and was in a Styrofoam container. He finished the last bite and set the container and plastic fork on the floor in the back seat. He balled up a napkin and tossed it in the backseat area as well. Messiness made him uncomfortable, but he would be able to clean it all up later.

Sitting behind the wheel, Reynolds glanced down at the photograph in his hand. "Yeah, that's him, all right."

Upon reaching the heavily traveled Soi 7, the man stopped. At that moment, a taxi came by and, at the man's signal, pulled over at the curb.

Cooper opened the glove compartment and lifted out the two-way radio transmitter. Holding it just below chest level to lessen the chance of some passerby seeing it, he depressed the transmit button. "All windows. All windows, this is window three. Rabbit has surfaced. He is entering a taxi heading east on Soi 7. A late-model gray Toyota. Over."

A burst of static hit the speaker, followed by a voice. "Uh, window three, this is window eight. That's a roger. We copy. Got him in our sights, and we'll take the 'a' position." It was Orville Harris, and it was clear that he was enjoying this.

Another burst. Then a voice with a Thai accent announced, "Window three, this window twelve. Roger, wilco, ten-four. We take 'b' position. This twelve out."

They were off: the gray Toyota taxi first, followed closely by Harris and Scharfenberg in the red Mercedes. The tan Datsun was next. Having just completed a U-turn, Reynolds and Cooper brought up the rear in the green Falcon.

"Okay, kiddies," Reynolds mumbled to no one in particular, "it's time to play 'follow the leader.'" Cooper found that strains of the song "It's A Small World" were running through his head. He made a brief and unsuccessful attempt at replacing it with "Viva Las Vegas."

Soon, all of them were well into the heart of the city, where the streets were wider and the traffic was heavier. Tall buildings surrounded them. Traffic circles and poorly timed stoplights confounded them.

"Uh, all windows. Uh, all windows, this is window eight." The major's voice again. "Rabbit is turning left on Rajadamri. Uh, we've dropped back three car lengths. Suggest you folks spread out some too. This is eight out."

A burst of static. "This window twelve. Roger, wilco, ten-four. This twelve out."

Don Cooper pressed his transmit button and spoke. "Eight, this is three. Would you like for us to slide over a block and take a true 'c' position to minimize the chances of being spotted? Over."

"This is eight. Ten-three on that. Hold your position for now. Let's wait a while to see how long he's going to continue in this direction. Do you copy? Over."

"This is three. Ten-four. Out."

Reynolds eased off on the accelerator, allowing two cars to pass. Out of the corner of his eye, he saw a sudden grimace come to his friend's face. "What is it, Don?"

"Oh Christ," Cooper moaned just then. "I've got it."

"Got what?"

"Bangkok belly." Cooper was doubled over in anguish.

"Oh man, you can't. Not now."

"Hell yes, now!" Cooper's features twisted in agony and he removed the plastic litter bag from its place below the dash and in front of the passenger door. He got it open just in time to bring it to his mouth and vomit into it.

Reynolds tightened his jaw. He made a left onto Rajadamri as the others had done, catching sight once again of the AFSC team in their tan Datsun, about thirty meters and four cars ahead. "Hold on, old buddy," he told Cooper.

Major Harris's voice suddenly filled the car. "Uh, all windows. All windows, this is window eight. Uh, we've been burned. Rabbit has definitely spotted us. We'll drop out and leave it to the rest of you to stay with him. Over."

Reynolds growled to himself through gritted teeth, "Well, what did you expect? You're driving a red goddamned Mercedes, for Chrissake."

One of the AFSC agents was heard from next, following a brief burst of static, "This window twelve. Roger, wilco, okay. We take 'a' position. Ten-four. Out."

Reynolds could see the red Mercedes occupied by Harris and Scharfenberg peel off to the left about a block ahead. They were out of it now. Glancing to his right just in time to see Don Cooper barf into the bag again, Reynolds clamped his hands tighter on the steering wheel and made up his mind to keep his eyes on the road and his thoughts on his work.

"Window three, this window twelve. Rabbit turning right on Ploenchit. We four cars behind. Over."

Window three's mic was resting on Cooper's lap. Don picked it up and said, "This is...oh...ohh...this is..." His attempt to get the litter bag to his mouth was late.

"Window three, this window twelve. Everything okay your location?" More static. "Over."

Ed Reynolds reached across, picked up the mic, gave it a quick wipe on the upholstery, and held it as close to his face as he dared. "Three here. Small problem, but we'll be fine. We're with you. Over."

"Roger, wilco, ten-four. This twelve out."

"Hey, Don," Reynolds said to his friend, "how about if I drop you at the next gas station and go it alone? You're obviously not at your best right now."

"No," Cooper insisted. "No, I'll be all right."

The AFSC agent's voice came over the speaker again. "This window twelve. We behind two buses. Rabbit ahead. "We... *Oi! Mai mii!* Buses pull over. Rabbit gone!"

Reynolds responded, "This is three. Suggest you take a left at the next intersection. We'll take a right. Maybe one of us will pick him up. Over."

"This window twelve. Roger, ten-four. Out."

The smell inside the Ford Falcon was beginning to turn Ed's stomach as he whipped the car around the next traffic circle, completing his right turn. Five minutes later, he spotted the gray Toyota taxi a few vehicles ahead. "Window twelve, this is window three. Have rabbit in sight. If you turn around, you might be able to catch up. Over."

"That good news. We catch up. Twelve out."

Out of the corner of his eye, Reynolds could see Don Cooper rocking back and forth. He was beginning to moan. Then, with startling suddenness, a green pickup truck loaded with vegetables backed out of a driveway less than twenty feet ahead of them. Reynolds stomped on the brake pedal, and they lurched forward as the brakes took hold.

The pickup stalled. The driver swore in Thai. The Falcon stalled. Reynolds swore in English. Horns blared. Tempers flared. Bystanders shouted. A little girl on the other side of the street cried. Cooper filled his pants.

CHAPTER THIRTY-ONE

When Marilyn Dunn was thirteen years old, the family cat died. Choo-Choo, a slender calico, was seventeen, having been with the family four years longer than Marilyn herself. Marilyn had never known life without him. In fact, it was recognized within the family that he had become her cat, for all practical purposes. And it was clear that he came to think of himself that way too.

To Marilyn, Choo-Choo was a friend, a playmate, a buddy, a father confessor. Because she had no sisters or brothers and had parents who were very skeptical of most of her would-be friends, the calico filled a void in her life.

People often say that cats are highly independent and even indifferent. And perhaps some are. But not so with Choo-Choo Dunn. This cat knew Marilyn well and, according to her mother, curled up each weekday and waited patiently on the small rug by the front door for her to return from school. And when she did, he came to life, following her, leading her, trying to anticipate where she might be heading next, rubbing up against her, sitting on her lap once she settled into a chair or the couch. He slept at the end of her bed. He ate food only if she was the one who dished it up.

Choo-Choo did not die quickly. He lingered in a slow, painful death, resulting from cancer of the stomach. The veterinarian had run out of treatment strategies and hope simultaneously. "Just make him as comfortable as you can, and give him one of these tablets twice a day to help with the pain," the doctor had advised, handing her a bottle. "That's all any of us can do."

It was around the middle of the day on a Thursday, a school day, that Marilyn's mother reached the conclusion that the calico wouldn't be able to hold on to life much longer. But as she described it later to her daughter, it was if he knew he *had* to, at least for a while. Lying on the rug by the front door, scanning the room frequently for Marilyn without finding her, it seemed that he gritted his teeth out of a determination to remain in the world until she returned and he could tell her goodbye. He seemed to understand the importance of that for both of them.

When at last Marilyn returned from school and lay down on the floor next to him, the calico opened his eyes in recognition, then closed them for eternity.

The Dunn family owned some property in the northern part of the state, ten acres, not far from Lake Shasta. The plan had been that they would build a cabin there someday when finances permitted, a family retreat from the workaday world of Sacramento.

When Choo-Choo passed on, they drove him up to the property. Selecting a site with an especially fine view of the nearby mountain, snowcapped and magnificent in its beauty, they buried him and erected a marker.

"Now he belongs to the ages," Marilyn's father announced.

Choo-Choo Dunn. Dead at seventeen.

To this day, whenever Marilyn thought of him, she found a tear coming to her eye.

During the next week, Mungchai Tisiwad was tailed by MI and AFSC agents in varying combinations to a movie theater, three restaurants, two department stores, a doctor's office, and a house of ill repute. Major Orville Harris insisted on personally verifying the authenticity of the latter establishment. He verified it for about forty-five minutes.

On the tenth of April, Marilyn Dunn and Doug Wilson had the surveillance responsibility, driving separate vehicles. As twilight approached, they followed Mungchai to the outskirts of town.

Marilyn depressed the button on her handheld mic and spoke into it. "Window seven, this is window ten. Over."

"Ten, this is seven. Over."

"Rabbit has just made a right turn onto Damri street. I seem to recall Damri is narrow and lightly traveled, and it dead-ends a couple of kilometers in, so we'd probably better ease off. Over."

"That's a roger. Dropping back now. You're right. Let's give him lots of room. Over."

"Good. Ten out."

Mungchai drove to a building in a small industrial complex and then went inside. Parking their Ford Falcons almost a block away and on opposite sides of the street, Dunn and Wilson waited in their cars.

Over the radio, she asked him, "Any idea what he might be doing in there? Over."

"Huh-uh. Can't even make out what kind of building it is." He surveyed the scene a bit more. "It looks like it might be a cluster of small factories. Wood carvings, furniture, tourist items, that sort of thing. That would be my guess. Over."

"Tell you what, window seven, I'll check out the building as soon as he leaves. Doesn't look like there's anybody else in there. I don't see any other cars around. You tail Mungchai. Sound okay? Over."

"Ten-four. But you be careful, ya hear? I'm kind of stuck on you, window ten. Over."

"I think you're pretty terrific too, window seven. And by the way, 'careful' is my middle name. This is ten out."

When Mungchai Tisiwad exited the building some twenty minutes later and then reentered the taxi, Doug Wilson followed him. Judging from his direction, it appeared he might be heading home. Wilson stayed close anyway, just in case the destination might turn out to be somewhere else.

With darkness settling fast, Marilyn Dunn got out of her car and made her way toward the building from which Mungchai had come. She was more than a little nervous.

It was a large ramshackle affair that had the look of a barn turned factory turned vacant building. Three stories tall, with girth comparable to height, its once brown hue had grayed considerably over the years. It could use a new coat of paint, Dunn noted. Hell, it could use a new coat of *wood.*

Dunn was surprised to discover that the building's doors and windows were new, installed most likely within the last few months. This gave the structure an element of security greater than first glance would indicate.

She peered through one of the windows, finding only darkness on the other side. Quickly inventing a cover story about searching for a lost dog, she went to the door and knocked. But as she had hoped, no one responded. A credit card from her purse—handy little devices, these credit cards—helped her make short work of the lock. And then she was inside. A smell caught her nostrils, a smell of filth and decay, causing her to think of rats and sewers and dead things. She suppressed a shudder.

Marilyn felt along the wall for a light switch. "Damn," she muttered when she found none. Moving cautiously toward the center of the room, she could barely see the outline of a light bulb and socket affixed to the ceiling and a string that hung from it. Pulling the string, she filled the room with light.

It was a smaller room than she'd imagined, a living room it would seem. Perhaps this barn turned factory turned vacant building had once been a house. One tattered couch and one decushioned armchair were the only furnishings. The walls were bare and badly scarred, as was the wooden floor.

"My kingdom for a roll of wallpaper," Marilyn said under her breath, surprised at how loud those softly spoken words sounded inside this ancient structure.

Gingerly, she stepped into another room, a kitchen. There she found a refrigerator, a stove, and a sink. She opened the door of the refrigerator—a Kelvinator, about twenty years old, she judged—and discovered that it was well stocked with food and drink.

In the fifteen minutes that followed, Marilyn explored the rest of the building, including the two upper floors. On the top floor, she found beds in three of the rooms. At the foot of one of the beds was a stack of cardboard boxes. Pulling back the flaps of one of them, she found it filled with pamphlets neatly rubber-banded together in batches. The print was Thai, but a likeness of Mao

Tse Tung on page one of each pamphlet left little doubt as to its contents.

Then she spotted something else. An address label was taped to the side of the bottom box, and the address on it was in English as well as in Thai. It was a Lopburi address—27 Saporn Road.

"Lordie, Lordie," she said as something clicked in her brain. She'd hit pay dirt.

When she returned to the offices of the 187th MI Detachment a short time later, she found Doug Wilson waiting for her. Everyone else had departed for home considerably earlier.

"Guess what, my gorgeous friend," she said.

"What?"

"I came up with an address...a *Lopburi* address."

Doug smiled. "Lopburi, huh?"

"Yep."

"It sounds like AFSC has some arrests to make."

The next day was a busy one for the AFSC people. Acting upon information provided by Doug Wilson and Marilyn Dunn, they apprehended Mungchai Tisiwad from his Bangkok home and brought him in for questioning. They dispatched a team of agents to Lopburi and the address on Saporn Road. A carefully executed raid netted several additional members of the Communist Party of Thailand. Khamon Pranii, Rapong Chansoo, and Prachar Keopraseurt surrendered after a brief exchange of gunfire.

A fourth CPT member, a Chinese woman, was more difficult to subdue. Leading a trio of AFSC agents on a chase through dense jungle, she fired back at them regularly with a small caliber pistol. Eventually, she ran out of stamina. Then she ran out of ammunition.

"You die, capitalist lackey dogs!" she spat at her captors, speaking in Thai.

One of the agents forcefully slapped a set of handcuffs on her wrists and said simply, "Shut up."

"In three months you all be dead!" she promised defiantly at the top of her voice. "The revolution is coming! The liberation of Thailand. It is already planned! Three months, imperialistic cocksuckers! Three months and you all be dead!"

When he learned the details of the capture, Doug Wilson could not help but wonder over the words of the Chinese woman. He asked Marilyn Dunn about it.

"Who knows?" she shrugged. "The meaningless ravings of a cornered lunatic, probably. I wouldn't put much stock in it." Changing the subject, she asked, "Did they find the scopes?"

"That's a big fat 'roger.' Telescopic rifle sights—comma—infrared—comma—US Army—comma—twenty crates."

Marilyn Dunn smiled. "Good."

CHAPTER THIRTY-TWO

"You haven't been following me, have you?" Ed asked her with a grin over lunch. He had been tailed much of the previous day. One of the USSR Embassy people cataloguing his activities, no doubt. Either GRU or KGB. Such things were common.

"Well, not me, personally. But that private detective I hired is costing me a fortune." Kanlaya was quick on the uptake.

"I suppose you know, then, about my eight other girlfriends?"

"The private detective counted twelve."

"No, no," he insisted, "that was *last* month. I'm trying to cut down. But it isn't easy."

"You just like women, that's all."

He shrugged. "You're on to me."

Someone accidently jostled Ed Reynolds's elbow, causing some of the beer to slosh out of his mug. The culprit turned out to be a listing Irv Bonner on his return from the men's room. "Sorry," he said.

"That's okay, Irv. Plenty more where that came from."

Bonner squeezed between Marilyn Dunn and Don Cooper to get back into his chair. On the other side of the table were Reynolds and Doug Wilson.

"I've never seen such a crowd in here before," Bonner observed. "Even in the rest room, they were lined up and waiting three deep at the urinals."

Reynolds agreed. "They're doing some kind of business here tonight. Even for a Friday. The place is packed."

Fat Raymond's was but one of many nightclubs lining Petchburi Road, a half-mile stretch of pavement usually referred to as "the strip." These establishments specialized in booze, loud music, and dancing. In a few cases, there was a bit of prostitution thrown in for good measure. Typically, the music was live, performed by energetic young Thai singers and musicians, belting out current rock hits from America. The clientele were predominately US Army types on R & R from Vietnam.

Cigarette smoke was thick at Fat Raymond's. It filled every corner of the brightly colored room, and it made Doug Wilson, a non-smoker with sensitive bronchial passages, cough occasionally.

The group had assembled this evening to celebrate the contributions of Dunn and Wilson in bringing the rifle scope and kidnapping case to a successful resolution. This was a much happier occasion than the last time they had gotten together here. That had been a few days earlier—April 5th, the day they'd learned of the assassination of Dr. Martin Luther King—a great American cut down in his prime by a crazed lunatic named James Earl Ray. That had been a sad day, indeed, and these five MI agents had felt the need to celebrate his life and toast his accomplishments.

"Damn! You guys are terrific!" Don Cooper was saying now to Marilyn and Doug. "You nailed those bastards." He refilled his mug with beer from the pitcher in the center of the table. The pitcher was getting low, so he signaled the waitress for another.

"Well, we did have some help from AFSC," Marilyn pointed out with modesty.

"They did the hard part," Doug added with a cough, recalling AFSC's account of the arrests, and also recalling the Chinese woman's ominous words.

Marilyn said, "In fact, when you come right down to it, there's plenty of credit to go around. *You* did *your* share." She nodded toward the other members of the group, each of whom had taken rotational surveillance duty.

"You must be referring to that memorable surveillance of a few days ago," Ed Reynolds commented. "Hell, I'm *still* trying to get the *smell* out of the green Falcon."

Don Cooper chirped, "Yeah, and Reynolds takes driving lessons from Mother Goose."

"Now, now," Marilyn said, "you kids play nice."

Reynolds volunteered, "Well, my vote for Most Valuable Player goes to the man in the bright-red Mercedes Benz. Major Orville Wright Harris."

A mixture of applause and laughter went around the table.

Don Cooper carried that thought a step further. "And here to accept the award on behalf of Major Harris, is his good friend and trusted associate, that renowned Gemini, Lieutenant Douglas Wilson."

More applause.

Wilson stood and made an abrupt bow, then spread his hands as if to silence the crowd. "Thank you, ladies and gentlemen, thank you. Major Harris regrets that he cannot be here this evening to share in this propitious event, but he asked me to express his warm appreciation for such a wonderful and richly deserved honor."

More applause. More silencing of the crowd.

Wilson continued, "And Colonel Morgan has asked me to say a few words on his behalf as well."

"Speech, speech," Marilyn Dunn chanted. "Speak on behalf of our beloved commanding officer."

"He wanted me to let you know that you're all guilty of undermining the mission, and that each of you is to report to the stockade at your earliest convenience."

"Oh, right, sir. Without delay, sir."

Reynolds raised his glass. "Here's to the stockade."

"To the stockade."

"To the stockade. Wherever that is."

They all clinked glasses and drank from them.

During the next few minutes, they found their attention shifting to the stage where a group called The Fantastic Five was singing "I Wanna Hold Your Hand." The lead singer was a young Thai woman with black hair that hung almost to her hips and who seemed to be everywhere as she frantically bounced around the stage. Three of her male backup singers plucked the strings of the guitars slung over their shoulders, while the fourth pounded away on a set of drums, collectively doing a suitable imitation of Ringo and the gang.

Irv Bonner picked up the conversational slack a few minutes later. "I understand *Valley of the Dolls* is coming to Bangkok soon. The Siam Theater, I think."

"That should be a good movie," Marilyn Dunn stated. "The book was great! Lots of terrific sex. I'll tell you, there isn't a novelist alive who can out-sex Jacqueline Suzanne."

Bonner smiled shyly. "I plan to be first in line at the ticket window as soon as it hits town." He felt himself blush.

"And I'll be right behind you."

Doug Wilson put his hand on Marilyn's wrist just then and asked, "How about a dance?"

She grinned and nodded. The two of them stood and worked their way through the crowd to the dance floor. There, they found a space among the masses and began "Twistin' the Night Away."

Reynolds, Bonner, and Cooper studied them a while from a distance, smiles on their faces. Ed finally spoke, "They make a great couple, don't they? Two really good people who deserve to be happy."

"Uh-huh. I just hope the world is ready for them," Cooper noted between belches. "And I hope they're ready for the world."

"The interracial thing, you mean?"

"Yep, that's what I mean."

Reynolds stroked the lower line of his jaw and furrowed his brow. "They'll make it, if that's what they decide they want."

Irv Bonner nodded his agreement.

Cooper stated, "They're pretty tough, at that." This was about as much philosophy as Don's blurred, beer-burdened brain could handle, so he lapsed into silence.

CHAPTER THIRTY-THREE

"I've located one," Ralph Owens's secretary announced at 1535 hours on April 14, 1968.

"A 1961 codebook?" Owens was excited.

"That's right. Our people in Paraguay have one. They've agreed to send it by special courier, as soon as they can spare somebody. It should be here in five or six days." She added, "Naturally, they expect us to reimburse them for his travel expenses."

"Bullshit."

"Excuse me, sir?"

"I said 'bullshit,'" repeated Ralph Owens, Central Intelligence Agency chief for Thailand operations.

PART SIX

THE EDMONDSON TRANSMITTAL

CHAPTER THIRTY-FOUR

"Oh, sweet baby, you've found one of my erogenous zones," Ed moaned as she eased her tongue into his ear.

"Mmm," Kanlaya responded, continuing to indulge her ear fetish.

"Of course, I have 258 of them. So your odds were pretty good."

"You are terrible." She clobbered him with a pillow.

"You are right."

As Ed Reynolds crossed out the number corresponding to April 19, 1968, on the short-timer's calendar on his desk, he took a few moments to wonder about his unwavering eagerness to get himself out of the army. Until this moment, he'd always taken it for granted as a perfectly normal and natural reaction, not really subject to question or debate. It certainly was a common enough sentiment, not only within the 187th, but also practically everywhere he looked in any unit in any branch of the service. Nearly everyone had a short-timer's calendar.

But from a purely objective viewpoint, Ed Reynolds's life in the army was not a bad one. In many ways, it was quite the opposite. He was living in a beautiful, exotic city of the Far East that he probably never would have even visited but for the army. His work was interesting and not too terribly difficult. To a greater extent each day, he was sharing his life with a wonderful woman—Connie Chanyangam. He'd never met anyone quite like her. And that too he owed to Uncle Sam. At least indirectly.

He was residing in a perfectly delightful apartment, complete with swimming pool and tennis courts. And air-conditioning that worked some of the time. Once housing, clothing, food, and overseas-duty allowances were added in, he was taking home about 550 dollars a month. Many of his friends on the outside—even college graduates like himself—were netting less than that. He'd opened a savings account a few months back and had accumulated over a thousand dollars in it. So it was even difficult for him to complain about his financial circumstances. Unlike most other military connoisseurs of short-timer calendars, his uniform of the day—every day—was civilian clothes. And he was assigned a government car. Not too shabby.

When you came right down to it, this whole special agent business was a pretty cushy deal. And a real boost to the ego. If he'd ever experienced feelings of self-doubt or lack of confidence, this situation certainly would have repaired them.

All things considered, this was a pleasant life. Why, then, the overwhelming urgency to abandon it? Why was he in such a hurry to escape? He sometimes asked himself that question.

Was it because of that great myopic bastard Colonel Morgan? The man who blundered his way from one fiasco to the next, leaving a trail of disaster particles Hansel and Gretel could have followed? Reynolds thought not. Reynolds was aware that many of Morgan's traits were shared by heads of civilian organizations. Even as a civilian, Reynolds could not be assured of immunity from the Spencer Morgans of the world. No, the colonel wasn't the reason.

Was it because of Major Harris? The man who had turned lunacy into a special kind of art form? The most ruthless of the ruthless? The man who at every key choice point in his life seemed to ask himself, "Now, what would an asshole do in this situation?" and then proceeded accordingly? The man who had truly cared about only two things in his entire life—himself and a bright-red Mercedes Benz? No, Major Harris wasn't the reason either. As strong as Ed's disgust was, he knew that through avoidance and sheer gritting of teeth, he could put up with Orville Harris for as long as he needed to.

There was, of course, the fact that the army had forced him to put on hold his plans for a career. That was a source of some frustration and had been all along, beginning with his first day of basic training. He was determined to become a successful journalist, to uncover important events and to write great stories about them. He yearned to set the world on fire with his journalistic abilities. The army was delaying the realization of that ambition, and certainly that was *a part of* his need for escape. He knew that. But it wasn't all of it. Not even close. Why, then, had the date of August 8, 1968, become so incredibly important to him?

One day the answer came to him suddenly! And it was so amazingly simple! He'd been remotely aware of it before—in some fuzzy, poorly defined way. But now it became clear. Control!

Or more precisely, the *lack* of it.

As a civilian, he'd been in control of his life. So even if it happened to be a shitty life—which it wasn't—he was the one in charge of it, and he was the one with the power to change it if he ever decided to do so.

Once he'd entered the army, Reynolds had turned over that control to someone else. Actually, to a whole *bunch* of someone elses. *They* decided what kind of work he was going to do. *They* decided where he was going to do it. *They* decided when he was going to do it. No recourse, No opportunity for debate or discussion. Just obedience.

His life was totally under the control of outside influences. And he didn't like it. He knew there were many people who felt differently about this issue than he did. He was glad of that, because he knew there needed to be a military. He wasn't in any way opposed to the concept. He simply wanted to be separate from it. And the sooner the better!

One hundred eleven days until separation. One hundred ten and "a wake-up," actually. If only he could hang on until then, all would be right with the world once more. He set aside the short-timer's calendar and smiled.

That afternoon Reynolds went out for drinks with Marilyn Dunn, Irv Bonner, Doug Wilson, and Don Cooper. There was but one topic of conversation—Lyndon Johnson's recent decision not to run for reelection. There was uniform agreement that this was good news. For her part, Marilyn was ecstatic, even jubilant! This obviously opened the door for Bobby Kennedy, who had announced his candidacy a couple of weeks before that. And it should be smooth sailing from here on out.

In unison, the group lifted their glasses and toasted Robert F. Kennedy, the next president of the United States.

There was a side to Ed Reynolds that few people were aware of. He himself was almost unaware of its existence. It was an illogical, irrational, right-brained side. It was a sentimental, romantic side. And from it, on the evening of April 21st, came the words, "I love you, Connie."

"I love you too," said Kanlaya Chanyangam.

Eyes closed and lips met.

At two thirty in the morning, the telephone rang, awakening both of them from a sound sleep. Ed reached out and picked up the receiver. And then he hurled it across the room, or at least as far as the coiled cord would permit.

As it lay there on the floor, Ed could hear a faint voice describing some sort of marmalade product. Ed and Kanlaya looked at each other through half-opened eyes and smiled. They snuggled together and went back to sleep.

CHAPTER THIRTY-FIVE

Lieutenant Colonel Spencer G. Morgan had nearly given up hope of ever learning more about the Edmondson transmittal when, on one of his rotational shifts in the van parked up the street from Ralph Owens's house, he heard the static-distorted voice of the agency chief as he said to his wife, "We've decoded it."

"The Edmondson report?" asked Eunice Owens.

"Yeah. Finally."

"Good. Congratulations."

"And is it ever hot stuff. It summarizes a Communist Party of Thailand plot that is scary as hell, I mean to tell you. The CPT intends to take over this country. And they have very specific plans for dealing with anyone standing in their way."

"Like you, you mean?"

"Exactly."

Silence for a moment, followed by, "That's terrible!"

A brief laugh. "I couldn't agree more." Ralph Owens's voice grew faint as he said, "Pour me a drink and I'll tell you more about it." It sounded to Colonel Morgan as though Owens was leaving the room and heading for another part of the house. It also sounded like what he had uncovered was incredibly bad news!

"All right. How about a Manhattan?" Eunice's voice too was becoming faint.

"Sure." Barely audible.

Morgan could pick up nothing more of that conversation. The next words he heard were more than three hours later. "Good night, sweetie pie." It was the voice of Ralph Owens.

"Good night, Ralphie. I love you. We'll get through this somehow."

"I love you too, honeybun."

Spencer G. Morgan was convinced he would go crazy if he didn't learn more about what was contained in the Edmondson report. He hoped he wouldn't have to wait long.

Two young Thai men and one young Thai woman hopped out of the gray pickup truck they had just parked in lot number eight. It was very late at night and the parking lot was empty. As nearly as they could determine, the entire campus of Chulalongkorn University was virtually deserted. Lights shone faintly in the distance on upper floors of a couple of the taller buildings on the far side of the campus, hinting there at the presence of cleaning crews or late-working professors. Other than that, the new arrivals were confident of solitude.

Despite the late hour, the air was warm, humid, and heavy, but a slight breeze made it more bearable. It blew through the jacaranda trees that bordered lot number eight, rustling them gently. The young woman watched while the two men dropped the gate at the back of the pickup and then vaulted up onto its bed. They walked forward to two wooden boxes that were held securely against the back of the cab by a sturdy hemp rope.

Unleashing the rope and tossing it aside, the young men picked up the two boxes, carried them to the rear of the truck, and carefully set them at the edge. Then they jumped to the pavement and once again lifted the boxes. They followed the young woman onto the sidewalk, the smell of jacaranda blossoms wafting sweetly into their nostrils.

Moments later, the trio of Thais came to a halt at the double-door entry of a two-story building. The woman produced a key, opened the doors, and led the men inside.

CHAPTER THIRTY-SIX

Reynolds was having a perfectly delightful dream about Major Harris drowning in an ocean of apricot marmalade when the telephone rang. He glanced at the clock. Two thirty. Of course. And two nights in a row! At least he was alone this time. He began swearing before his hand even made it to the receiver. "Hello, goddammit, Finsky, you prick!" he shouted into it.

Specialist Fourth Class Finsky chortled, "Apricot marmalade."

"English muffins and apple jelly, you goddamned son of a bitch!" Reynolds barked.

"That's my boy," Finsky said in a melodic tone. "And by the way, the CO is really pissed about your no-show last night. He's considering disciplinary action. You know, Article 15 stuff. UCMJ. Be here in fifteen minutes, okay?"

"I'll be there when I damn well feel like it."

"Right. Fifteen minutes. See ya."

Reynolds slammed down the receiver and got dressed. He was surprised to find himself among the first to arrive at the office. Only three others were ahead of him. One of them, First Sergeant Barnett, was wearing fatigues, while the other two were wearing customary garb of slacks, short-sleeved white shirt, and narrow, diagonally striped necktie.

When everyone was present, Colonel Morgan assembled them in the conference room. "Find a seat, people," he instructed. "This is not a drill. This is the real thing."

"Does this mean we're taking to the jungle, sir?" Barnett called out from the third row, his voice brimming with obvious excitement.

"Afraid not, First Sergeant. I've just come from the Officers' Club at the Chao Pya Hotel. A little late-evening refreshment." The

Chao Pya catered to the US military, having established an Officers' Club and a special gaming room filled with slot machines. The one-armed bandits accepted only US coinage, and it was widely known that they received plenty of it.

Morgan continued, "General Wolfe was there. Over his sixth or seventh martini, he let it slip that he's planning to pull a surprise inspection of our outfit at 0830 hours this morning."

A concerned buzz filled the room.

"Well, *we're* going to be *ready* for him. During the next five-and-a-half hours, we are going to GI this place from stem to stern, from top to bottom, and from head to toe. And speaking of heads"—a wicked smile came to the colonel's face—"I'm putting Sergeant Reynolds in charge of the men's latrine. And the women's too. Maybe that will convince him to take these apricot marmalade exercises more seriously in the future."

There were chuckles and snickers.

"And I want them spotless, Sergeant. I want everything to glisten. I expect to be able to eat off those commodes."

"I'll see what I can arrange for you, sir."

"Good," Morgan responded, either missing or ignoring the innuendo. "Now, everyone will be responsible for cleaning his or her own office or cubicle. In addition to that, Sergeant Cooper will straighten up the ready room, and Specialist Finsky will do the corridors and the open areas, including waxing and buffing the floors. Naturally, I'll need someone to take care of my office while I oversee this operation. Sergeant Dunn, that will be you. It never hurts to have a woman's touch in these matters."

Marilyn Dunn grimaced, almost said something, but held back.

"Can anybody think of anything I've overlooked?" Morgan asked.

As Ed Reynolds was aware, it was characteristic of Orville Harris that his eyes narrowed and his brow furrowed whenever something significant was on his mind which, fortunately for all, did not occur often. "Sir," Harris said, eyes narrowing, brow furrowing, "I think it might be a good idea for me to hold a preliminary in-ranks inspection at 0800 hours, just to be on the safe side."

"Sort of a dry run, you mean."

"Yes, sir."

"Excellent idea, Major. Do that."

By 0800 hours, the facility was clean, cleaner than it had been in months. Reynolds found the glare from waxed floors and polished desks to be nearly blinding, especially when they confronted eyes that were still droopy from lack of sleep.

The members of the detachment were assembled once more, this time in formation. Everyone, that is, except for the colonel, whom Reynolds believed to be snoozing in his office, as evidenced by the distinct sound of snoring coming from that direction.

"Ten-hut!" Orville Harris said to the group.

The members of the group snapped to attention, their .38 revolvers tucked inside their belts and civilian pants and/or skirt, immediately to the left of the buckle, as had been instructed and diagrammed minutes earlier when Captain Scharfenberg had issued the appropriate revolver to the appropriate trooper. First Sergeant Barnett, the lone exception, was still dressed in fatigues. Because of an overhang problem, it was difficult for Reynolds to tell if the first sergeant was carrying the required revolver.

"Dress right, dress!" Major Harris barked. Left arms were extended, establishing the proper distance between troops, and eyes looked right. "Ready, front!" Arms were dropped. Eyes refocused straight ahead.

The major was enjoying this, Reynolds could tell. Far too much.

Harris continued to conduct his preliminary inspection, Al Finsky trailing a step behind to record any deficiencies. Finsky too seemed to be enjoying these early-morning activities.

In order, Finsky recorded:

Bonner—2 gigs (unshined shoes, tarnished belt buckle; "but sir, it's tough to polish a civilian belt buckle." "That's *your* problem, Lieutenant."); Dunn—2 gigs (no reason given); Wilson—1 gig ("Stand a little closer to your razor next time, Lieutenant." "Yes, sir."); Barnett—1 gig (the first sergeant was gigged on general principles when Harris was unable to get a line of sight at the first sergeant's belt buckle to determine whether it needed polishing); and Reynolds—8 gigs ("No explanation necessary.").

"Could we make that an even 'ten,' sir?" Finsky asked the major. "It'd be easier for record-keeping purposes."

Harris silenced him with a scowl and then moved on to Don Cooper. "Let me see your weapon, trooper," he instructed.

In two crisp movements, Cooper removed the .38 from his belt and presented it to the major. Harris examined it carefully, flipping open the cylinder, studying the chamber, peering down the barrel.

"Filthy. Absolutely fucking filthy," Harris announced. To Finsky, he said, "Three gigs. A soldier's first responsibility is to his weapon. That goes *double* for special agents... So you'd better make that *six.*" He returned the weapon to Cooper.

Finsky noted it, chortling audibly. Ed Reynolds was reminded of the fact that Finsky was a prick.

Before dismissing the formation, Major Harris delivered a lecture on the importance of getting haircuts at precise seven-day intervals, which of course was ridiculous in that not one of them, other than First Sergeant Barnett, had been anywhere near a barber for the past seven *weeks* and few had any intention of seeing one for the *next* seven. Reynolds, who as a civilian had worn his hair in a style that could best be described as "Beatle-length," was planning his next haircut for some time around Memorial Day.

At 0828 hours, General Wolfe arrived and was met at the front door by Colonel Morgan. Wearing dress greens and campaign ribbons. Nathan Wolfe, commanding general of US Army Support, Thailand, was a tall man with the trim, athletic build of one who works out regularly. His hair was black on top, gray along the sides, and his hairline was securely anchored at the top of his forehead despite his advanced age. With a powerful, attention-commanding face, Wolfe had the look of a man destined for recognition on Mount Rushmore. And when he walked, it was with a bearing that was profoundly military.

As soon as Major Harris officially called the group to attention, the general strode over to stand in front of Ed Reynolds.

Reynolds, who had never met the man before, was surprised that when the general opened his mouth to speak. A tiny, wispy, high-pitched voice came out. "Let me see your shot record, son," he said.

"Yes, sir." Reynolds produced his wallet and fished out a folded-up white card. This was his official US Army shot record, a complete account of every immunization Reynolds had received since entering the service. All members of the military, including MI, were expected to keep their shot records with them at all times.

General Wolfe examined the card and each entry on it. "I see you're past due for a typhoid shot, son." He handed it back.

"I'll take care of it right away, sir," Reynolds responded. He hated shots, not to mention the strange doctors at the 603rd Medical Dispensary. On the other hand, they were probably preferable to typhoid.

Wolfe made his way through the group, individually checking everyone's shot record. There was no in-ranks inspection, nor was there any inspection of the facilities that now shined more brightly than ever before. It was obvious to all, other than the general, that Major Harris was keenly resentful of this slight. He had the look of a thundercloud about to rain.

Prior to departing, General Wolfe said a few quiet words to Colonel Morgan and then centered himself in front of the group. "It is important to remember that this is not a sanitary country," he began solemnly. "Nothing about it is hygienic or clean. That, good people, means germs. *Lots* and *lots* of *germs*. *Germs* can be an even more deadly enemy than communism. At least you can see communists. Germs are invisible. *Germs* are deadly. *Germs* can *kill.*"

That struck a responsive chord with Don Cooper, who nodded vigorously.

"Now, there are only two ways to combat germs," Wolfe continued. "Keeping those immunizations current is the first."

Cooper was not just current with his immunizations, but he was also three months ahead of schedule. He took considerable pride in that.

"The second has to do with cleanliness. Keep yourselves clean at all times, no matter what circumstances you may find yourselves in."

Cooper was so clean, he squeaked.

"Now, there's one more word to the wise I'd like to leave you people with. And that concerns the women of this country. They may be pretty, but they are bad news. Stay away from them. They can give you diseases you've never dreamed of."

On the contrary, Cooper dreamed of them constantly.

"I've heard, and I believe it to be accurate," the general went on, "that there is a strain of VD here in Southeast Asia that is so virulent and so resistant to penicillin that it is completely incurable. In fact, in many cases, your...um...your...uhh...hammer falls off... in the advanced stages." Then, noticing Marilyn Dunn in the audience, he amended, "If you're a fellow, that is."

On this note, General Wolfe did an about-face and departed. An eyewitness report had it that he stopped off in the men's room just long enough to wash his hands, and then went across the street to the hardware store owned by the elderly Chinese couple, where he bought a can of Lysol and sprayed himself all over with it.

The next morning, setting aside prior promises he'd made to himself, Don Cooper made for the 603rd Medical Dispensary to see Captain Doctor Swanson. He was met with "Well, Trooper Cooper it's you again. What is it this time?"

"Venereal disease, sir. And I think it may be the virulent kind."

CHAPTER THIRTY-SEVEN

The following morning, the telephone on Spencer Morgan's desk rang. "We need to meet," said the voice on the other end of the line. Although the man didn't bother to identify himself, Morgan knew that the voice belonged to Ralph Owens, and it carried a strong note of urgency.

"All right. When?"

"Today. This afternoon, if possible. My office."

"Okay," Morgan agreed. "How about 1530 hours?"

"Fine."

"See you then."

Morgan's level of anxiety was sky-high by the time he made the turn onto Wireless Road that afternoon and caught sight of the embassy. His gut was telling him that life was about to become very complicated. His gut was right.

Seated in Owens's austere office in an uncomfortable chair a few minutes later, Morgan crossed his legs, ankle over knee, and awaited the words of the CIA man.

Ralph Owens stated, "This is about the Edmondson transmittal. We've decoded it. We now know what it says."

Morgan was tempted to remark, "Well, it sure took you long enough." Instead, he simply said, "Oh?"

"We had some trouble locating the proper codebook."

No sense pissing off the CIA needlessly, Morgan reasoned, by saying what he really thought about the inadequacies of the organization and the universal ineptness of the people running it. "Sometimes codes can be more trouble than they're worth."

"You're probably right about that. Anyway, it looks like Edmondson was really on to something. And it means big trouble for both of us."

"What kind of trouble?" Spencer G. Morgan had enough problems already. He sure as hell didn't need any new ones.

Ralph Owens picked up a two-page document from his desk,
glanced at it briefly, and passed it across to Spencer Morgan. "I think
you'd better read it for yourself."

Leaning forward in his chair, Morgan focused on the neatly
typed, recently decoded report. He read silently, with increasing perplexity, the document that was destined to change his life
forever:

TOP SECRET

CIA CHIEF, THAILAND   **EYES ONLY**

AGENT REPORT ON INSURGENCY ACTIVITIES IN NORTHERN THAILAND FOR NOVEMBER 1967 (U)

1. (U) Consolidated Agent Report submitted in accordance
    with Agency Directive 94b, dated August 17, 1966.

2. (C) Reference is made to para 9 of cons agt rep for
    September 1967. No change.

3. (C) Reference is made to para 10 of cons agt rep for
    September 1967. No change observed.

4. (S) On November 8, the head man of the Karen hill tribe
    nearest Chiang Rai was assassinated, presumably by mem-
    bers of the Communist Party of Thailand (CPT), and
    threats have been made against other tribe members who
    have been outspoken in their views against communism.
    Two of them have fled the area in fear for their lives.

5. (C) On November 16, three US airmen on R & R from
    Vietnam were fired at from a speeding automobile in
    Chiang Mai. The automobile was a late-model dark-blue

Toyota. No injuries were sustained. Although this is presumed to be the work of the CPT, local authorities are also checking out a "jealous husband" theory.

6. (TS) Reports indicate that equipment and weapons from China and the Soviet Union are now in use in the northern sector. On November 23, plastic explosives of Soviet make were discovered in three of the abandoned CPT supply dumps uncovered by the Thai Border Patrol Police (BPP). Officials of the Armed Forces Security Center (AFSC) and the BPP maintain that the explosives are of a new type and are significantly more devastating than anything seen in this sector to date. A further, more comprehensive description of these materials will be provided in report form as soon as it becomes available.

7. (TS) A most reliable source has disclosed that a CPT espionage network of unprecedented scope has been established. It hatched in Chiang Mai, evidently during the early months of 1967. However, because of the rapid growth of the Bangkok contingent, a shift of the network center is anticipated, probably by early January. The source of that information is an insider, an agency subagent who successfully infiltrated the ring in September 1967.

8. (TS) Within six (6) months of the shift to Bangkok, a major coup is planned, a complete overthrow of the Thai government. It is being referred to as "The Liberation of Thailand." Indications are that this action is to begin with the assassination of the king, the queen, and the prime minister. The coup is to be spearheaded by the network principals already located in Bangkok: Chaisin Panomvana, the deputy prime minister; Tawan Chanyangam, well-known Chulalongkorn University professor of foreign languages; and Kanlaya Chanyangam, the professor's daughter.

9. (TS) Upon completion of the initial round of assassinations, the deputy prime minister will assume control of the government, declaring himself head of state and declaring the regime a communist dictatorship. Several key members of the Thai military have already pledged their support.

10. (TS) Once that phase is concluded, opposition leaders are to be swiftly arrested, tried, and executed. Included in that group will be the ranking official for each of the following organizations: the Armed Forces Security Center; the Border Patrol Police; the Central Intelligence Agency; the Office of Special Investigations; and Military Intelligence. In addition, all other members and agents of each of these entities have already been identified. Once their agency chiefs have been arrested, they will be targeted for systematic elimination.

11. (TS) Approximately eight (8) months after the Thailand coup, a similar strategy is planned for Laos. Preliminary strategies are already under way to set the stage for that action. Optimism is high among group members that this strategy will prove successful.

12. (S) It is imperative that steps be taken immediately to curb these plans.

Harold Edmondson
AIC, Northern Sector

Spencer Morgan finished reading the document but then took a moment to review paragraph ten. Yes, it really did say what he thought it said. Attempting to ignore a sudden, massive wave of nausea, he returned the report to Owens. Beads of sweat had formed at his temples. "Wow," he said quietly, swallowing hard, "this is...this is—"

"No shit."

"Wow," Morgan said again. His brain wasn't working right. All he could think about was what it must be like to be swiftly arrested, tried, and executed. He'd already begun planning the menu for his final meal when Owens spoke again. "Kind of fucks up your whole day, doesn't it?"

"Uh-huh."

"There's something else you need to know," the agency man said, sounding surprisingly calm.

"Oh?"

"We conducted a quick investigation this morning of the three conspirators named in paragraph eight of the report, and we found out something very interesting about the woman—Kanlaya Chanyangam."

"What'd you find out?"

"She's romantically involved with a young man named J. Edgar Reynolds...one of your agents, I believe." The expression on Owens's face was almost one of smugness.

"Jesus!" Morgan swore, discovering that fear was giving way to anger. "Reynolds! I might have known. He's probably in on it with her. That communist! He's been trying to undermine the mission since the day he arrived in Thailand, the son of a bitch!"

"We found no evidence to suggest collusion between the two of them. We don't believe Reynolds is directly involved, or even knowledgeable of the situation. In fact, we're not even sure that she was trying to pump him for information. It may be nothing more than a simple romance."

Morgan folded his arms. "Humph. Maybe."

"At any rate, we've got our work cut out for us. We have to take action, and we have to do it very quickly."

"What kind of action did you have in mind?" Morgan had a peculiar feeling that he wasn't going to like the answer.

"We've got to beat them to the punch."

"What do you mean?"

"The only logical course of action is for us to assassinate the deputy prime minister...and to do it soon." Ralph Owens's tone of voice was so matter-of-fact it was probably the same one he would have used to describe the need for removal of a speck of lint from a dark suit. "When you come right down to it, we really don't have a choice."

Morgan, momentarily stunned, asked finally, "Couldn't we just alert the prime minister and the king and queen? *They* could handle the deputy prime minister. They're targets too, just like us. I'm sure they'd be anxious to deal with this."

Owens shook his head. "They wouldn't believe us. Not until it was too late. They'd think we were grandstanding. Or just trying to stir up trouble. Chaisin Panomvana has been a part of the ruling hierarchy of this country for nine years. They trust him completely. Me, on the other hand, they've met a total of two times at government-sponsored cocktail parties. And *you*, they don't even *like*."

"What about the US ambassador? They'd believe *him*."

"Well, that would be a dandy idea. Except for the fact that the ambassador just started a three-week vacation in Brazil. He's fulfilling a childhood dream—paddling down the Amazon with just the bare essentials—a change of clothes, a razor, and a toothbrush. No, this is something we're going to have to handle ourselves."

"There must be some other way." Morgan's stomach was churning. He had killed on a few occasions over the years. In battle. Back in his days in the artillery branch of the service. From a distance. Without premeditation. But cold-blooded murder? That was different.

"Hm-mmm. Believe me, I've studied this from every angle, and there is no other way."

Morgan pinched the bridge of his nose and then unsuccessfully tried to rub away the tension of the moment. "Oh god," he moaned.

"We owe it to Thailand to attend to this matter," Ralph Owens stated. "In fact, we owe it to the entire free world. And besides, if we don't get him, he'll get us."

That remark jolted Spencer Morgan into a nod of agreement. "Okay," he said.

"Good."

"But what about the rest of the network? Even if we manage to take care of Chaisin Panomvana, the others might still pull off the coup…and the executions."

"Not a chance. Without his power and his influence with the military, the whole thing'll fall apart. Without its head, the snake dies."

Morgan considered that for a moment. "I suppose you're right," he mumbled finally. His words were spoken so softly, he could barely hear them himself.

"I *know* I am. Just the same, we'll want to have AFSC pick up Professor Chanyangam and his daughter for interrogation. With any luck, they'll clue us in to the other members of the ring. I'll set the wheels in motion as soon as you and I finish here."

"Okay, but let's make it an interagency effort. Obviously, AFSC needs to formally make the arrests, but MI and the CIA should assist and be part of the interrogation."

"Good idea. You supply an agent, and I'll supply an agent."

"Yeah." Morgan cleared his throat. A lump seemed to be forming there. "And what about the assassination?"

"The sooner the better. I'd say we ought to aim for Monday." This was Friday. "You and me. A team."

Since their first meeting, and even before that, Morgan hadn't liked Owens. He sensed that Owens felt the same way about him. The thought of the two of them becoming a team for something as important as this brought back Morgan's nausea.

"I'll put together a plan," the agency man went on. "We'll meet on Sunday to go over it and smooth out any rough edges."

Morgan didn't like being dictated to. He was tempted to insist that *he* be the one to put together the plan, or at least that he be a part of the process. But unable to find the will or the energy at this point for a confrontation, he simply said, "All right."

"Same time, same station on Sunday?"

"Okay."

Morgan stood and walked slowly from the office. He still didn't like it. Not a bit. Once he returned to the 187th, he would confer with Lieutenant Wilson. Maybe the lieutenant's astrological advice would put this whole situation in a better light.

He located Wilson just as the members of the unit were preparing to wrap things up for the week. He wasn't comfortable sharing the specifics of his predicament with the lieutenant, so he spoke only in general terms. Unfortunately, Wilson's astrological assessment did little to help. Morgan was sure he wouldn't be getting much sleep the next few nights.

Chapter Thirty-Eight

In Thailand, as in many parts of Asia, there are few things as important as saving face. This fact sometimes causes motorists to flee the scene of an automobile accident rather than to stay and deal with the shame and embarrassment that would otherwise follow. It has been known to prompt card players caught cheating to go into hiding in remote parts of the country, taking on new identities. And sometimes it even causes arguments to turn into gunfights. Almost anything is better than the humiliation of losing a debate.

Even something as natural as baldness can trigger a loss of esteem. In Thailand, it is sometimes said, "The longer a man's face becomes, the more face he loses."

Despite a postgraduate education in Moscow, and despite his mastery of three western languages, not the least of which was English, Professor Tawan Chanyangam had never managed to shake this singularly far-Eastern value. The need to save face at all costs was deeply rooted within him.

It was not a conscious choice he had made at any point in his life. It was simply a fact. It was a part of him. He had lived with it, as he had lived with a long jagged scar on his left shin, a souvenir from a boyhood soccer match. It was as natural to him as the green of the grass and the blue of the sky.

"The Armed Forces Security Center knows of your involvement with the Communist Party of Thailand," an informant—a long-time plant within AFSC—had told him a half hour earlier. The informant had located Professor Chanyangam in the latter's office on the second floor of the Foreign Languages Building at the Chulalongkorn University campus. It was Saturday. The professor had come in

255

during this quiet time on the campus to catch up on some paperwork and to correct a batch of exams completed two days ago.

The professor's eyes had narrowed in momentary disbelief at hearing this news.

The informant, a young man named Romchai Sapanakit, had continued, "They know of the plan to overthrow King Bhumibol and Queen Sirikit and the prime minister."

"You are certain of this?" It was alarming news indeed!

"There is no doubt, Professor." Romchai Sapanakit spoke solemnly. "You are to be arrested within the hour."

"But how could they have found out?"

"Someone in our organization must have turned against us. It is the only possible explanation. Probably someone in the north. As a group, they have seemed to be less trustworthy."

Professor Tawan Chanyangam's hands clenched slowly, then banged as one on the desk. "This is disastrous! This is a calamity! It was all proceeding so well!"

"Yes."

"So smoothly. Our strategies. Our timetables. Our objectives were within reach."

"I know, Professor... But it is not to be." The young man's voice broke on the last few words. "I am so sorry."

A terrible sadness came over the professor as he came to fully realize the impact of what he had just heard. He was distraught that a brilliant plan of which he had been the primary architect was about to be thwarted. A plan that he had proposed successfully to Deputy Prime Minister Chaisin Panomvana. A plan that would have served Thailand so well. About to dissolve...like so much smoke.

As the young man had said, it was not to be. An American quotation came to mind, although not clearly—something about "the saddest words of mice and men."

Then too there was the fact that much shame was headed his way. The professor knew *that* with the utmost certainty. The shame of arrest and handcuffs. The shame of a trial. The shame of prison and, perhaps, even execution. The shame of knowing that he would be remembered as a traitor. And a murderer.

His countrymen, he was aware, would fail to appreciate the purity of his motives. They would fail to understand the nobility of his cause and the extent of his patriotism. They would remember him simply as the killer of Harold Edmondson, CIA operative. They would remember him as the mastermind behind the theft of twenty crates of infrared, telescopic, rifle sights. They would remember him as the man who arranged for the murder of Mason McElroy, US Special Forces sergeant co-opted in the rifle-sight theft and later determined to be expendable. They would *not* remember that he loved his country deeply and that everything he did was undertaken with only that love of country in mind.

"You must run, Professor," the informant pleaded moments before his own departure. "There is still time. You can escape."

"And where would I run? How could I hide? I am too well known. My photograph is in the newspapers almost weekly for one reason or another. Strangers call me by name as I travel about. And besides, I am too old for that. No, to run would be pointless."

"But you must try."

"I cannot. It would be foolish. And it would be futile."

"For the good of the cause."

"I cannot," the professor repeated, folding his arms. "But you must do one more thing for me, my friend. You must locate my daughter and warn her that they will be coming for her as well. She has no telephone, so go to her at this address." With hurried strokes, he wrote it on a slip of paper and held it out to Romchai Sapanakit.

The young man accepted it with an unsteady hand.

"Go to her," the professor persisted. "If she is not at home, find her wherever she is. She has youth and enthusiasm on her side. She has the energy and the vigor and the heart to flee, and then to fight again. Go to her and warn her."

"Very well, Professor. I will do as you ask."

"Thank you, my friend."

"It is my great honor to serve you in any way I can."

Romchai Sapanakit then departed to do the professor's bidding, casting a mournful look over his shoulder as he reached the doorway.

As the minutes ticked away, Professor Tawan Chanyangam sat at his desk and considered his options. Escape, he was still convinced, was out of the question. Quite impossible. But what about some sort of plausible explanation to the authorities? An intricate, carefully woven scheme of lies that would address all the facts and yet make him out to be nothing other than a loyal Thai citizen?

He sighed. Even if possible, such an approach would be hypocritical. Reprehensible! He could not betray the principles and philosophies in which he believed so firmly. Whatever kind of life might follow such a betrayal would surely be hollow.

For the first time, Tawan Chanyangam considered the alternative of death. The thought lingered. An honorable death. By his own hand. In a manner of his own choosing. A form of escape different from that suggested by the informant but infinitely more effective. Martyrdom. The sudden allure of this thought was so powerful it made him straighten in his chair. His feet flattened on the floor, and he inhaled sharply without intending to.

And then he relaxed. A wave of calmness came over him. A calmness more profound and complete than any he could remember. The calmness that comes from facing up to and moving past a difficult decision. And he welcomed it.

But how to bring about this ultimate escape? How to make it a reality? He owned a .45 caliber automatic pistol, the pistol he had used to kill Harold Edmondson barely in time to keep him silent. But he kept it in the nightstand in the master bedroom of his home. Realizing he had no time to engage in even the briefest of travels, he dismissed that idea. Something more immediate was needed.

Tawan Chanyangam eyed the closet about eight feet away from his desk. Memory of the closet's contents brought a slow smile to his face. Just three nights ago, Kanlaya and two other members of the CPT had arrived in a pickup truck and, while the campus was deserted and still, had carried in two boxes of carefully packaged explosives. They'd stored them in the closet, preparatory to their eventual use at the Palace in the takeover.

The explosives, Professor Chanyangam recalled, were Soviet made, primarily of the plastic variety—a recently developed, highly effective hybrid called RD-490. Kanlaya had described it to him in some detail, had even explained the detonation procedure.

Kanlaya. What a fine daughter she was! What a blessing to him! What a blessing to Thailand! At least she would escape. She would find a way to revive the cause. That thought pleased him greatly.

He was grateful that this was Saturday and the Foreign Languages Building was empty. That made it all so much simpler.

In a driving rain that had seemingly sprung from nowhere, a gray AFSC Datsun sedan pulled into a space at one end of parking lot number eight on the Chulalongkorn University campus. Inside the automobile were three AFSC agents, all young and eager. Also inside were a CIA agent named Mark J. DeSilva and an MI agent named Irving P. Bonner. This was to be a team effort. An interagency arrest and interrogation.

All four doors of the Datsun flew open simultaneously, and the five agents exited, moving swiftly toward the two-story structure straight ahead, which they knew to be the university's Foreign Languages Building. Fallen jacaranda blossoms, purple and now wet from the rain, covered the sidewalk, sticking to it.

When the five men were within forty meters of the building, an attractive young Thai woman carrying an umbrella and a briefcase appeared at one side of the structure, having approached from the opposite end of the campus. Nearing the entrance, she seemed not to see the five men through the sheets of rain that separated her from them. Briskly, she hurried toward the door, and collapsing the umbrella, she stepped through it.

Even from this distance and through the rain, Irv Bonner recognized the woman as Kanlaya Chanyangam. Several times Bonner had shared breakfast or lunch with Kanlaya and Ed Reynolds. He'd enjoyed those occasions immensely, not having a clue then as to Kanlaya's secret side. Reynolds still didn't know. No one had been in any hurry to tell him. Even Colonel Morgan had shown restraint, forcing Bonner's reluctant admiration.

"It sure is wet," Bonner mumbled to the other agents, pulling himself down further into his lightweight, waterproof jacket.

"It sure as hell is," mumbled Mark J. DeSilva in response.

One of the Thai agents inadvertently stepped into a deep puddle and, in coming out of it, nearly lost his shoe.

Explosion!

With a suddenness that froze the five young men in their tracks and seemed to make the rain halt in its descent, an eruption of fury and flame violently pushed window glass outward from all sides of the building on both levels!

Another explosion a few seconds later, even more powerful than the first, rocked the building to its foundation, shaking the ground beneath the feet of the agents!

In the next instant, flames were everywhere, the conflagration erasing for Bonner the image that had lingered on his retina of the young woman entering the Foreign Languages Building. A structure that was now an inferno.

He was stunned! He was horrified! Immediately sick to his stomach, his knees went to the wet pavement, creating pain in his kneecaps and shins that he would not feel until much later. Face dropping to his hands, he cried like a child. Then, without warning, he vomited.

Irving P. Bonner knew that he would never be the same again.

Chapter Thirty-Nine

"Two down and one to go," Ralph Owens announced, nibbling at the end of an index finger. "And our plan is ready."

"Oh?" Spencer Morgan was still reeling from the tumultuous events of the previous day, and it was difficult for him to mount any enthusiasm for an assassination plan. After all, this wasn't an idea he had been thrilled about in the first place. Lieutenant Wilson's subsequent astrological advice hadn't been supportive of the notion either, warning that important activities should be deferred until the stars were more favorably aligned.

"I think the deputy prime minister's death should appear to be a communist-inspired act," the CIA man said. "That way we can kind of kill two birds with one stone...so to speak." The corners of his mouth turned up. "You can see the beauty of that, can't you?"

The colonel agreed somberly that this would be a good goal.

Owens continued, "The most common assassination technique used by communist terrorists is a small bomb, usually thrown rather than planted. So that's the approach we're going to use."

"The agency has an explosives expert, right?" Morgan asked, recalling Lieutenant Bonner's unsettling account of the Chulalongkorn University events and wishing to avoid getting too close to anything with the potential to go *boom*. "Couldn't he handle it for us?"

"Unfortunately, we lost our explosives expert a couple of months ago," the CIA chief confided. "He hasn't yet been replaced."

"Killed in the line of duty?"

"Not exactly. While stopping in the middle of a crosswalk to scrape some dog shit from his shoe, he was hit by a bus. Not quite as dignified a way to go out as he might have liked, but..." Ralph Owens gave a shrug.

"I'm sorry to hear that."

"It was very sad, actually. I delivered the eulogy at his funeral. Of course, I had to change my talk to make the dog shit something a little more socially acceptable."

"Naturally."

Leaning back in his chair to create enough room for him to cross his legs, Owens shifted the conversation to a new topic. "Tell me, Colonel, can you ride a bicycle?"

Morgan, puzzled by this new tack, said, "I think so. It's been a while, though."

"It'll come back to you, I'm sure. Now, by tapping into some key contacts in the local government, we've been able to get the lowdown on Chaisin Panomvana and how he spends his time. Everything he does during the course of a weekday, Monday through Friday, is part of a very exact schedule. He arrives for work precisely at nine o'clock, leaves for lunch at precisely twelve in a chauffeured limousine, arrives for lunch at precisely twelve ten. He always lunches at The Polynesian Restaurant."

"Interesting."

"Chaisin enjoys fresh air, so he always insists that the windows of the limo be rolled down."

"Oh?" Morgan couldn't quite see where Owens was headed with this line of thinking.

Owens took in a breath and then went on, "If the two of us were dressed like Asians, and we just happened to be riding a couple of bicycles past the restaurant at the very same moment the limousine was pulling up in front of it, we could—"

"Oh right." Morgan had it now. "We could toss the bomb into the car."

"Exactly."

Ralph Owens and Spencer Morgan spent the afternoon in the "tech room" located on the embassy's third floor at the end opposite from Owens's office. Between the two of them, aided by a CIA explosives textbook complete with diagrams, they were able to create a small portable explosive device. It relied on five sticks of dynamite for its punch, and a sophisticated timing mechanism—straight from the textbook—to cause the device to explode exactly three seconds after activation.

Slipping the device into an innocent-looking purple plastic bag from the Thai Damaru department store, Ralph Owens tied a cord around the opening. "It's in the bag," he joked.

Morgan didn't laugh.

At 1130 hours on Monday morning, Morgan and Owens were ready to make their move. Wearing dark wigs and blue silk shirts and pantaloons, they had donned broad-brimmed straw hats tilted low, and large sun glasses covering much of their faces. They looked as Asian as it was possible for them to look, which both of them had to admit wasn't particularly Asian at all.

A lifelong Catholic, Spencer G. Morgan made the sign of the cross. It couldn't hurt, he reasoned, and it just might help. It was time to set the plan in motion.

On Sukhumvit Road, they rented two bicycles from Tommy's Rent-It Shop, after a vigorous round of negotiating over the cost. Once outside, Owens instructed Morgan, "Tie the bag to your handlebars."

"Okay." Carefully, the colonel did so. Then the pair pedaled off in wobbly fashion.

At Rajadamnern Boulevard, they made a right turn. They stayed on Rajadamnern for several blocks, obeying the frequent traffic signals, maneuvering past the occasional traffic circles. These were important blocks to the two cyclists, because they took advantage of that opportunity to get the feel of their machines and to develop the balance necessary to operate them effectively when it really counted. Movements were becoming smoother, more fluid. Confidence was growing steadily. They checked their watches, discovering that they were right on schedule.

"Good luck, Colonel!" Owens shouted across the four feet of pavement that separated them.

"Thanks! You too!" He gave a thumbs-up sign.

They turned the corner at Kasawangse Street and instantly recognized The Polynesian Restaurant on their left, a large peach-col-
ored building with angular, pointed arches of varying heights. The
Polynesian was generally considered one of the finest restaurants in
Bangkok, offering a broad range of cuisines at exorbitant prices, and
appealing to the wealthiest and most influential clientele of the city.

Their timing could not have been better. The deputy prime
minister's limousine had just rolled to a stop when the Americans
arrived, side by side on their bicycles. Spencer Morgan drew in a long
breath, more to quell the butterflies in his stomach than out of any
particular need for oxygen, and pulled the bag from the handlebars.

"Now, Colonel!" Owens shouted.

Pulling alongside the sleek long black automobile, adrenaline
pumping through his arteries at a record rate, Spencer Morgan main-
tained one hand on the handlebar grip and used the other hand to
remove the device from the bag and activate it.

As casually as he could, he tossed the bomb at what he took to
be an open window. He was wrong.

The device bounced off the glass and tumbled back into the
middle of the street as Morgan and Owens pedaled furiously to make
their getaway.

Three, two, one, explosion!

Some paint chips were gouged from the rear door of the limousine, although its occupants scarcely heard the noise. The chauffeur
swatted at the back of his neck, as though shooing away a mosquito.

A small chunk of cement was torn loose from the street near the
center stripe. A passing motorcycle policeman was thrown from his
cycle, badly scraping a knee. A prostitute on the corner was knocked
off her feet and into a large wooden vegetable stand. Cursing all the
way, she disappeared among a hundred heads of lettuce as the stand
collapsed. A moment later, a hand worked its way up through the
lettuce to make an obscene gesture.

Morgan and Owens were two blocks away before it occurred to
anyone at the scene to chase them. Then the policeman wrapped a
handkerchief around his now-bleeding knee, righted his motorcycle,
and took up the pursuit.

Although they realized that the mission itself had been a failure, the Americans were confident that at least they had made a clean escape. Even so, they didn't dare slacken their pace for so much as an instant. And they began to alter their course—a turn here and a double-back there. "Better to be safe than sorry, Colonel!" Owens shouted over to Morgan.

"Right!"

"Pedal faster, Colonel"

"Right."

"Pump those legs, Colonel!"

"Right."

"Pretend this is Thursday afternoon, Colonel, and you're on your way to meet Maureen Meadows!"

How the hell did he know about that? "Right."

Owens said nothing more. He just grinned and pumped his legs.

It was clear that they had outfoxed or outmaneuvered the motorcycle policeman. He was nowhere to be seen.

A short time later, however, they inadvertently zipped past two parked, but occupied, police cars. Instantly, with a show of flashing lights and sirens, both cars took after them, pulling them over for speeding. Thirty kilometers per hour in a twenty-five zone.

The Americans attempted to "make things right" by offering a generous donation to the policemen's ball or any charity of their choice. They were unsuccessful. Carted away to the police station, they were charged accordingly. Speeding and attempted bribery.

During the twenty-seven days it took for the US authorities to arrange for their release, four important things happened: (1) the king, queen, and prime minister were advised by the US ambassador, fresh from a delightful vacation in South America, of Chaisin Panomvana's CPT involvement; (2) to the surprise of representatives of the CIA and MI, the ruling triumvirate accepted the information at face value, arranging for Chaisin to be arraigned on charges of treason; (3) in exchange for promises of no execution and a reduced prison term, Chaisin agreed to tell all he knew, resulting in the roundup of key members of the network; and (4) Spencer G. Morgan contracted an intestinal virus from the prison water supply which was to stay with him—in recurring form, causing intense abdominal pain in each instance—for the rest of his life.

When at last they were released from their adjoining cells, Spencer Morgan of Military Intelligence and Ralph Owens of the Central Intelligence Agency stormed off in opposite directions, each vowing that he would never have anything to do with the other again. After all, they really never liked each other anyway.

Chapter Forty

Even though it had been more than a month, Ed Reynolds wasn't over Kanlaya. Vivid memories lingered stubbornly. He wasn't over her death or the tragic circumstances surrounding it. He wasn't over the void in his life that had been created by her absence from it.

And he still hadn't managed to sort everything out. He had no explanations. She had cared for him. He was sure of that. No one could be *that* good an actress. And yet, she'd been a communist agent. A member of the CPT. That too was clear.

Had she been using him? He didn't think so. She'd never attempted to get information from him, even though he'd never kept his line of work secret from her. Had she been setting him up? Biding her time? Waiting for just the right moment to make her move? And if so, what might that move have been?

Ed never would know any of these things with certainty. But on the last day of May 1968, lying on his bed late in the evening, he made a decision. He decided how it was that he was going to remember Kanlaya Chanyangam. He would remember her charm and grace. He would remember her wit. He would remember her beauty. He would remember the way her face lit up whenever she smiled. And he would remember the fact that she *always* smiled whenever she saw him.

He would remember too those times when she had looked up at him and said, "I love you." And he decided, whenever he heard those words in memory, he would believe them.

Romchai Sapanakit, the informant who had served as Professor Tawan Chanyangam's steady source of information regarding activities of AFSC, the Thai intelligence agency, and who had informed him that his arrest was at hand, had somehow escaped detection himself. Watching the network collapse around his ears when the deputy prime minister had buckled and told all he knew, Romchai had felt certain the collapse would take him down with it.

Although the deputy prime minister had not known Romchai's identity—only the Chanyangams, father and daughter, had known that—there were others in the CPT network who were very much aware of the existence of an informant operating somewhere inside AFSC. If that fact had come to light during the investigation, Romchai was doubtful that his record and his various activities in recent months could have withstood close scrutiny. But so far, at least, he was a free man.

And he was an *angry* man, as well. It was an anger born of the events that had resulted in the suicide of the professor, a man he admired greatly, and the accidental death of his daughter.

Two weeks after the event, Romchai managed to pinpoint the leak in the CPT network. He determined the name of the individual who had furnished information to Harold Edmondson, information that had signaled the ultimate destruction of the network and, yes, of the professor himself. Soong Pitak, one of three members of the network other than himself not to be picked up during the flurry of arrests recently concluded, protested his innocence at first.

"It was not me, I swear it. I have been true to the cause."

Romchai continued his intense questioning, now at knifepoint. "I want the truth. I demand it!" The tip of the knife scratched the side of the other man's neck just enough to draw blood.

"All right. All right," Soong said, sighing deeply. "Yes, I knew Harold Edmondson. I…gave him information…in exchange for money. I had much need for money."

That had been enough for Romchai Sapanakit. Moving the knifepoint down the body of the confessed traitor, he searched out a soft spot between the man's ribs and drove the blade home. An hour later, he disposed of the body in a tributary of the Chao Pya River. Soong Pitak, a man of few familial and friendship connections, would probably not even be missed.

Now the time had come for Romchai to turn his anger in another direction. Toward the Americans. The countrymen of Harold Edmondson. He would begin with the individual who was the lover of Kanlaya Chanyangam. Romchai had followed this person on several occasions. Many times Romchai had warned the professor of the imprudence of permitting such a romance to continue. "He is an American agent, Professor. The *enemy*. This is a dangerous thing. No good can come of it."

"It troubles me also," the professor had admitted. "But she loves him, and I want her to be happy. She deserves happiness. And *that,* my young friend, is the good that can come of it."

"Very well," Romchai had said with a shrug. "Perhaps it will run its course in short order."

"Perhaps."

While Kanlaya was alive, Romchai Sapanakit had found Professor Tawan Chanyangam's perspective reasonable. Now that she was gone, and the professor as well, it meant absolutely nothing.

CHAPTER FORTY-ONE

Late for an evening appointment, Ed Reynolds took the elevator to the ground floor of the Chairanee Building, hurried out to the parking lot, climbed quickly into his green Ford falcon, and raced off in the direction of the Chao Pya Hotel. He had a routine interview to conduct with Captain Neil Montgomery, who was billeted there, as were many of the US Army officers assigned to one form of duty or another in Bangkok. The army had made arrangements with hotel management for special rates.

The only time Montgomery had been available for the interview was a half-hour period beginning at 1900 hours. So Reynolds had decided to stay around the office until a few minutes before then to catch up on some overdue reports.

In addition to its function as a billeting facility, the Chao Pya served as the officers' club for the US military establishment. Montgomery was a junior officer in the administration of the club. Reynolds himself had used the excellent and attractive facilities of the club on several occasions. With his credentials and his uniform of civilian clothes, gaining admittance was not difficult. Colonel Morgan, however, frowned on the notion of his enlisted personnel fraternizing with officers. So far, Ed had managed to keep him from finding out. Of course, there had been a few close calls resolved by a few quick exits.

Reynolds's interview with Montgomery, a slender, dark-haired chain-smoker, was brief. The man was a fast talker who stayed on the subject and avoided extraneous speech. Even his habit of lighting one cigarette from another scarcely slowed his replies to Ed's questions.

"Thank you for your time, Captain, I now have what I need and I'd better be on my way. And I realize you have other commitments."

"Happy to help." The two shook hands.

Downstairs in the crowded lobby, Ed stopped to buy a newspaper. He preferred the *Bangkok World*, but all he could find this late in the day was the *Bangkok Post*, so he settled for that. Both were printed in English and both did a reasonably good job of capturing the news and presenting it intelligently, fairly, and accurately.

A tingling sensation along the back of his neck made him stiffen. It came from a sudden and distinct feeling that he was being watched, that one pair of eyes out of all those around him had singled him out for special attention. Casually, he scanned the faces that were within view. Finding none that looked familiar or seemed unduly interested in him at this moment, he shrugged. Evidently it had been his imagination.

But on his way out to the car, with darkness falling, he had the feeling again, even stronger this time. When he turned to check on it, a figure fell back into a shadowy alleyway. A coldness gripped Ed Reynolds. He was definitely being followed. He didn't like it.

Passing by his Ford Falcon, Ed ignored it and continued along the sidewalk, wanting to give his adversary a chance to reveal himself. He was more than a little curious about who it might be. Walking past a trash receptacle, he jammed the newspaper into it.

The first time Ed could recall being tailed was about a month and a half after his arrival in Thailand. His tail, as he learned later, was a KGB agent assigned to the USSR embassy, cataloguing him: a couple of photographs; his home address; the make, model, and license number of his car; and a list of his closest friends.

Reynolds had been uncomfortable then, and in a number of similar situations since. And he was uncomfortable now, standing at the corner of Sri Ayudhya and Ramsin, waiting for the stoplight to change, pretending to be calm. Reynolds gave a silent curse and then, while the light was still red, made a dash across the street, dodging around a Toyota and a Chevrolet.

Looking back over his shoulder, he got his best look yet at his surveillant as the man too darted quickly through the crosswalk. An Asian, tall with a slender build, the man was dressed in a light-blue shirt and dark-gray trousers.

An awareness came over Ed that this man might have more in mind than simply observing and recording his activities. That sprint out into the open on his part would be a bold move for someone whose only objective was to take notes and write a report later. An attempt on his life was unlikely, Ed concluded, but possible. And he found that possibility disturbing.

He was at the next intersection now, arriving just as the light turned to green. With long strides, he crossed. A block farther along, he turned left, then right a short time after that, then left again. The man behind him was hanging back, but he was still there. Each time Reynolds tried to spot him with a rapid glance over the shoulder to get a clearer picture of him, the man instantly stepped back into a doorway or managed to merge into a crowd.

If he couldn't identify the man tailing him, maybe Reynolds could do the next best thing—lose him. Nearing a large department store that still was open, Reynolds saw his opportunity. He ducked inside and rushed down the main aisle, slipping through the clientele with the moves of a broken-field runner. Noticing a rear exit, he adjusted his direction and headed for it.

Outside in the darkness was an alley, and speeding feet made short work of that. At the end of it, Ed found a second alley branching to the right and he turned the corner.

Then he heard hurried footsteps that were not his own. The man was still behind him! Son of a bitch! The guy was good.

Darkness was total now. Ed could barely see his shoes beneath him, slapping against the dirt surface of the alleyway. A cardboard box suddenly appeared in his path, and he hurdled it, nearly losing his balance on the other side as he landed unevenly on some rocks and debris. Stumbling, he bounced off a stone wall, then righted himself.

The darkness made everything fuzzy, but an end to the alleyway was coming quickly into focus, a dead end. A large trash dumpster on the left side was just a few feet from the high wall at the very end.

"Oh, Christ," Ed muttered, just loud enough for his own ears to hear.

His brain churned, searching for alternatives: Turn and fight? With what? No weapon. Turn and rush past his pursuer? What if the man was armed? Giving him a target at point-blank range didn't make a lot of sense. Scale the wall? It was at least twelve feet high! And Ed was no climber anyway.

More from instinct than decision, Ed hurled his body around the far side of the dumpster, temporarily, at least, putting a barrier between his adversary and himself. A shield for the moment.

He let his body slide down the side of the building that formed one boundary of the alley, the dumpster brushing against his right shoulder, until he was sitting on the ground. His back was wedged into the corner created by dumpster and building. His legs were extended in front of him.

They were tired legs, he realized, looking at them. He could see and feel them shaking slightly. His arms were tired too, as though he had been lifting concrete blocks for several days without a rest.

Minutes passed. Or was it only seconds? He couldn't be sure. Whatever the time span, Ed used it to bring his breathing under control. This had the favorable side effect of improving his hearing.

It was then that he realized there were no footsteps approaching. He'd assumed the footsteps he'd heard earlier would continue, ending only at the moment of confrontation.

And yet, Ed knew the man was back there somewhere. There could be no doubt of that. He would have no reason to quit now. Not with his prey so clearly cornered.

Then it came to him! Whether or not the man himself was armed, he had no way of knowing for sure that Ed wasn't. For all this man knew, Ed could have a revolver tucked inside his shirt. Ed put his mind to work in an effort to turn his surveillant's uncertainty into some kind of tactical advantage.

Crrack! A bullet slammed into the shielding end of the dumpster. The impact caused an echo inside the metal cubicle that bounced around for what seemed to Ed an eternity.

Loud noises! Damn, how he hated loud noises! It wasn't enough that he was about to be murdered behind a bunch of garbage in a deserted alley, but it was to be a noisy death at that.

"Hey, pal!" Ed shouted, "can we talk about this?"

Silence.

"Maybe we can work something out! Whattaya say?"

More silence.

"Really, let's be civilized about this, okay?" Then Ed attempted a Thai version of this suggestion, in case the man didn't understand English.

That was answered by another gunshot! The flash of it lit up a short stretch of the alleyway. The sound of it pushed against Ed's eardrums with hammer-like force.

Yet another gunshot! Louder than the other two, Ed was sure of it, smashing into his senses.

A fourth gunshot! It seemed somehow louder yet, echoing in the confined space of the alleyway. Ed Reynolds was vaguely aware of his knees drawing up to his chest and of his arms pulling them in even tighter.

A fifth gunshot! Striking the dumpster once again, creating that horrible metallic sound that lasted approximately forever.

Then, a different noise. Footsteps. Moving slowly. Cautiously. Closing in, like a hunter stalking a deer. Getting closer to the dumpster. Twenty-five feet away now, Ed guessed. Then twenty. Then fifteen.

A stumbling noise! The man must have tripped over something in the dark.

That sound. That irregularity. That distinctive reminder that his tormentor was imperfect. A human being with frailties.

Hope sprang from that sound! Hope that started in his toes and sprang up to his chest and shoulders. Hope that jolted his senses to life and awakened his brain.

Suddenly, he knew he could beat it. This "loud noises" thing. At least this one time, by god, he could beat it! And he could beat this man coming for him. Fear was replaced by a calm fury, a quiet rage. How dare this sonofabitch do this to me!

Ed raised himself up about three-quarters of the way and turned so his back was positioned squarely against the dumpster, knees bent slightly, feet a little more than shoulder-width apart. With every ounce of strength he had now or could borrow from the future, Ed pushed backward.

It took just over two seconds for muscle groups to engage fully and to overcome the inertia of an aged dumpster with a half load and rusty wheels. When it finally did move, it moved fast and hard! Ed Reynolds's driving legs gave it no choice. In the next instant, it smashed into something, knocking it to the ground, climbing over the top of it, crushing it, grinding it into the earth.

It was, Ed knew, a man. A slender one, judging by the angle of the dumpster.

Moving carefully around the dumpster and bending down, Reynolds saw that the gun had come free, and he picked it up. Just then, he heard the faintest and briefest of moans.

He pulled the man's arm away from the dumpster, which had pinned most of his body, and checked the wrist for a pulse. Nothing there. Reynolds tried again. Nothing. He reached across to the man's throat and placed two fingers alongside it to take another measurement. Still there was nothing. It became clear to him that the man was dead.

It puzzled Reynolds how the impact of a rolling dumpster could kill someone. He explored the area, using sight as much as possible, but touch even more.

The man's head, now about a foot and a half from the wall of the building, oozed blood from an open wound. Reynolds rubbed his sticky fingers together upon making that discovery. It made sense now. The impact of the rolling dumpster had knocked the man over and forced his head into the wall, hard enough to do him in.

Leaving the body where it was, Ed Reynolds made his way to a telephone and called the police. Speaking in Thai, he explained what had happened and provided his name, address, and phone number, in case they might have follow-up questions. Then he went home, showered, and climbed into bed.

CHAPTER FORTY-TWO

Marilyn Dunn noticed that her fingernails needed work. She'd let them go for too long. She stared at them, resting her fingertips on the desk, making a mental note to give herself a manicure sometime soon. Or maybe she would treat herself with a visit to one of the many professional manicurists who made their living in Bangkok, and who were very talented and relatively inexpensive.

"I know it's rough. As a matter of fact, it stinks," Ed Reynolds was saying, seated on the other side of the desk. It had been his lot to break the news to her, he himself having found out only moments earlier. The front page of the newspaper was filled with it. And there were photographs. *Chilling* photographs.

Marilyn nodded, her mouth going dry. So dry that words would have been impossible, even if she'd had words to say.

"It hit me hard too," Reynolds went on. "But I guess that's one of the potential hazards these days of being in politics and the public eye. That doesn't make it *right*. Or *fair*. It's just an unfortunate fact of life. Look what happened to John Kennedy. And then Martin Luther King two months ago. The world is becoming a sick place. A *dangerous* place. None of us likes that. But we're probably better off if we learn to accept it."

Damn! Did he have to get philosophical on her?

"We have to pick ourselves up and dust ourselves off and get on with the business of living."

Philosophy on an empty stomach. Yech!

"You'll be surprised at how quickly you can bounce back from something like this." Ed smiled a friendly smile, well-intentioned, no doubt. "Hell, just look at me. Living proof."

Marilyn Dunn decided to forgive her friend's feeble attempts at commiseration. The poor guy had been through a lot lately, himself, and it was obvious that he was just trying to help. But it was equally obvious that he wasn't going to be successful. This was simply too great a hurt. Yesterday, June 6, 1968, the world had been shaken by an assassination, reminiscent of another that had occurred some four-and-a-half years earlier, with names and initials only slightly different. This one had taken place at the Ambassador Hotel in Los Angeles. Marilyn Dunn was devastated!

She was conscious of Ed's voice. "We've all lost a great human being. A great contributor to American society. He would have been a fantastic leader for the country. These are difficult times, and he would have made things better."

"Yeah," she whispered, "he would have made things better."

"C'mon," Reynolds said, tugging at her hand, "let's get out of here. I'll buy you a drink. You look like you could use one."

"You're wrong," she corrected. "I could use *ten*."

About an hour later, sometime after her second scotch and water, Marilyn Dunn began to sense an unusual presence. It was not Ed Reynolds. He was seated across from her, jabbering away about the advantages of being young and having one's whole life in front of one and the importance of getting the proper perspective on things. My god, her friend was turning into Dr. Joyce Brothers right before her very eyes.

No, this was something—or someone—entirely different. And it was right next to her. And from it came soft, warm words. Wise words. Words that Marilyn had heard before. "Some men see things that are and say 'why.' I dream things that never were and say 'why not.'"

Then, for no fathomable reason, Marilyn remembered a yellow house in Sacramento, a yard so beautifully green and landscaped that people drove from miles around to see it, a bright room with yellow wallpaper, a large flaxen-haired doll, and a lonesome only child who was slow to make friends and whose closest companion was a calico cat.

A shudder came over her just then. She took a moment to envision a world free of war, free of bigotry, and free of hatred. And when she asked herself "why not?" no answer came to her.

Chapter Forty-Three

Orville Harris knew that he was not well-liked. He was aware that most members of the 187th gave him a wide berth. He knew about the parties he wasn't invited to. He was aware of being left out of plans for lunch or drinks after work.

But then, it was tough to win popularity contests when you were busy being an outstanding operations officer and the best goddamned intelligence operative on the planet! That was a very big job, indeed!

It bothered him sometimes, this not-being-liked business. He would have to admit, though, it wasn't anything new. Occasionally, he would reflect over his childhood days, recalling similar feelings and experiences.

Growing up in Great Falls, Montana, had soured him some. Not that he had anything against the town itself. It was a pleasant enough little burg. It was just that someone with his talent, with his drive, with his ambition, deserved a chance to mature and develop in the proper place. New York or San Francisco—either of those cities would have been more fitting. His abilities were wasted in Great Falls. He knew it, and he resented it.

Orville Harris wasn't popular in high school. A spokesman for a group of his classmates had gone so far as to tell him, "I've been elected to inform you that you are one arrogant and obnoxious son of a bitch."

"It's a free country," Orville had pointed out correctly.

"Yeah? Well, *nobody* in *any* country has a right to be as obnoxious as *you* are."

Orville ran for president of the junior class and then vice president of the senior class, being soundly defeated in both cases in record voter turnouts.

He'd had a total of three dates during his high school years, with three different girls. Three different girls who didn't know each other. Each of them, in turn, immediately told everyone she knew to "stay away from that jerk." Word sure could get around quickly in a small school. There were no more dating opportunities in high school.

Orville's introduction to sexuality had come at the hands of a professional, a bleached-blond prostitute who'd demanded twice her usual fee. "You're weird," she'd told him. "I charge extra for weirdos."

She upped the ante again when he insisted on painting her red, white, and blue. "And you can bet your ass I'm gonna send you a bill for the paint remover!" she'd screamed at him as he left.

Advancing precariously into adulthood, Orville Harris managed to adjust to his lack of popularity, substituting other things for it—drive and determination, guts and grit, perseverance, power prestige, and pride. It was clear to him at every stage that his life was going to be a success!

And then, just to prove it, along came West Point, thanks to a favor owed his father by a Montana senator. And he made it through, somehow, despite rocky beginnings. Yes, sir, Orville Harris was an officer in the US Army—a West Point man, no less. He had shown them all!

Four Buddhist monks with shaved heads and orange ceremonial robes stood on a corner in downtown Bangkok, awaiting the opportunity to cross at a busy intersection. As they waited, they talked of theology and philosophy and hopes for world peace. After a heavy, early-morning, mid-June rain, the skies finally had begun to clear, and the monks gazed upward, welcoming gratefully the return of the sun.

Just as the traffic light changed and the four orange-clad men stepped from the curb, a bright-red Mercedes sped past. Its tires hit the edge of an expansive puddle as if by design, sending up a vast spray of water in rooster-tail fashion. Instantly, the religious men were drenched.

One of them, the oldest of the four and a chronic asthma sufferer, found himself gasping for air, just then catching a glimpse of the Mercedes's dark-haired, crew-cut driver grinning broadly. Moments later, the gasping monk watched the bright-red Mercedes turn into a small parking lot just less than a block away, immediately adjacent to what appeared to be the Chairanee Building. Then it backed into a parking space. The monk put his hands on his knees and attempted to catch his breath.

Ed Reynolds had just finished pouring himself a cup of coffee in the break room, the last cup the pot had to offer. He was leaning against the wall next to two corner windows, blowing on the coffee to cool it. Delicately, he took the first sip and eased it down his throat. With Colonel Morgan out sick today—some sort of recurring intestinal virus—Reynolds was more relaxed than usual. The presence of the colonel, who was always eager to find some reason to accuse Reynolds of undermining the US mission in Thailand, sometimes made him a bit tense.

Ed found his gaze shifting to one of the windows and the scene outside. He was pleased to see that the sun had come out. With roots in the Pacific Northwest, where the term *overcast* was the mainstay of the meteorological vocabulary, he always had been one to celebrate the arrival of the sun.

Then he saw off to his left an orange-clad Buddhist monk suddenly appear and march across the intersection, along the sidewalk, and into the little hardware store owned by the elderly Chinese couple. What, Ed wondered, would a monk need from a hardware store? His curiosity grew as he took another sip of coffee, this one a bit carelessly. It burned his upper lip.

His question was answered momentarily when the monk reappeared carrying a sledgehammer. Reynolds refocused his eyes. Yes, it really was a sledgehammer. With a twelve-pound head, he judged, and a handle about the length of a croquet mallet, it *certainly was* a sledgehammer. A sledgehammer—no question about it. *A monk with a sledgehammer.* Yes, indeed.

Fascinated, Ed watched from the eighth floor as the monk headed directly for his building, the Chairanee, and then, just before reaching it, veered to the right. By sliding over to the other window, Ed was able to continue observing as the orange clad figure strode into the parking lot. The monk stopped squarely in front of the major's freshly waxed Mercedes. The brightness of the sun seemed to enhance the redness of the car, giving it a sheen that nearly made Ed squint.

Suddenly, Ed Reynolds realized what was about to happen, and he sprinted out of the room to see who else might be nearby, coffee splashing from his cup as he ran. Some twenty feet outside the door, he found Dunn and Cooper engaged in conversation. "Marilyn," he said. "Don, get in here. Right now. You two have to see this."

"What?"

"Yeah, what are you talking about?"

"Quick. Don't ask questions."

They followed him into the break room and then over to the window. The three of them arrived just in time to see a diminutive monk lift a sledgehammer high over his head, pausing for a moment, poised over the hood of the Mercedes as though he was at a carnival preparing to ring the bell and win a prize. Marilyn Dunn was so startled by the sight of it, she sucked in her breath involuntarily.

"Shall we call the police?" Cooper asked.

"Are you kidding?" Reynolds laughed.

The monk brought down the sledgehammer with such force it lifted his feet off the ground. The hood buckled under the weight of the blow, and a thud could be heard from eight floors above. The holy man did it again, creating even more damage this time.

The monk pivoted his body slightly, taking aim at one of the headlights. With two quick, short-arced pokes, he demolished it. Apparently in the interests of symmetry, he moved across and did the same to the other headlight.

By the time he moved over to the side of the Mercedes, he had attracted a small crowd. A dozen or so people had gathered. Slack-jawed, they looked on, but no one interfered. A few of them even began to cheer, likely unaware of why he was doing this, but evidently impressed by his resolve to do it well.

A solid smash to the driver's-side door caved it in convincingly. The little orange-clad fellow seemed to have fallen into a nice comfortable rhythm. The roof was his next target, and he positioned himself carefully. Three rapid blows lowered it by a good four inches.

"I love this," Marilyn Dunn mumbled, several stories above the commotion.

"Me too," Ed Reynolds agreed.

Don Cooper began to laugh. He couldn't stop. His legs gave way and he sat on the floor. Rolling onto his back, he cackled hysterically.

Dunn said to him, "Hey, you're missing this."

The windshield disintegrated beneath the next blow of the holy man's hammer. Glass flew in every direction.

"I'm surprised the little guy didn't get cut," Reynolds said.

"Must be divine intervention" was all Dunn could think of to say. Then she too fell down in a fit of laughter.

When the monk moved around behind the car and went into his wind-up, preparing to wreak havoc on the rear window, Reynolds collapsed onto the floor. He laughed until his belly hurt, and then he laughed some more.

Just then, Major Orville Harris appeared at the doorway. "What the hell is going on in here?" he demanded. "First Sergeant Barnett complained to me about the noise. What are you clowns up to?"

Reynolds picked himself up and made a show of dusting himself off. "Uh, it's Special Agent Dunn, sir. She just told us the latest traveling salesman story. It's a great joke, sir. You'd love it."

"That's right, sir," seconded Cooper. "It is one funny story."

"Get back to work, goddamn it. All three of you. I *know* you have things to do. You can tell your silly little jokes on your own damn time." Controlling their laughter as best they could, they filed past Harris and out of the break room.

The trio returned to their desks. Reynolds leaned back in his chair and chuckled softly. The vision of Major Harris's treasured red Mercedes being reduced to a pile of rubble at the righteous hands of a Buddhist monk gave Reynolds a lift such as he had not experienced in a long time. How tremendously satisfying! Maybe there is justice in this world after all, he thought, as an ever-widening grin took hold of his face.

Reynolds wondered if the major was planning to use or wax his car anytime soon. He certainly hoped so.

Author's Note

As indicated elsewhere, this is a work of fiction. However, it is quite obvious that some of the references in the book are to real events and real people. The Vietnam War was real, of course, and so was the Tet Offensive of January 1968, as but two examples. The second Super Bowl was also real, and the Green Bay Packers really did beat the crap out of the Oakland Raiders, much to the chagrin of two of this book's main characters—Ed Reynolds and Doug Wilson.

Obviously, President Lyndon Johnson, President John F. Kennedy, Senator Robert F. Kennedy, General William Westmoreland, and the Reverend Martin Luther King, Jr. were real people. Also real, unfortunately, was James Earl Ray, the man who assassinated Dr. King.

I feel compelled to offer some insights regarding one of the characters in the book—Bernice Wiggins. A missionary in a remote part of Thailand, Bernice has many fine qualities, but included among her *not-so-fine* traits are: she is narrow-minded and loquacious, and she suffers from an overactive libido. This should in no way be read as a disparagement of missionaries in general.

Although I am not particularly knowledgeable on the subject, my distinct impression is that missionaries are, by and large, a noble group, selfless and motivated to try in their own way to make the world a better place. I respect that. Bernice Wiggins is an entirely fictitious character, whose only function in the book is to be entertaining. It should be noted that Tradit, her village of residence, is also fictitious, as is the neighboring town of Boonalok.

Lon Orey

ACKNOWLEDGMENTS

I would like to thank my friends Mark Nordlie, Frank Kastelic, Terry Hobbs, Anup Patel, Scott Houston, Les Brenno, and Skip Williams for their encouragement and suggestions during the writing and re-writing of this book over the years. I also want to express my appreciation to Stacy Tatters, Publication Coordinator, for her patience, perseverance, and professionalism. I'm grateful for her steady hand in working through the many elements of bringing this book to life. Most importantly, I would like to thank my wife Shirley Barnes for her love and support throughout this process, and throughout life in general.

CPSIA information can be obtained
at www.ICGtesting.com
Printed in the USA
LVHW112242210921
698404LV00005BA/8/J